BANGKOK FILE

A Danny McKenna Novel

Phil Ribera

This is a work of fiction. Names, characters, places and incidents are the product of the author's imagination and are used fictitiously. Any resemblance to actual persons, living or dead, events or locales is entirely coincidental.

Bangkok File. Copyright © 2020 by Phil Ribera. All rights reserved. Printed in the United States of America. No part of this book may be used or reproduced in any manner whatsoever without written permission except in the case of brief quotations embodied in critical articles or reviews.

ISBN-13: 978-0-9962103-8-6
ISBN-10: 0-9962103-8-5

Published by Phil Ribera

Learn more about the author by visiting: www.philribera.com

THE NOTE

ELAINA,

THE FIRST TIME I TOOK A LIFE, I WAS SICK TO MY STOMACH. NOW, I KILL WITH AS MUCH EMOTION AS IT TAKES TO SWAT A FLY.

I AM NO LONGER THE SWEET LITTLE BROTHER YOU ONCE KNEW; I'VE BECOME A COLD-BLOODED MURDERER

YOU WILL NEVER SEE ME AGAIN, AS I HAVE DECIDED TO LEAVE THE AREA FOR GOOD. IT WOULD BE IN YOUR BEST INTEREST TO FORGET YOU EVER KNEW ME.

TAKE ALL OF OUR PARENTS' INHERITANCE AND USE IT TO MAKE THE MOST OF YOUR LIFE.

LOVE YOU, SIS

JOHNNY

CHAPTER 1

It wasn't the first time one of my cases began with a note, but I'd seen fortune cookies with more information than Johnny's goodbye letter.

"This is all he left?"

"That's it," she said. "My brother used to tell me the less I knew about his life, the better."

I set the note down. "When was the last time you saw him?"

"Just over a week ago." Her emerald eyes dropped. "He came back for the funeral and then left before it was over. My parents recently died in a car crash, did I mention that already? Anyway, I haven't seen Johnny since their service."

"And no word from him after he left?"

"Nope, only the letter. It came in the mail two days ago."

I turned the envelope over and studied it. The stamp was U.S., but the postmark was too smudged to read.

"Where does he live?" I asked.

"I don't know."

"Do you know where he works?"

She shook her head. "I don't even know what he does for a living."

"What about a wife, girlfriend, partner, anything like that?"

"Not that I know of."

"Close friends?"

Elaina shrugged.

I motioned toward his letter. "It says he's killed people. What's that all about?"

Another shrug.

"Does he have a criminal record?"

"I don't think so."

"Drugs, mental disorders, health issues?"

Elaina shook her head again. "He was always a good kid. Never got into trouble, made good grades in school, was pretty much your all-American boy next door. Joined the military after college, then sort of disappeared once he got out."

"What do you mean, disappeared?"

None of this was making any sense to me, and another one of her shrugs helped to make up my mind. "You know what? I'm going to have to take a pass on your missing brother case. I'd really love to help you out, and the extra money certainly wouldn't hurt, but I'm not getting a good feeling about any of this."

The young woman's eyes widened. "No... Please!"

"Not that you would intentionally mislead me, but the story of your brother's disappearance isn't really adding up. There's got to be something more to it that either I'm missing or you're not telling me."

Tears welled in her eyes as she fanned her face and tried to blink them away. "Please Mr. McKenna, I'm telling you everything I know. I realize it's not much to go on, but you have to understand; I just lost my parents, and now I've also lost my brother. You're the only person I can turn to."

I let out a sigh, wondering how the neighbor she just met could possibly be *the only person* she could turn to. On the other hand, if her brother really was some kind of murderer, it might be a rare opportunity for me. Catching a serial killer wouldn't only be a boon for my PI business, but I'd be headline news! And this time it would be for something good, which would have a lot of people eating crow. My wife, for one, and the idiots who ran me out of the SFPD.

I looked back at Elaina. Her face was like an Ivory Soap model, and her taut body smoldered with the vitality of youth. I figured her to be in her late 20s, which put me somewhere in that gray area between *old enough to be her father,* and *a seasoned gentleman who young women often find desirable.* Despite all that, I wasn't about to exploit her situation. The girl was in a bad way—still grieving over her mom and dad, and all broken up about the brother she'd just learned may be some kind of depraved killer.

In any event, I've always been a sucker when it comes to a woman's tears. She needed me, and I couldn't just turn my back on her. At least that's what I told myself.

Suddenly, my head was nodding and I heard the words leaving my mouth. "Okay, I'll take your case."

CHAPTER 2

I stepped off of Elaina's sailboat—a sleek Beneteau 423—to find Cliff pacing the dock with his hands in his pockets.

"Well? Did ya check on her? Is she okay? What did she say?"

I steadied Cliff with a hand on his shoulder. "Yes, I checked on her. And yes, she's okay."

"Then what's the problem?" He glanced toward her boat. "I've heard her crying in there for the past couple of nights."

I frowned. "You'd have to be pretty damn close to hear that. What'd you do, press your ear to the hull?"

"Not exactly." His face flushed with embarrassment. "But as the harbormaster, it's kind of incumbent on me to keep an eye on things 'round here."

"And you do a great job at that," I said, ushering him back up the ramp. "Elaina just has some family issues that she's dealing with. No need to worry or involve yourself, buddy. She'll be fine."

I waited until Cliff was inside his office before heading back across the marina to Wanderlust—my thirty-two-foot Island Packet sailboat. Night had fallen, ferrying with it a chilling breeze. I went down to the galley and put a frozen Lean Cuisine dinner in the oven.

I'd recently seen a doctor about my bad knee, and he told me I could stand to lose a few pounds. Got a cortisone injection for my trouble, which helps with the pain but seems like a quick fix for the symptoms and doesn't really address the cause. He told me to come back in six months and he'd give me another shot. Anyway, the Chicken Parmesan isn't too bad, and comes in at only 340 calories.

After dinner, I put on a jacket and went topside to smoke a cigar. I don't smoke them often, but sometimes it'll kill the craving to throw in a second frozen meal. I'd normally have a scotch with the cigar, but I'm also trying to cut back in that department.

Pulling out the note Elaina had given me, I sat there rereading her brother's cryptic message. With so little to go on, I tried to dissect the only clues I had at my disposal. There were essentially three parts to his letter, the first being an admission of sorts that Johnny had turned into some kind of killer. The second section implied guilt and self-loathing as he advised Elaina to forget she ever knew him. Lastly, he mentioned their parents' inheritance—which I interpreted as him relinquishing his portion to her.

It had crossed my mind to ask Elaina how much *inheritance* we were talking about, but I'd decided to table that for later. I hoped it was at least enough to pay me, which was yet another thing we hadn't discussed.

My sense was that missing adult cases weren't all that difficult. Unlike with kids, adults generally fell into one of three categories: Medically dependent lost, victim of suspicious circumstances, or voluntarily missing. Elaina's brother wasn't senile or medically ill, as far as I could tell, so I eliminated that one. And since his note implied that he was leaving of his own accord, I figured him for the adult runaway. And considering the references to murders he's committed, he probably had good reason to hit the road.

This was going to be a game of hide-and-seek, which would probably simplify the investigation even more. No matter where Elaina's brother went, he'd have to eat, sleep, and get from place to place. That meant leaving a paper trail. Driver's licenses, auto registrations, Social Security number, bank cards, cell phones—all goldmines in a missing person case.

I booted up my laptop and punched in the name Johnny Teagan. His wasn't the most common name, but it certainly wasn't unique. My choices included a nine-year-old soccer player in Idaho, a school custodian in Massachusetts, a Rhode Island accountant, and a self-described warlock from England. There were 29 pages of people with the same name. I then tried John and Jonathan, but the results were equally random and equally numerous. Nothing really stood out or obviously pointed to Elaina's brother.

Before calling it a night, I left myself a short to-do list:

1) Find out about Elaina's inheritance
2) Get more info about brother Johnny
3) Have Shanay print out contract
4) Send Doris her support check

CHAPTER 3

The neighborhood was quiet, only a jogger and a couple of dog walkers. Although it was his family home, JR went in through the back door to keep from being seen. It would only take one phone call from a nervous neighbor, and he knew that the cops would have him in handcuffs. From there, it would be a simple exercise of connecting the dots, he thought. The locals would call the feds, and they would have him in lockdown before the end of the day.

It was the first time JR had been to the house since the funeral, but it already felt tired, vacant, and unlived in. Smelling of dust and old wood, each sound echoed like an empty church.

He climbed the stairs to his old bedroom. They had cleaned and painted it, dressed it up. The room now looked like it belonged to Marcia Brady.

A feeling of dread suddenly swept over him as he glanced around the spartan room. It swiftly turned to panic as he imagined Mom and Dad tossing out all of his important papers. Anxiety drained away once he finally located his things in a box on the closet floor.

About to drag it out into the light, he was suddenly drawn to the window by the sound of closing car doors. A Jeep that hadn't been there when he arrived was now parked in the driveway.

JR couldn't see anybody, but he heard voices near the back door. The car wasn't police, but he thought it could belong to undercover detectives—or worse. And JR couldn't risk being seen, especially not now.

Rushing out of the room, he took the stairs two at a time. He heard the patio door latch turn just as he reached the ground floor. JR quickly ducked into his father's study and threw open the window.

He was trim and agile, and was able to climb over the sill and drop quietly onto the concrete landing below. Finding himself behind the house now, JR crouched near a gate that led onto a side street. He waited quietly as he listened for the sounds of rushing footsteps or speeding vehicles. There were only muffled voices of two people who were now inside the house.

JR finally raised his head up to peer down the street. It was clear, and after another minute or two he opened the gate. He wasn't as afraid as he was curious. Still wanting to know who was inside, the young man started to make his way through the garden toward the front of the house.

His buzzing cell phone sent him scrambling back against a row of thick bushes. It was Mai.

"Hey," he whispered into the phone.

"John, it's me."

"I couldn't get to my things," he said. "Someone showed up at the house and I had to bail out of a window."

"Are you okay?"

"Yeah, but I'm glad you didn't come out here with me. It's still too dangerous."

Mai was quiet on the other end of the line, and he knew she was doubtful.

In some ways, her predicament was as bad as his. Maybe worse. But she had only given him bits and pieces of her past, and the little he knew of it wasn't good. They'd met while he was still in the service, and Mai had left her job to be with him. The uncle for whom she worked had come looking for her. Though Mai rarely spoke about him, her fear of the man was evident. JR sensed that the dynamics of her employment and her subsequent departure, had caused Mai a tremendous amount of anguish and stress.

"I'm not just being dramatic," he said in his defense. "This shit's getting real out here."

As JR listened to more silence, he began to wonder if his girlfriend was right. Perhaps he had overreacted a bit. He'd been hypervigilant ever since the funeral, and maybe he'd let fear warp his perception of reality.

After a few seconds, he sighed. "I don't know, maybe--"

That's when the first shot rang out, stopping JR mid-sentence.

The crack of the rifle echoed over the neighborhood, taking John immediately back to boot camp training at MCRD San Diego.

Mai heard it over the phone. "John! Are you there?"

There was no response.

CHAPTER 4

It was a cool morning in Alameda. Not really what I would call a wind, but the air wafting off the bay carried a slight chill.

Sitting topside with my coffee and the latest copy of *Seaworthy*, I noticed Elaina making her way toward me across the dock. She wore a moss green hooded sweater, white denim jeans, and white tennis shoes. I pretended to be too enthralled in my magazine to notice.

"I have you to thank," she said. "Last night was the first decent sleep I've had in a week." Then she offered me a foil wrapped loaf of banana bread—which, although not part of my new diet regimen, I accepted.

A minute later, I climbed up the companionway with a couple of paper plates, a knife, and a mug of coffee for her.

The night before, Elaina had mentioned that she couldn't stay in the family house after the death of her parents—too many reminders. She'd also told me that she had purchased her new sailboat, outright. I remembered seeing her moving her belongings in a week or so prior—struggling with the gate as she carried cardboard boxes down the ramp.

"So, tell me about the inheritance."

Elaina gave me a strange look, but I figured why beat around the bush?

"Well, there's Mom and Dad's house in the Berkeley hills." She squinted out across the gray estuary. "And Dad's auto dealership, once it's sold. And then there are Mom's retirement IRAs, their stock portfolio, and--"

I'd heard enough. "So, they left you and your brother in good shape."

She nodded. "Except it sounds like Johnny doesn't want any of it."

"Why do you think that would be?"

She shook her head. "No idea."

"And you're sure you want me digging around in your brother's life? I mean, we have no idea at this point what he's into. He could be an assassin-for-hire. A wealthy assassin-for-hire, who doesn't need his parents' money."

"I don't care about that. I just want you to find Johnny. Whatever it costs, I'll pay it. I just want you to find him."

I certainly liked the sound of that. And with a couple of my old law enforcement connections still intact, I'd probably be able to run him down in no time.

"Worst case," I said with a pained grimace, "he could be dead or in prison."

She flashed the look again, so I moved to the next item on my list. "I'll have my secretary print out a contract for your signature. And I'll need you to write down everything you know about Jimmy."

"Johnny."

"Sorry, Johnny. Including his birthdate, height, weight, known addresses, and any ID numbers you can find; social, driver's, medical, military. Oh, and I'll need a recent photo of him."

Elaina looked overwhelmed. "Most of that stuff, if it even exists, is going to be in storage somewhere in my parents' house."

"Can you get into their place?"

She nodded. "I think they had a hidden key."

While Elaina went back for her purse, I called the office.

"McKenna Investigations, Executive Assistant Shanay Moore speak'n."

"Hey Shanay, it's me," I said. "Anything going on?"

"Nope. Same as always."

"What's with the 'Executive Assistant' thing?"

She coughed out a laugh. "Yeah, I decided to give myself a little promotion. Sounds a lot better than plain ol' secretary."

"Huh. Well, I need you to fax a standard contract to me on my boat. The client's name is Elaina Teagan, that's T-e-a-g--"

"Yeah, I got it. So, what kinda case we got us, McKenna?"

"Missing person." I said. "It's her brother, Johnny Teagan."

"I think I just nodded off for a second. Seriously, McKenna? You couldn't find us someth'n juicier, like an espionage case or a murder?"

"Just fax me the form. Thanks, Shanay."

Sha Nay Nay Moore was a drugged out street informant of mine when I worked the Bayview-Hunters Point beat. During the roughest time of my cop career, when the powers that be ran me out of the department, she was one of only a handful who stood by me. So, we kind of stuck together and I ended up giving her a job in my little PI office in Oakland. She's been clean for almost two years, and is raising a little girl on her own. I figure if she wants to change her name to Shanay and call herself my executive assistant, what do I care?

An hour later, Elaina and I turned onto Tanglewood Road in Berkeley—a stone's throw from the stately Claremont Hotel. Being near the campus again brought me back to my college days at Cal, and I was about to mention my football scholarship to Elaina when she pointed to the left.

"It's that house," she said. "You can pull into the driveway."

One look at the place and I wanted to kick myself for not having charged her more. But she'd already signed the contract, so I kept my mouth closed and just followed her up the walkway toward the palatial estate.

She checked around the door frame, under a flower pot on the porch, and then around the side of the house to a brick patio. Again she lifted the plant containers, finally locating the spare house key.

We stood in a large foyer, with a living room to the left and huge dining room to the right. Both had high ceilings with heavy chandeliers, hardwood floors, and built-in oak bookcases and wall cabinets. Farther to the left was a large kitchen and butler's pantry, with French doors leading out to a small patio.

"The bedrooms are upstairs, but what I think you're looking for might be in the cellar."

She led me past an office, then down a narrow stairway to a musty basement. One entire wall held a workbench full of tools, many of which were suspended from hooks around the room. A rack with cardboard boxes looked promising, until I saw they were labeled with things like Christmas lights, extension cords, tax records, and family pictures. Elaina dug through the photo box and came up with a 5x7 of Johnny in his Marine Corps dress blues. She said the picture was a few years old, but that he still looked the same.

I asked her to hold it under the light and I took a picture of it with my phone. Might come in handy later, I thought.

"What about your brother's bedroom?" I asked. "Could he have kept important paperwork there?"

"Possible." She turned out the lights behind us as we climbed the stairs to the main level. "But I'm pretty sure my parents emptied and repainted it when he left for college."

The first floor study was off to my left, and I noticed an open window. Closing it out of habit, I knew that burglars sometimes use obituaries and death notices to target unoccupied homes. Though it contained mostly antiques, I figured a place like theirs could be a thief's treasure trove.

As we ascended the main staircase, I noticed a chair on a track that ran all the way up to the second floor.

"It's a Stair Lift," said Elaina. "My dad had it installed after my mother's hip replacement."

I wanted to try it out to see if it would help my knee, but I resisted the urge.

In the hallway at the top of the stairs was a framed, autographed photo of Bill and Hillary Clinton, which I assumed was a testament to how well connected Elaina's parents had been.

Johnny's room was off to the right.

"It used to be a mess in here," Elaina laughed. "He had his drum set over there, a mountain bike on a rack on this wall, and he even had a weight bench and all his weights in the room."

You wouldn't have known it. The space now had a feminine bedroom set, and the walls were adorned with white wainscoting against periwinkle blue flowered wallpaper. Nothing of Johnny's had been spared during the remodel.

We were about to leave when I noticed a closet, partially obscured by the open bedroom door. Inside, sat a solitary plastic container about the size of a carry-on suitcase.

I looked at Elaina.

"Bet that's it," she said.

Dragging the box to the center of the room, I opened it to find a half-dozen neatly indexed folders and envelopes. They stood upright, so it seemed a simple task to locate and pull out those that appeared important.

The files held nothing more recent than old military enlistment papers. Stuffed in a small box at the bottom of the container was a red, white, and blue military ribbon—the kind that sits over the uniform breast pocket. Having no idea what it signified, I unclipped it from the tiny plastic box it was set in, and snapped a photo of it on my phone. Then I clipped it back into the box.

Another file held paystubs from years past, and a third contained high school and college transcripts. Both of them yielded Johnny's Social Security and driver's license numbers—which officially secured my investigation into the *piece-of-cake* category.

His social would show recent employer information, and the driver's license would list his current place of residence. Not quite as momentous as bank statements, but still good news for me.

Trying to conceal my exuberance, I frowned around the rest of the room as if there was more to be found. My biggest challenge was going to be not finding the kid so quickly that I screwed myself out of a big payday at the end of the job.

Then, as I stood up, I heard the tinkling of breaking glass.

CHAPTER 5

The shattering window was followed a fraction of a second later by the crack of a rifle shot. I reacted even before I'd consciously made sense of what was happening. "Get down!" I yelled, bear hugging Elaina to the floor beneath me.

Suddenly, the room erupted in pandemonium. The rat-tat-tat of automatic weapon fire reverberated off the walls as broken glass and pieces of sheetrock flew in every direction.

Seeing an ornate chandelier dangling precariously above us, I bulldozed Elaina across the floor away from it. Seconds later, another volley of gunfire blew it into a hailstorm of leaded crystal shards.

With all of my weight on Elaina, I took out my cell phone and dialed 9-1-1.

"What's happening?" cried Elaina.

"Somebody's shooting at us."

The emergency call-taker was on the line now, and had heard my response.

"Who?" came her voice in my ear. "What's your location?"

"Tanglewood Road," I said. "Number 26. Rifle fire coming from the northeast into the second floor of the house."

Another volley of gunshots peppered the walls and a bookcase in the hall. More shooting followed, which I'm sure the dispatcher could hear. The rounds left a trail of holes across the wall and out into the hallway where the Clinton photo now lay shattered on the floor.

"We're on our way," she said. "Can you describe the suspects?"

I paused, not about to stick my head up to look. "Uh, no. But I don't think they're Democrats."

Elaina turned to look at me, but said nothing.

"Stay right where you are," ordered the dispatcher. "And don't go outside."

"No shit."

Sirens sounded in the distance, and that was about when the shooting ceased. By the time I gathered the nerve to glance out the window, the attackers were gone. Neighbors cautiously inched their way out of their homes, like turtles from their shells, to see the first of many police cars skidding into the area.

I didn't want us to be victims of friendly fire, so I told Elaina to stay on the ground until the cops cleared the house.

Once satisfied that the threat was gone, an ambulance and fire engine that had been staged on Claremont Avenue were allowed up to the driveway. By that time, the police had searched through the house, finding me and Elaina dogpiled on the bedroom floor.

As they walked us outside to be checked for injuries, I whispered into Elaina's ear. "Don't say anything to them. Just act like you're too traumatized to answer their questions."

"It won't be an act," she said.

Elaina played her part to perfection and never said a word. Furnishing all of the answers myself, I stuck to the story that I was Elaina's neighbor, there to help sort through her deceased parents' belongings.

"So, you can't think of any reason someone would try to kill you?" asked a plainclothes detective.

I shrugged. "Nothing."

He and his partner were clearly frustrated, and finally gave up after nearly an hour of questioning. I saw in their eyes that they knew there was more to it and didn't believe a word I'd told them. I certainly would have felt the same back when I was a cop.

A team of crime scene technicians had descended on the place by then, and were setting up camp like they'd be there for a while. Elaina gave the detective the house key and asked that they lock up when they were done.

I realized that in the confusion of the shooting, I had left the papers up in Johnny's room. Without them I'd have none of the identifying numbers I needed. The only thing I'd actually taken was his military service ribbon—which I had inadvertently stuffed into my pocket when the shooting started. The ribbon was useless to me, but the paperwork I'd left upstairs meant everything.

"I need to get back inside for a sec," I told the detective. "Forgot something upstairs in the bedroom."

He shook his head. "It's a crime scene now. You'll have to wait until we've finished."

We stared at each other, and I knew this was payback of sorts for not being truthful during questioning. Nobody had been killed, or even injured, and he could have let me through if he wanted to.

I stared, and he stared back—two rams about to butt heads. Then I smiled and nodded, and he returned the nod.

Whether or not he knew I was a former San Francisco cop, I couldn't be sure. But they had copied down my ID, and by this time had likely run the license plate of my Jeep parked out front. A simple Google search would have given the detective the whole sordid story of my ousting. It's what I would have done if I were him.

As we drove out of the neighborhood, I noticed a foursome of investigators standing on the hillside behind a house across the street. My guess was that they'd located the sniper's nest, from which the shooters had launched their attack. The hill was heavily treed, which would have afforded ample cover, concealment, and ease of escape. *The suspects definitely had training*.

Heading back to the yacht harbor in Alameda, I found myself eyeing Elaina the same way the detective had eyed me—wondering what she was holding back. There had to be much more to this case than she'd let on.

I decided not to mention it to Elaina, but I had every intention to go back alone for the papers I'd left inside her parents' house.

CHAPTER 6

JR instinctively took cover behind the brick retaining wall next to the house. It gave him the time he needed to identify where the shots were coming from.

The rapid bark of an automatic weapon had been accompanied by shattering glass, yet he could see nothing from the back side of the house. Realizing the shooters were on the Tanglewood side, JR sprinted through a pedestrian path on Garber Street heading in the opposite direction of the threat.

JR's long dormant military training had taken over, as if his brain had been pulled apart. Suddenly it felt as if he had one foot in his old neighborhood and the other in Kabul. His mind flashed back to July 17, 2014—his 23rd birthday.

His unit was detailed to provide a security escort for the Afghan Airforce during an early morning troop transport. Their course took them on *Route Irish*, the military's nickname for Darulaman Road—the most heavily traveled artery from the military training center in the south to Kabul Airport.

It was still dark when the convoy approached airport grounds. The early morning stillness was suddenly rocked by a car bomb, immediately followed by a barrage of gunfire. The airport and the transport convoy were under heavy attack by the enemy, who had barricaded themselves in a construction site the night before.

The ensuing firefight lasted four hours, and only ended when all five insurgents were killed—one blowing himself up in a bomb vest and the others shot by coalition forces. The battle was the most intense action JR saw. Only a few months after that, his transfer came though taking him out of Afghanistan.

JR finally slowed when he got to a small park a few blocks from his parents' house, called Monkey Island.

Having lost phone contact with Mai when the shots rang out, he sat down next to an oak tree to call her back.

"What happened?" she asked.

"Somebody was shooting."

"At you?"

"I'm not sure," he said. "But they must have been." He paused as two police cruisers rushed past the park with lights and sirens. "I don't know exactly what's going on or why, but it's time for me to get out of here."

"Good. I don't like being back here alone--"

JR was deep in thought, still trying to figure out what had happened. "They had to have been coming after me," he interrupted. "It couldn't have just been a coincidence. I'll get to the airport and try to catch the first flight back."

"Then what?"

"Then... I don't know. I'll think of something."

"If they found you in California, they can probably find you just as easily back here." Mai was generally soft spoken, almost to the point of subservience. But she could also be direct, even insistent, especially when it came to protecting JR. "I'm not going to stand-by and let you turn yourself in, if that's what you're thinking of doing. You're being hunted, and I don't trust anybody with your safety."

It wasn't the place or time for this discussion, thought JR, even though he knew she was right. And there was still another looming issue—one he hadn't yet broken to Mai.

"What?" she asked, as if reading his thoughts. "You're quiet, and that means there's more. Something you're not telling me."

JR had started up Avalon Avenue toward his parked rental car. "It's nothing. We'll talk once I get back."

She was about to press the issue, but stopped herself. It wasn't in her nature to nag, yet she was determined to get it out of JR upon his return.

Several police cars and a fire engine had knotted traffic further up Claremont. JR could see officers on foot, checking driveways and yards but he was far enough from the activity that nobody paid him any attention.

During the drive across the Bay Bridge toward SFO, JR thought about his predicament. There were so many aspects to it, not the least of which were his feelings for Mai. He had fallen hard for her, and he knew she felt the same about him. JR didn't want to be with anyone else, and couldn't see himself in a life without her—which made the discussion he had been avoiding all the more crucial.

She would be waiting when he got off the plane. JR knew that Mai would be as eager for the answer to her question as she'd be to welcome him back. Probably even more so. That gave him the five-hour flight to figure out what he was going to tell her.

With luck, she would be the *only one* waiting for him.

CHAPTER 7

It was after 8 p.m. when I stepped quietly out of Wanderlust onto the dock. I paused halfway up the ramp, glancing at the buttery light reflecting off the water beneath Elaina's boat. Continuing through the gate, I hurried from the marina into the parking lot before she could spot me.

The Berkeley cops would have finished collecting evidence and diagramming the crime scene by now, and I knew that the day shift had signed off-duty for the night.

Parking my car near a sandwich shop two blocks away, I flipped up my sweatshirt hood and strolled casually past the house. It was dark and quiet, which I hoped was a good omen.

I took one last look up and down the block before ducking into the driveway. Checking under the flower pots, I came up empty. It was then that I remembered Elaina giving the detective the house key. *Son-of-a-bitch!*

Thinking back, I didn't recall an alarm in the house. So after ringing the doorbell to make certain nobody was still inside, I used my elbow to smash a 4-inch square of glass out of the patio door. I waited in the dark for any sign of activity in the house or from the neighbors, but reassuring stillness hung in the air.

Silently, I reached through, unlocked the door, and let myself in. I stepped carefully through the dark house, then felt my way upstairs. The floor was still littered with debris from the shooting, which made it all the more difficult to navigate in the dark. At one point I stumbled on what felt like a broken length of doorjamb, twisting my bad knee. Cursing under my breath, I was equally annoyed for having forgotten to put on my brace before leaving the boat.

Streetlamps in front of the house provided ambient light in Johnny's room, allowing me to discern the outline of his file box. The flashlight app that Shanay had loaded onto my cell phone made it a simple task to locate the paperwork I'd forgotten earlier. As long as I was there, I decided to take another look through the container—which worked to my benefit. In the last unmarked file folder, I found a single manila envelope that read: Wells Fargo.

Stepping over to the window—or what was left of it—I stared up at the spot on the hillside where the police had searched. It still eluded me as to how the shooting might be connected to my missing person.

Stuffing the papers and the envelope into the back of my pants, I turned off the cell phone light and limped out of the room.

On the track at the top of the stairs sat the chair lift, which, in my impaired condition, proved more than I could resist. Reactivating the flashlight feature, I found a small remote, sat down on the seat, and pressed the down arrow.

The backward facing chair began its gentle slide down the track, doing the work that my sore knee would have had to do.

I had just begun the slow descent when my phone rang. Seeing that it was my wife, I answered it. "Hello, Doris? I meant to call you."

"Oh?" I couldn't tell if it was a sarcastic 'oh', so I waited for her to say something else. "I haven't gotten my check yet," she finally said.

"Yeah, it's on my *to do* list. I promise. In fact, I'm sending a little bit extra for Bridget's birthday. I wasn't sure what to get her, so I figured cash is always--"

"You're not going to see her?" It hadn't taken Doris long to start in on me—no surprise there. "Thirteen is a big deal to a young girl," she said. "Do you think sending her money is going to make her feel valued and loved?"

"I know. Yes, I mean no, I'm not *just* sending her money. I'm planning on seeing her, too." I took a breath. "I just--"

"Where are you, Danny? What's that grinding sound?"

I quickly used the remote to stop the chair. "It's nothing. Anyway, I'm in the middle of a job. Can we talk about this later?"

"Fine, whatever. Just remember to come by on Sunday to see Bridget. It would mean a lot to her."

I gave Doris my word that I'd be there for the party.

She hadn't been keen on me just stopping by the house in the past, so I knew this was important—maybe to Doris as much as to Bridge. But I felt like it could also be an opportunity for me. As I sat on the motorized chair, paused halfway between the first and second floor, I imagined the possibility of moving back home. I pictured us being a family again.

Maybe Doris was starting to soften to the idea.

Switching the remote back on, the lift continued its downward trajectory. It was definitely an unhurried ride, and I figured that I could have gone up and down the stairs twice in the time it was taking. Even with my bum knee.

As I approached the bottom, the gentle whirring of the motor grew louder under my weight.

Unfortunately for me, it had drowned out the sound of someone entering the house through the French door I'd broken.

The ride came to a cushioned stop at the foot of the stairs. Still facing backwards, I used the handrail to pull myself to a standing position—just in time to hear footsteps directly behind me.

I wheeled around, and was immediately blinded by a powerful beam of light. I realized that the shooters must have still been watching the house, and were now going to finish the job they started.

With my hands outstretched in a futile attempt to block the light, I tensed my body in anticipation of a bullet.

CHAPTER 8

"Don't move," commanded a voice behind the beam of light.

I squinted toward him, but all I could see were ghostly yellow shapes that had been burned into my retinas.

Then other voices all at once:

"Interlace your fingers behind your head!"

"Is there anyone else in the house?"

"Keep your hands where I can see them!"

"Do you have any weapons?"

"Turn around!"

"I said don't move!"

Confusion—the telltale sign of cops. Somewhat relieved but not wanting to be another shooting statistic, I decided that it was best to do nothing. A second later I was steer wrestled onto the ground.

"Watch the knee!" I yelled, but to no avail.

When my vision returned, I found myself standing handcuffed in the foyer. Three uniformed Berkeley officers were staggered around me; one calling in my ID on his radio, another holding a flashlight under his arm, and a third seemingly captivated by the first edition books on the shelf next to him.

"I was the victim of an assault earlier today," I said. "I'm sure the detective in charge will verify that I have permission to be here."

Although ignoring me, they must have gotten through to somebody who pulled the prior incident report. I heard a monotone voice reciting my personal information as well as Elaina's over the air. The dispatcher also mentioned a Detective Nate Howard, which I made a mental note of.

One of the cops dialed a number on his cell, and I assumed he was calling Howard at home. But I was wrong.

"Hello, is this Elaina Teagan?" (pause) "This is Officer Velasquez, Berkeley PD. We have a Daniel Patrick McKenna detained inside your parents' home on Tanglewood Road." (pause) "Yes, he's alone." (pause) "Uh, no, apparently he was riding a motorized lift down the stairs."

I rolled my eyes.

"No ma'am, we believe he broke a window to gain entry."

Stretching my head toward the officer's phone, I yelled, "It was only one small pane of the patio door!"

An angry tug yanked me backward.

"Yes, I see." The officer glanced at me. "Yes, I understand. Thank you."

He ended the call and nodded to the cop standing behind me. I felt the cuffs release, and sensed a downward notch in their bearing and attitudes.

"You can go, McKenna."

My sweatshirt had covered the paperwork stuffed into my pants, and the officers hadn't noticed them when checking me for weapons. I nodded my *see-ya-later* as I hustled out the door, then down the driveway and back to my car.

It was just after midnight when I entered my passcode at the gate and stepped onto the ramp. I could see Elaina's outline, wrapped in a heavy jacket, waiting for me on the deck of my sailboat. She'd have questions, and I needed to come up with some quick answers.

"I think I need a drink," I said as I climbed aboard. "You want to come out of the cold and join me?"

She flipped a lock of her hair back, then followed me down the companionway in silence.

Tossing the papers onto the table, I said, "I wanted to get back there before this stuff got seized or misplaced."

"Look, McKenna," she started.

"You can call me Danny."

"Okay, *Danny* . . . If we're going to trust each other, I also have to know that you're telling me everything."

I raised my palms. "No, no, it's nothing like that. I would have told you what I was doing, but you had been through enough for one day. Plus, I wasn't about to put you in any more danger."

"What about you?"

"It goes with the job, Sweetheart," I said, giving it my best Bogart impression. "Besides, it's what you're paying me for."

Her gaze shifted to the envelope lying next to the papers. "And what's this?"

I shrugged. "Could be something helpful, or it could be nothing." I dumped its contents onto the table. "Looks like banking papers, maybe an account or something. Wells Fargo in Oakland." I shook the envelope again and a single key dropped out.

"It's for a safe deposit box," Elaina said.

I glanced over the papers again. "Says box number 259 is rented under your brother's name."

She frowned at the key. "Won't do us any good without Johnny there to sign for it."

It was true. Bank procedure generally required the box renter's ID and signature, which got me wondering about what mitigating circumstances could alter their policy.

Pouring each of us a drink, I joined Elaina at the table. It's a tight galley and the L-shaped bench seats barely fit two adults comfortably. After a short silence, we both started to say something at the same time and then stopped. Suddenly my cell phone chimed a text message alert. I glanced at it then quickly put it back in my pocket.

"Ex-wife?" Elaina asked.

"Yeah. Well, not exactly. We're only separated."

She nodded.

"By the way," I said. "How did you know that?"

"Mr. Phillips, the harbormaster."

"Cliff. That figures." I laughed, but wondered in what context the subject had come up. Had she inquired to Cliff about my status and availability? Maybe Elaina's mourning was over, and maybe I wasn't too old for her after all.

CHAPTER 9

March weather in the Bay Area can be unpredictable, and I awoke in the middle of the night to the sound of rain pelting the deck above me. I also awoke alone, and with a tinge of a headache.

After having only one drink together, Elaina had chosen to return to her sailboat. In hindsight, we were both all the better for it. To be perfectly honest, she hadn't really given any signals that there could be something more.

With little else to do, I'd poured myself another glass and stayed up until 3 a.m. looking through Johnny's transcripts and employment records. I had checked his name again, this time using his birthdate and middle name, but still had no luck. No social media accounts, and nothing on any of the search engines.

I was in no hurry to get out of bed that morning. Once I was finally up, I called the office to let Shanay know I wouldn't be coming in. My second call was to my old partner, Linh Phú, who was now assigned to the Bay Area Drug Task Force operating out of the Federal Building downtown.

"Hello, Inspector," she answered. "It's good to hear from you."

I told her that I'd been meaning to call her sooner, but that work had been a real bear. I don't think she believed me. Then I mentioned the case I was working on, and sheepishly asked if she could run the guy for me.

"That'll cost you lunch," she said with a laugh. "Or at least a cup of coffee."

"You have my word," I said. "So, the name of my missing person is Jonathan Roy Teagan. Also goes by Johnny." I gave Linh his birthdate, driver's license number, and social. I also told her there was a good chance he was wanted by the police, or at least had a substantial criminal record.

"Not a problem," she said, agreeing to call or text me as soon as she came up with anything. Then, almost apologetically, she added, "Oh, and we just got word that Mike Prowse has been promoted to captain."

I groaned. "Yeah, my lovely wife texted me the news last night. Do you know where he'll be assigned yet?"

"That's the worst part," said Phú. "He'll oversee the inspectors, which means he's now my new boss."

It felt like a double gut punch. The guy had worn his lips raw sucking up to Greg Dowd, who was now Chief of Police. But Prowse had been in Internal Affairs for as long as I could remember. He'd spent almost no time in uniform, and he'd never investigated anything other than cops. Between the two of them—Prowse and Dowd—they had effectively bounced me out of the department. But that wasn't the worst part. Mike Prowse had started dating my wife after we split up.

I hated the guy.

"Inspector McKenna, are you still there?"

"Yeah, Linh. I'm here." I tried to shake off the anger. "Anyway, I truly appreciate your help on this. And we'll get together for lunch as soon as I wrap up this case—which shouldn't take more than a few days."

I sat in the cabin after we hung up. As I listened to the rain, I thought about how cruel and unfair life was. I'd been unjustly railroaded out of the police inspector job that I had worked so hard to attain, and the two cockroaches who did it both got promoted.

Dropping down to the floor, I started doing pushups. I kept doing them until my arms turned to spaghetti and I couldn't lift myself off the ground. The pushups hadn't burned off all of my frustration, so I rolled over and began doing sit-ups. When my stomach ached and I thought I was going to heave, I stopped and took a shower.

Around 10 o'clock, Elaina came over. "Danny, are you up?"

"C'mon down," I yelled.

I was sitting at the table, going over Johnny's paperwork when she made her way down the steps.

"That's where you were when I left," she said. "I hope you haven't been there all night."

I laughed. "I'm just waiting for word from one of my old partners. Do you want some coffee?"

Just as she told me no, my cell phone vibrated across the table. Linh Phú's name was on the screen, and she started before I could say hello.

"Inspector?" She said. "I ran your guy Teagan, and something's not quite right."

"What do you mean, 'not right'?"

"I mean, there are no records."

"Of course there are," I said. "I gave you his Social Security and driver's license numbers."

"Yes, but there are no records that show those numbers ever existed. Are you certain that you read them accurately?"

"Uh-huh, in fact I double checked them. They have to be in the system. He's used them for college, and for jobs, and even to get into the military."

Linh was silent. "Unless they've all been deleted."

After I got off the phone with Phú, I relayed the conversation to Elaina.

"How can that be?" she asked with a blank expression.

"I don't know, but it isn't what I had expected." I thought for a minute. It would be next to impossible for a person to have all of their government-issued identification expunged. An entire lifetime of personal records and documents, gone? *Absurd.*

"Maybe there is a logical explanation in his safe deposit box."

"But neither of us are authorized to access it."

"True," I said. "But I had an idea last night when I was looking over his papers."

I went into the stateroom and dug through my drawers. Finding the elastic bandage that I used on my knee before I bought the brace, I returned to the dinette table. Then I pulled out Johnny's papers, which now included a small notebook of mine. I flipped it open, and Elaina stared down at my writing. On the pages was line after line of her brother's name.

"I copied your brother's name exactly as he'd signed it on his enlistment papers: John R. Teagan."

She twisted her head to see both his original signature and my attempts to copy it. Then she lifted one eyebrow. "To the average person, your forgery doesn't look too bad. But these bankers are trained to spot frauds."

I nodded. "That's what the ACE bandage is for. Grab his papers and the deposit box key. You're coming with me."

CHAPTER 10

That particular Wells Fargo branch was in Oakland's Montclair District, an upscale neighborhood in the hills above the Warren Freeway. We sat in the lot until lunchtime, figuring that more employees would be on break and lines would be longer.

With the elastic bandage wrapped in a figure 8 sling around my right arm and neck, we hurried through the rain and into the bank. Adding a bit of a limp once inside the door, I hoped for an extra touch of sympathy. Elaina held my other arm to guide me to the back end of the customer line. When it was my turn, I stepped slowly up to one of the two manned windows.

"I'd like to access my safe deposit box," I told the young woman.

She smiled and then eyed the line of customers behind me. Then glancing behind her, she said, "I'm so sorry, but if you can wait ten or fifteen minutes the operations officer will be back from lunch. She'll be more than happy to help you."

I grimaced. "I'm afraid that won't work. Unfortunately, I don't have that kind of time today."

Her jaw clenched as she tried her best to maintain the smile. "Certainly, sir. What's your account number?"

Glancing at Johnny's bank papers, I read off the number to her.

She frowned at the screen. "I show that account closed, sir."

It was a hiccup I hadn't anticipated. "Uh, yes." I motioned with the papers. "I had to close my account, but I kept my safe deposit box. It's box number 259."

She nodded. "Mr. Teagan?"

"Yes, ma'am."

"I see you paid for the deposit box in advance for the next ten years?"

I swallowed and nodded.

She smiled again, sliding a card and pen across the counter. "I need a signature here, and I'll need to see your ID."

Giving it a labored effort, I signed the card. "Sorry, it's the best I can do," I said, nodding toward my sling.

"I understand." She turned to the next teller. "Eric, I'll be helping a customer with his safe deposit box."

Eric frowned up at the line of customers. Clearly unhappy, he said nothing.

She slid her window closed and motioned me toward the far end of the bank. Elaina hadn't said anything up to that point, and took my arm to guide me across the lobby.

"Maybe she forgot about the ID," Elaina whispered to me.

But when we arrived at the solid access door to the safe deposit vault, the teller turned to me. "Your ID, sir?"

Offering a disarming laugh, I said, "Unfortunately, my wallet was stolen last night. That's why I need to get into my box."

Her face twisted, and I could see the derailment coming in her eyes.

"We've just come from the police department," said Elaina. "They have the robbery report, if you'd like to call them. I mean, seriously, hasn't Johnny been through enough?"

I held up the box rental receipt and the key. "All I need are my insurance papers out of the box so I can get medical attention."

She looked back at the line of customers, then at Eric—the solo teller she'd left to help them. Then she studied the signature card again.

"Fine," the teller finally said. Leading me inside the vault room, she motioned with a hand for Elaina to wait in the lobby. The teller used her master key to match mine in the box's lock, and then she slid the narrow canister out. Setting it on a table in the center of the room, she said, "I'll be right outside. Just press the buzzer when you're done."

I thanked her and waited until she'd left before opening the lid.

"What the hell?" I said to myself as I stood there staring into the box. "I don't get it."

A different teller let me out of the vault room—apparently back from her lunch break. I nodded my thanks, and crossed the lobby to Elaina. She was seated on a couch, reading a magazine. I'd tucked everything into my pants pockets, so there was no outward sign of what I'd removed from the box.

"Well?" said Elaina.

"Let's get out of here first."

We got into my Jeep and I pulled out everything that had been in the box. She stared at it with the same bewilderment as I had.

"His passport," I said, setting it on the dash. "And his wallet." I opened it. "...containing his driver's license and all of his bank cards."

Elaina examined each one, setting them next to his passport. "Why in the world would Johnny rent a safe deposit box for ten years in advance, and then leaves all of his identification inside it?"

I thought about it for a minute, the windshield wipers beating rhythmically back and forth. "The only thing I can think of is that Johnny doesn't want to be found."

CHAPTER 11

That night I tried the Swedish Meatballs with pasta. I was pissed about the extra calories I'd allowed myself the night before, and figured that this diet dinner would make up for last night's scotches.

Afterwards, I turned out the galley lights and put on some soft jazz music. Lying on my sofa—which doubled as a bed when Bridge stayed over—I thought about the case, which was getting more and more confusing by the minute. It wasn't turning out to be the *slam-dunk* I'd anticipated.

I imagined the reasons that someone would want to disappear, the most obvious being that he had killed someone or maybe even a lot of someones. So, it would make sense that he's running from the police. Or, perhaps the guy is avoiding a scorned lover or a paternity suit. My musings were suddenly impinged upon by a new realization.

Throwing on my jacket, I carefully made my way across the wet dock. I called out to Elaina from dockside and she motioned me into the cabin.

"What did you figure out?" She passed me a hand towel, which I used to wipe myself down before taking off my jacket.

"Did you say that Johnny left right after your parents' funeral?"

"Actually, he took off in the middle of the services," she said.

"And then you got a letter from him a couple of days later?"

Elaina nodded.

I scratched my head. "How was Johnny able to travel without any credit cards or identification?"

"I wouldn't think he'd be able to," said Elaina.

"Hmmm." I leaned back and closed my eyes—the raindrops tapping at the hatch like a gameshow clock. "Did Johnny ever go by any other names?"

"No, never."

"I guess he could have pre-booked his travel," I said. "Before he dumped his bank cards. But ever since 9/11..."

"He'd still need his ID to fly, right?" Elaina gazed across the cabin at me with the innocent curiosity of a doe.

"Right." I checked the time and it was only 8 o'clock. Scrolling through my phone's contact list, I found Sarah Brooks' number and hit dial.

"As I live and breathe," she answered. "Please tell me you're not in jail again."

"No way," I said. "How have you been?"

Brooks laughed. "Cut the shit, McKenna. You're not calling me at this time of night to find out how I've been. What can I do for you?"

Now I laughed. "Fair enough. I'm actually working a case that's got me stumped."

I explained how all of Johnny's identification records appeared to have been purged, and that we suspected he'd gone into hiding under an assumed identity.

"If I give you a name, can you access TSA records to see if he flew out of San Francisco or Oakland on . . ." I turned to Elaina. "What was the date of the funeral service?"

"Saturday, March 28th," she said.

"The 28th," I repeated into the phone. "I assume that the services were held in the morning . . ."

Elaina nodded.

"So I'm guessing that his flight would have been sometime that afternoon or evening," I said to Brooks.

Elaina nodded again.

I spelled out Johnny's full name and gave Brooks his date of birth. I also told her that I had very little to go on, and that this was only a vague hunch.

"It's all good," she said. "I'll run the dude eight ways to Sunday, and see if we can't find out what he's up to."

After we disconnected, Elaina said, "You sure know a lot of police people."

"Sarah's actually an investigator with U.S. Customs and Border Protection."

"Oh." Her eyes widened.

"Yeah, we worked a big case together back when I was with SFPD." I saw that Elaina was impressed. "International theft ring, multiple homicides, the works."

Elaina grimaced and shook her head, and I realized that it was too graphic for her affluent Berkeley upbringing.

"Sorry," I said. Then changing the subject, "Fingers crossed that Brooks can come up with something to help us locate Johnny."

In addition to his mysterious actions, there remained the overarching fact that someone had tried to take out me and Elaina—which I still hadn't been able to fit into any of this. Except that now I felt fairly certain, whoever it was had mistaken me for Johnny.

I had given my TSA records hunch about twenty-to-one odds, but if Brooks struck out, I had absolutely no plan B.

CHAPTER 12

I lingered in the main salon, trying to make something more of the conversation with Elaina. I'd hoped that she'd reciprocate the offer of a drink, but she only yawned and glanced at her watch. I finally got the hint and left. Hustling back through the rain, I reasoned that she'd done my calorie count a favor.

The weather had improved by morning, enough that I was able to have my coffee topside. Other than Cliff trying to sweep the wet leaves off of the fuel dock, I was the only one out.

My phone's muffled ringtone shook me out of the tranquil moment, and I hustled down into the cabin to get it. Because of the unpredictable reception at the marina, I'm complacent about keeping it with me. Anyway, I was thrilled to see that Sarah Brooks was already calling me back.

"Sarah," I said, "give me some good news."

"You were right about this Teagan guy. He's a freak'n ghost."

"Right?" I sat down.

"And there's nothing in any of our databases that show he ever existed. Even his passport information has been erased."

My mind was spinning, trying to grab onto something that made sense. "Have you ever seen anything like that before?"

"Only once," she said. "It was a woman in witness protection."

I was silent again.

"So, that got me thinking." I could hear Brooks tapping on a keyboard. "Ran the dude on STILLS, under the name you gave me--"

"STILLS?"

"*Secure Travel Identity Linking System*," she said.

"Huh? Never heard of it."

"NSA implemented it after 9/11." More keyboarding in the background. "Yeah, it's supposed to automatically match passenger IDs with method of payment. Apparently it culls through bank accounts, credit cards, PayPal, money orders, whatever, to make sure we don't have another *Mustafa al Shithead* taking over one of our planes."

"So you found him on that system?"

"Uh, no." Brooks paused. "But, here's what I know about new witness protection identities. They usually have the protected person keep their original first name, so as not to make them too confused. Sometimes even their same initials—first and last."

"Okay." I was hoping this was leading to something.

"So, I ran another check using every combination of Johnny Boy's initials and came up with a possible... I repeat, it's only a possible."

"I'm listening," I said.

"Fella by the name of JR Travis left out of SFO that Saturday night at 10:30 p.m., United flight 1137 nonstop to Baltimore/Washington International. Arrived 6:54 the next morning."

"Uh-huh, and the guy has the same three initials," I said. "Is that it?"

"C'mon, McKenna. Give me some credit." Papers shuffled in the background. "Here's where STILLS comes in handy. It flagged the dude, because the tickets were not purchased on his credit card. They were bought by... Who-do-ya-think?"

"John Gotti?"

"The U.S. Marshals Service," she said. "The same agency that administers the Federal Witness Protection Program."

I thought for a second. "They also have a fugitive detail that hunts down wanted suspects. Could they have taken him into custody for something and are bringing him back to face charges?"

"Well, I guess that's possible too," she said. "But there's one other tidbit you might want to factor in. I've been told that the witness protection program has an indoctrination safe house where every protected person and family starts out. A secure building in a highly secretive location that only a handful in the Marshals Service know the exact location of."

"And?"

"It's rumored to be in Washington D.C."

I thanked Brooks for starting her day early for me, and for going the extra mile. It wasn't a certainty that JR Travis was Jonathan Roy Teagan, but if nothing else it was an intriguing coincidence.

Grabbing the photo of brother Johnny in his marine blues, I slipped out of the marina before the lights came on in Elaina's boat. It wasn't that I was hiding anything, but I did want to do some of my own investigating. Besides, where I was headed was going to be a crap shoot as to how welcome I'd be. And if things didn't go well, I didn't want to embarrass myself in front of Elaina.

Forty-five minutes later I pulled into the parking garage at SFO. Even though the airport is nearly ten miles outside of San Francisco, the SFPD provides security and has a bureau there. My hope was that I might still be able to find a friendly face.

On the third level of the parking garage is a fenced section—free to law enforcement, which I sheepishly took advantage of. I then headed for the International Terminal where I milled around until I spotted a young uniformed officer on a police bicycle.

Introducing myself as a former SFPD homicide inspector, I asked if he could escort me past security, to the 5th floor Field Operations office. He radioed someone for permission, and they must have approved it.

While I waited outside the glass partition, I saw a photo of the deputy chief in charge of airport operations. Tiffany Blythe had been Park District watch commander the morning of my first homicide case. It looked like the recent SFPD promotional dominos had fallen in her favor.

Blythe swaggered out to greet me in her trademark John Wayne manner, and I remembered to prepare myself for her grip.

"Not sure if you remember me," I said. "Danny McKenna."

She laughed heartily. "The homicide in the park," she said. "And who could forget the headlines when you were arrested for murder?"

I tried to laugh, though it didn't come out as hardy. "The murder I was cleared of," I reminded her.

"Right. So, what can I do ya for?" She braced her hands on her hips.

I explained that I had since started a private investigations business and was looking into a missing person case. It would have been a mistake for me to mention anything about the witness protection angle, because she would have frozen solid in her tracks. So, I simply gave her the name JR Travis.

"We believe he may have boarded United 1137 on March 28th at 2230 hours," I said.

Blythe hesitated, and then brought me inside to her office where she made a call. A minute later a young man stepped in. He was tall and thin, and wore a loose fitting suit.

"Walter Pang," he said, shaking my hand.

Blythe said, "Walt is the sergeant in charge of the Threat Assessment Unit. I assume you'll want to take a look at the boarding area CCTV footage."

I nodded.

"Then Walt's your man," said Blythe.

I thanked her and followed Pang down the hall to a large room with cubicles arranged in tiers similar to stadium seats. It was dark, lit only by the glow of monitors at each workstation. At the front of the room were two giant screens. Both were black at the moment.

Pang had slipped on a headset when we entered the room and was already talking into it, repeating the flight information that I'd given to his boss.

He turned to me. "Flight in question departed out of Terminal #3. It was delayed fourteen minutes, and took off on runway 1R."

I started to search my pockets for a pen and paper.

"Not to worry," said Pang. "I'll have it all printed out for you."

"And the video footage?" I asked.

"Main screen left," he said. "Coming up now. CCTV of Boarding Area E, Gate 65, beginning at 2200 hours."

Slipping Johnny's military photo from my pocket, I held it at my side as I scanned the stationary view of the passengers. After a few minutes, I spotted someone in the second boarding line with similar physical characteristics.

"There," I said, pointing. "Boarding group B, third guy in line."

Suddenly the camera angle changed. It was a closer shot, facing back at the passenger line from the ramp entrance. I could see a rear view of the lady scanning the tickets, and the faces of each passenger as they passed.

"Freeze it there," said Pang into his headset. Then he turned to me. "Is that him?"

CHAPTER 13

Elaina studied the hotprint they'd made of the still shot.

"I'm, like, 99% sure," I told her. "It's just that he's wearing a baseball cap and sunglasses. That's the only uncertainty."

She set the photo down. "I think that's Johnny."

The midday sun had worked its way through the clouds, and the warmth of it felt nice as we sat on the deck of my sailboat.

"If it is your brother, that would answer a few questions." I ticked them off on my fingers. "The Marshals Service paid for his flight, which probably means he's going into protective custody. It also explains why he would leave his identification and bank cards in the safe deposit box. Maybe most importantly, it partially answers the question of why someone opened fire on us."

"We were next to the window in Johnny's bedroom," said Elaina. "Whoever my brother needs protecting from, probably thought we were Johnny."

"We need to find out what he got himself into." I reclined back on the deck chair. "He must have been involved in something pretty bad. Bad enough that the U.S. government needs him alive long enough to testify."

Elaina turned away and gazed out at the glistening water. "I'm less concerned with what he did, and more concerned with finding him alive. I won't rest until I can hug my brother and make sure he's okay."

While she went below to use the restroom, I sat thinking about her brother. I had hoped that getting a photograph of him boarding a flight to D.C. was tantamount to finding him, but it was becoming clear that Elaina wanted me to actually deliver the kid to her in a neat package with a ribbon on his head.

"It's not going to be easy," I said when she returned. "Especially if Johnny is in protective custody. The Marshals will never even admit that they have him, much less allow someone from his past to connect with him."

"What do you think it would take?"

I shrugged. "Short of going back there myself..." I glanced up to see her little doe eyes staring back at me. "Look," I said, "I have this *thing* about traveling. Did it a lot when I was a kid, and now I avoid it like the plague."

I briefly considered telling Elaina about my daughter's birthday on Sunday, but she didn't need to know details of my personal life.

"Besides," I added, "it would be a complete waste of money for me to go poking around in Washington."

"But it's my money," she said. "And we have a signed contract. I'm not paying you to tell me that you're 99% sure he's somewhere in the vicinity of the nation's capital. I'm paying you to actually find him." Suddenly, Elaina's doe eyes looked more like a Grizzly Bear's.

"Under one condition," I said. "I go alone."

She started to object and I cut her off. "I know you're a hands-on type of client, and you want to be involved in every step. But I'm going to have to approach this with shrewd, fleet footed know-how. And that can't be accomplished if you're with me."

An expression of hurt took over Elaina's face, and I saw that her hopes were being crushed.

"I promise I'll call you the moment I find something. Anything at all."

She finally agreed, and I thought I'd lift her spirits by reminding her that she owed me a drink. It seemed a lighthearted way to get her off of the discouragement track and onto the McKenna train. But she asked to take a raincheck.

Elaina left, and for the second night in a row I sat alone on my sailboat with my tail between my legs. I took a dinner from the freezer and set it on the counter. It was called Farmer's Market Pizza, and the picture on the box looked like crap. Nothing like Stefano's, our family's favorite.

Tossing it back in the freezer, I poured myself a drink instead. *Why did I ever take this case?*

CHAPTER 14

My alarm went off at 3:45 a.m., and I thought I'd died and gone to hell. After a shower, I dressed and packed a few clothes along with my trusty binoculars. Stuffed everything into a carry-on, ordered up an Uber, then scuttled up the ramp to the parking lot.

It was dark and cold and damp. There wasn't a sound in the marina except riggings clinking against sailing masts. A blue Saturn sat idling in the lot, a young man behind the wheel. Twelve minutes later, I was standing with my bag in front of Oakland Airport's Terminal 1.

My 6 a.m. flight on Delta was still scheduled for an on-time departure, so I grabbed a cup of coffee and a sweet roll. As I sat in the boarding area, I wondered how many calories it would cost me if I only ate half of it. My trip to Washington was going to be short, and I figured I could cut back on meals while I was there. Maybe my hotel would even have a gym.

Who was I kidding? My timeline was already going to be tight enough if I was going to make it back in time for the birthday party. Finding Johnny that quickly would take plenty of energy and probably a shitload of luck.

Something I'd told Elaina still troubled me. It wasn't as if I could just walk into the Marshals Service and ask if Elaina's brother was in witness protection. Even if I were still a cop, they wouldn't tell me. The key, I realized, was their indoctrination site for new protectees. Sarah Brooks had mentioned that it was somewhere in D.C.

If I could somehow find that safe house, then I could watch the place and eventually locate Johnny.

As I sipped my coffee and finished the second half of my roll, I began wondering about the information Brooks had found on the NSA's system. It occurred to me that the file may have included an address, which would definitely get me started. Still too early to call Brooks' cell, I dialed her office number instead, and left a message.

"Sarah, it's McKenna...again. I'm headed to D.C., and I need a little more help from you. The payment for JR Travis' airline ticket. I need to know the billing information, if you have it. Specifically, the address listed on whatever U.S. Marshals account his airline ticket was charged to. I'll be in the air when you get this, so leave a message or text if I don't answer. Thanks again. I owe you."

I also left a message for Shanay, letting her know that I would be in Washington D.C. for a quick meeting, and that she could leave at noon if the office was quiet. A meeting sounded more professional than what it actually was; a fishing expedition.

My last call was the one I dreaded. Staring at Doris' programmed number on my screen, I ran the script of what I would say to her. My trip to Washington was going to be short, just an overnighter, and I could book the Saturday night redeye back. I'd be in the Bay Area by Sunday morning—plenty of time for Bridget's party.

So, why did Doris even need to know that? She would just assume that I was laying the groundwork for an excuse to miss it. And then she'd berate me for even going on the trip.

I decided not to make the call.

About to turn my phone to airplane mode, it started buzzing. "Sarah?" I answered.

"No, sorry. It's Walt Pang at SFO."

The early morning fog hadn't cleared from my mind, and it took me a few seconds to place him. "From the hidden camera, closed circuit TV, whatever..."

"Threat Assessment Unit." Pang cleared his throat. "I'm calling to let you know that your missing person was identified through facial recognition on a more recent flight."

I struggled to my feet, nearly spilling my coffee. I'd have to return my ticket and purchase another for the new location. "Go ahead, I'm listening."

"We found what we think is the same guy, JR Travis, arriving on an inbound Southwest flight the morning of April 6th and then taking an outbound Southwest flight the following afternoon."

"Where to?" I was next up at the counter to exchange my ticket.

"It was roundtrip. D.C. to SFO, and back to D.C. again."

I quickly stepped out of line. "So, he's still in D.C.?"

Pang hesitated. "Well, that was three days ago. Your guy could be in Katmandu by now. Captain Blythe just wanted me to let you know that the flight last month on the 28th wasn't his most recent."

Thanking Pang for the information, I stood in the crowded hall staring up at the massive arrivals and departures board. Pang was right, Travis could be anywhere. But I guess knowing he was in D.C. three days ago is better than thirteen days ago.

Now, the big question was if JR Travis and Jonathan Teagan were really one and the same.

CHAPTER 15

The rental car idled in the Motel 6 parking lot before slowly backing into the stall directly in front of their room.

The driver, a young woman, got out and loaded the bags into the back seat. Pausing in the shadows of the 2nd floor landing, she carefully scanned the lot. Once certain nobody was watching, she opened the car's trunk and signaled with three sharp taps on the motel room door.

He came out and immediately climbed into the trunk. She gently closed it and then gave the grounds another quick glance before getting back behind the wheel.

The lot dipped as the car pulled onto 4th Street NE, causing it to bounce slightly. Worried about bruising her precious cargo, the woman continued slowly through the intersection and onto New York Avenue NW. It was Friday afternoon, and the 30-mile drive would take over an hour in the heavy traffic. Stopping only once at the toll booth, the young woman drove in the slow lane and at the speed limit so as not to stand out.

Once off of the 267, Mai pulled the car onto a dirt shoulder just off of the rental car return drive. Standing at the back of the car until traffic thinned, she then opened the trunk.

JR Travis now wore a grey knit cap and sunglasses. Dressed in an olive drab shirt, faded blue jeans and high-top tennis shoes, he hoped that nothing would draw attention or identify him in any way.

Quickly scrambling out of the trunk, he walked alone to the bus shelter while Mai got back in the car and continued to the Avis drop-off line.

She joined him at the bus stop after returning the car, and the two huddled together as they waited for the shuttle.

"Are you sure we weren't followed?" JR asked.

"I looked in the mirrors," she said. "There was nothing out of the ordinary."

He nodded, still glancing around. Others began to crowd the shelter as the next bus approached. JR's pulse quickened when they were suddenly sandwiched between passengers.

"We'll stand toward the back and keep our bags with us," he said. "Just follow me, and don't say anything."

They stood together at the rear of the shuttle bus, and Mai kept her head down while JR peered through his sunglasses at the other passengers.

The bus pulled to a stop at Terminal B, and the driver called out the airlines served. JR and Mai grabbed their bags and stepped off.

He reflexively gripped Mai's hand when he saw the man approaching. A big guy who seemed to be scanning the crowd with intensity equal to his. JR dipped his head and continued toward the departure doors with Mai in tow. Feeling the doubt of paranoia, JR wondered if he was losing his mind. Still, he was somewhat relieved when the man continued past him and boarded the bus heading back to the car rentals.

JR and Mai separated when going through security—a strategy that JR had come up with in the event that his new passport was questioned, or if he was detained for any other reason. They remained separated at the boarding gate as a precaution.

Mai held her passport and airline ticket tightly at the gate. Following JR's instructions to the letter, she sat alone, avoided eye contact, didn't speak to anyone, and did nothing to attract attention.

When Mai's boarding group was called, she approached the attendant with her documents in hand.

The man checked them and handed them back. "Enjoy your flight, Ms. Nakhon."

As Mai headed down the jetway, she wanted to turn around and see if JR had made it through. He had been worried that something would go wrong before they boarded the flight, so Mai kept with the plan and did not risk glancing back.

Finally, as she made her way to her seat, Mai felt JR's hand lightly touch her shoulder. "Don't worry babe, we're almost in the clear."

Her body finally relaxed. She had intentionally purchased tickets that kept them separated, her by the window and him on the aisle. A businessman took the seat between, and though he slept most of the flight, Mai did not speak a word during the entire ten-hours to Istanbul. JR also continued the act of being strangers, though he once allowed his hand to brush hers as she squeezed past him to use the restroom. But he remained on high alert throughout the flight, watching for anyone who might have followed him onto the plane.

It wasn't until their layover that they ducked into a modern lounge just off of the terminal, away from the bustling travelers, that they finally spoke.

"Please tell me what happened," she said. "Why did we have to leave so suddenly?"

"First they killed my parents in order to draw me out. Then they were waiting for me at their funeral. Now, they've staked out my parents' house hoping to get another shot at me."

Mai gasped. "But the Marshals were supposed to protect you."

"It's my fault," JR said. "They warned me not to go back for the services."

"What about the evidence? Were you ever able to get it from the house?"

He shook his head. "Someone showed up before I could even make it upstairs. I heard them coming through the patio door and I had to jump out of one of the windows."

"So you left it there?"

"I had to," he said. "Couldn't risk it falling into the wrong hands."

Her intense eyes urged him to continue.

"Like I told you on the phone," he said. "There was shooting, and the cops were coming, and I couldn't chance going back inside to get it."

She tenderly stroked his cheek. "I'm just glad that you're safe and we're finally together."

"Witness protection wouldn't have worked anyway," said JR. "We would never have been able to stay together in the program."

"Because I am not a U.S. citizen?"

He nodded. Mai had already extended her tourist visa once, and that six-month extension period was quickly coming to an end. They both knew she wouldn't be able to remain in the U.S. any longer.

"Couldn't the Marshals help to intercede with Immigration?"

He shook his head. "I asked. Wrote a letter outlining the risk to you if I were to testify."

"And? What happened?"

"It's what I've been wanting to tell you, but couldn't," he said. "My protection handler denied the request. They said I would have to go into the program alone." He sneered. "Hell with that. Things will be better for us once we get to Thailand."

"Bangkok might not be as much *'better'* as you think," she said. "You may not be hunted there, but people are still looking for me."

JR's palm pressed into his forehead. "I don't know what else to do, Mai. It's a place that we both know, and it's also where I still have some connections."

CHAPTER 16

With a plane change in Salt Lake City, I didn't land in D.C. until 3:40 p.m. local time. It was in the low 40s and windy, which made me wish I'd packed more than just a sweatshirt to keep me warm.

I walked out of the terminal building toward the car rental shuttle. My eyes darted in every direction, as there suddenly seemed to be half a dozen men who could have been Elaina's brother. One in particular, a guy in a beanie cap and sunglasses, stared at me as he got off the bus. But he was with a young Asian woman, so I ruled him out.

I realized that the chances of running into Johnny Teagan in a city of 700,000 people were, well, 700,000-to-one. I needed to focus on finding the safe house for protected witnesses.

The first thing I did was check my phone, but there were no messages from Sarah Brooks. It had been nearly eight hours, and I had expected to hear something by the time we landed. That sent me down the path of irritation which only got worse.

The car rental companies had almost nothing to choose from, and I ended up in a Honda Fit. If I thought Doris' Civic was a pain, this car was about half that size and it just about ruined my knee for good. Then, as I left the rental lot, I saw only brake lights and cars inching along like snails. In my hurry to get this case into fast gear, I hadn't taken into account the Friday evening commute in and around the Capitol.

Inching north along the Richmond Freeway, I saw a whole new channel of cars funneling in from the Pentagon—everyone trying to get across the 14th Street Bridge into D.C. None of this was working for me, so I took the first off-ramp I could. Dropping onto 15th Street, I crossed under the freeway and pulled into a motel parking lot.

Just then Sarah Brooks called.

"Sarah," I said with a sigh of relief. "I thought you were going to text me."

"McKenna..." Her voice held none of its familiar, playful sarcasm. "Decided to call and actually speak with you, so that nothing is lost in translation."

"Sure, okay."

"I get that you want to find this guy and all," she said. "But I'm telling you, you don't want to fuck around with the Marshals Service."

"Of course not, no, not at all. My only intent is to--"

She cut me off. "Save it, McKenna. I'm not stupid. I know what you're up to, and I know how you operate. Once you get a wild hair up your ass, you're off to the races. Now, having said that, I'll text you everything I've got. But don't say I didn't warn you."

"Appreciate it, Brooks." I rubbed my tired eyes with my free hand. "If I can just figure out where their safe house is..."

"Yeah, good luck with that. It's one of the most highly guarded secrets in the federal government, and probably better protected than Fort Knox." She paused a few beats. "Just keep your head down, McKenna."

As I started to thank her, the line clicked off. A second later I got her text, which consisted of only one line: *7600 Ora Glen Drive #113, Greenbelt, MD.*

I stared at the address for some time, having no idea where Greenbelt, Maryland was. It definitely wasn't in D.C.

The freeway was still as clogged as my daughter's shower drain, and I wasn't likely to figure out this witness protection thing right then. The motel I'd stopped in front of was on the cheesy end of the quality scale, but given the choices it was good enough.

After renting a room for the night, I ordered a large sausage and mushroom from Extreme Pizza and watched a King of Queens rerun while I waited for my dinner to be delivered.

Later, after I'd eaten and gotten my fill of network TV, I tried to sleep. Problem was that my room faced the freeway, which I could have reached out the window and touched. And the fact that I was still on West Coast time didn't help. My mind kept going over the notion that the Marshals maintained some sort of indoctrination safe house in the nation's capital. Something about that gnawed at me, until I finally figured out why. Thinking as a cop, I realized that the logistics of securing an apartment house in a huge inner-city would be a nightmare. Transporting protectees in and out, teams of security people, government vehicles, all of it drawing the attention of neighbors. It would be too obvious. It would never work.

Getting dressed again around midnight, I went down to the lobby to find the business center. I hadn't brought my laptop, and between my crappy eyesight and the tiny phone screen, searching things on my cell wasn't going to cut it.

"We'd be happy to print something for you," said the night clerk, "but we don't have a computer workstation for our guests."

I'd seen a large hotel from the freeway when I drove in, so I braved the now colder wind and walked two blocks to the Crystal Gateway Marriott. Fortunately, they not only had a 24-hour business center, but I was able to access it without a Marriott keycard.

Entering the Greenbelt address that Brooks had given me, I was eager to see where Johnny's flight was billed to. I felt optimistic that my luck was about to turn.

"What the...?" I stared at the results: *USPS*. "It's a damn post office box," I said. Then, bringing up a map search to confirm it, I punched in the same address. Sure enough, a handsome brick post office building on a bucolic treed lot. *Son-of-a-bitch!*

The trip had been a complete waste. I had traveled all the way to Washington D.C. to look for a mysterious safe house full of federal protectees, and found only a post office box. What in the hell was I thinking? If it was that simple, anyone could look it up. Witnesses would be killed all the time, and the Marshals wouldn't be able to boast their perfect record of keeping protected folks alive.

Out of options, I considered throwing a Hail Mary pass. If I were to pay a visit to the Marshals headquarters, perhaps they could at least give me something to pacify my client. Maybe it would be enough for Elaina to know for sure that her brother was safe and in good hands.

A search for U.S. Marshals Headquarters came back with an address on S. Clark Street in Arlington, VA—a fortuitous coincidence, since I was already in Arlington. Enlarging the mapping icon, I was amazed to find that their main office was just across the freeway about eight blocks from my hotel. *Maybe my luck was beginning to change after all.*

I was about to click off when I noticed a second red location bubble on the map. Zeroing in on it, I realized that it pinpointed another Marshals Service facility. Listed as their *police department*, it showed an address on Cherrywood Lane in Greenbelt, MD.

"Huh...Greenbelt again." Then, looking up directions from there to the post office address that Brooks had given me, I saw they were less than two miles apart.

Browsing the City of Greenbelt website, I saw that it was a quiet suburb twenty miles north of the Capitol. As I perused the images, it struck me that Greenbelt would be a much better tactical choice for a safe house than D.C.

Still a fantastic longshot, I felt that the Greenbelt angle still gave me better odds than a cold-call to the Marshals' headquarters.

It was 4 a.m. when I got back to my motel room. Not wanting to get bogged down in a phone call to Elaina later in the morning, I elected to update her with a short text instead. The timestamp on the message would also guarantee that I was hard at work.

It may have been a little bit of an overstatement, but I wrote: FOLLOWING LEAD IN GREENBELT MD, WILL CALL LATER WITH UPDATE.

CHAPTER 17

It was no use. With my mind now spinning with investigative strategies, there was no way I'd be able to sleep. I went down and checked out of the motel—the night clerk probably wondering why I had bothered to get the room in the first place.

I bought a large black coffee to go at a place called Dunkin', then hit the 395. The inky sky was tinged with the first rays of daylight as I continued across the Potomac, surprised at the amount of traffic on a Saturday morning. The previous afternoon wind had blown away the smog, providing me with a sparkling peek at the Capitol dome as I passed the outskirts of D.C. Other than that one section, my view from the freeway consisted of construction barricades, a hodgepodge of colorless buildings, and cement sound walls covered with graffiti.

The scenery turned more colorful once I hit the Maryland border, and I made it into the city of Greenbelt in under an hour. Starting with the Cherrywood Lane address, I thought I should take a look at the Marshals' police department first. Not that I expected this super-secret safe house to be there, but it would make sense that it might be close by.

The area itself was a peaceful commercial development, with mostly modern structures scattered among rolling green hills. I found the Marshals building set back from the road in the Capital Office Park. It was a big place, about fifteen floors, with smoked blue glass that reflected the sun and clouds. I'd thought about going inside, but decided against it after noticing several exterior cameras.

I drove around the parking lot taking photos from differing angles with my phone. I'd just started to pull back onto Cherrywood, when I spotted an unmarked street blocked off by a rolling security gate. A low marble sign in front bore the words: United States Courthouse. Parked just inside the gates was a black Ford van with blacked out windows. Even with my binoculars, it was impossible to tell if the van was occupied. Again, my mind went into overdrive.

A federal courthouse this far out in the sticks surprised me. It was neither befitting to its rural surroundings, nor convenient to the D.C. metropolitan area. What it would be convenient for, is the swift and secure transportation of federal witnesses providing testimony. And here it was, a stone's throw from the Marshals building. Snapping a few photos of the courthouse, I continued on so I wouldn't be noticed.

Now some things began to fit for me. A secure safe house somewhere out here would not only be protected by the Marshals police, but would be close to the courthouse. In addition, the area was sparsely populated. A building to secretly house witnesses in this sector would be difficult to detect and easy to secure.

I spent the rest of the morning driving around the business park. Starting on the street between the Marshals police building and the courthouse, I drove in slow concentric circles—continuously widening as I worked my way outward. The way I figured it, the safe house would have to be within a mile or two of the center. But after an hour, I'd found nothing that even hinted at a covert government facility. I began to worry that I'd been barking up the wrong tree all along. After all, what did I know about the ways of the federal government?

Expecting a call from Elaina by that time, I was glad that she was finally giving me some space. Except, I wished I had better news for her when she did decide to call.

By the afternoon, I'd given up. It was time to let Elaina know that I had struck out, and then catch a flight back to my harbor paradise. Checking my watch, I realized I'd still get back in plenty of time to make it to Bridget's birthday party.

I wanted to get some cash for the return trip, and spotted a bank just on the other side of Ivy Lane. Hoping that the ATM wouldn't pinch me for a ridiculous service charge, I also prayed that I hadn't yet drained my account dry. But as I approached the mouth of the driveway, I came to an abrupt stop.

Across the parking lot was what looked like a business office, but something about it stuck in my craw. As it began bubbling up my gullet, I realized what it was. A concrete wall surrounded the ground floor. Decorative in appearance, I realized that the wall could also double as a protective barrier. A gap at the front of the building revealed a set of double doors set behind a low planter box.

It was different enough in appearance from the surrounding buildings, for me to take a second look. I skipped the ATM and circled around the lot, checking out the structure in more detail.

Seven stories high. No physical address. And no windows on the ground floor, only the concrete barricade. Then I noticed the security cameras—twenty or more, covering every conceivable angle of the building's exterior.

As I backed the car to better view the upper floors, I spotted the clincher. A half-dozen radio towers and microwave dishes ringed the roof like a crown of jewels, in the center of which stood an orange windsock on an elevated platform. It was a helipad, no doubt about it. I circled the building again, taking photos from each side.

Going over it in my mind, the place ticked all of the boxes. It was within easy reach of the Marshals' patrol force, not more than a minute from the courthouse, heavily fortified, and inordinately monitored. The place was plenty large enough for at least half a dozen families, with ample housing for protective details, even a tactical team, and possibly a few offices. The kicker was its seclusion.

Around the backside of the building were dual roll-up doors, which I imagined being the secure access points for protectees. I envisioned armored vans like the one I'd seen in front of the courthouse, ferrying mob bosses and their families in and out. The best part was that nobody would ever notice it out here. It was the perfect setup.

Remembering that it was Saturday, I realized that the area was probably quieter than usual. In fact, the only other vehicle in the parking lot was a beat up truck belonging to a couple of landscapers—both of whom zig-zagged across the pavement with their leaf blowers thrumming.

I stopped the car at the front. Next to the glass doors was a sign that read: *Gerald & Shur Realtors.* It certainly seemed to be an awfully big building for a two-partner real estate firm. Getting out of my car, I casually sauntered over to the entrance. What had appeared to be normal glass doors were actually as thick as a bank teller's window.

Inside was a wide stone counter set on a concrete half-wall. Behind it sat two men wearing sport coats. One of them walked to the window.

"The building's closed today, sir," he said.

"I saw your sign when I was at the ATM." I motioned toward the bank across the lot. "Will the realtors be in on Monday?"

He waved me away. "Not taking any new clients."

I'll bet they're not. I headed back to my car and pretended to drive away. Pulling to the curb once out of view, I entered the real estate company's name into my phone's search app. There were no returns of the property-for-sale nature. But under further searching, I found the name Gerald Shur—a DOJ attorney credited with creating the original Federal Witness Protection Program in the mid-1960s. The guy had long since retired and was probably dead, but I was certain the bogus firm on the door was someone's clever homage to the program's founder. In any case, it was way too much of a coincidence for me. There was no real estate company in the building, and no other reason to have that level of security in an average commercial office building.

Backing into a shaded spot near the bank, I had a perfect view of the entire site. Sometimes I have a certain feeling when I know I've gotten something right, and I definitely had it now. I'd solved the mystery. This was, without-a-doubt, the top secret safe house.

I sat there all day, waiting for someone to come or go. But office park was as quiet as a tomb, except for the drone of the leaf blowers. Then, as the late afternoon sun dipped behind the buildings of downtown Bethesda, the time change and my lack of sleep began to catch up to me.

I closed my eyes, only for a second, then forced them open. As I struggled to stay awake, the exhaustion finally overtook me and then I felt them close again.

CHAPTER 18

"Hey, you can't park here!"

I opened my eyes to find a large mustached security guard peering into my driver's side window. "This is private property."

The sun had disappeared from the sky and I could no longer hear the buzzing leaf blowers. I had nodded off, but couldn't tell how long I'd been out. Wiping my moist cheek against my shoulder, I held up my hand to signal that I'd gotten the message.

His car was stopped cockeyed in front of mine, so I wasn't able to leave just yet. As my eyes adjusted, I saw his partner standing on the passenger side of their car talking into a handheld radio. I realized from the door emblem, that they were actually Greenbelt cops.

"If you move your car a bit," I said, "I'll be able to--"

"Step out of the vehicle, please." His face was set, and his mustache downturned.

Rolling my eyes, I took in a breath and let it out slowly. Then, leaving one hand on the steering wheel where he could see it, I opened the door with the other. My left foot had just stepped onto the pavement when the blast came.

It knocked me backward into the car, my upper body twisting halfway across the passenger seat. The first thought to cross my mind was that I'd been shot. There was smoke, tiny bits of glass, and my ears rang so loudly that I couldn't hear anything else. Completely disoriented, everything felt like I was under water.

The cop was no longer standing there. As I used the steering wheel to pull myself up, I saw that he was on the ground and not moving—a thread of blood trickling from his mouth. My next thought was that he had also been shot. But the whole area was engulfed in a dusty cloud of smoke, and it was then that I realized there had been an explosion.

The bank windows had been blown out, and an alarm blared in tandem with the one in my ears. My eyes scanned toward the police car where his partner—a woman—was on her hands and knees coughing. She seemed to be a little better off than the cop next to me, and I realized that my car door had partially shielded me from the blast concussion.

Kneeling on the pavement next to the cop, I turned him onto his side so he wouldn't aspirate. He was unconscious, but at least he was breathing.

Then I grabbed the radio from his belt. "Officer down, Old Line Bank off of Ivy Lane!" I yelled into the mouthpiece. Unable to hear the dispatcher's response, I repeated it again, this time adding that there had been some sort of an explosion and two of their officers had been injured."

Holding the speaker to my ear, I heard her say, "I copy your radio traffic. Emergency personnel are enroute. Who is this transmitting? What is your ID?"

My instinct was to give my old SFPD call-sign or badge number, but instead I answered, "I'm a civilian."

Sirens wailed almost immediately. As the haze began to dissipate, I saw that the building I'd been watching—my suspected safe house—was even worse off than the bank. The explosion had blackened the entire south wall, blowing a chunk of concrete the size of a bus out of the cement barricade. The smoking crater left by it reminded me of news footage I'd seen of terrorist attacks.

Debris from the building, scorched car parts, and pieces of foliage were strewn hundreds of yards in every direction. Such that police and fire vehicles had to weave their way around these obstacles to get into the scene.

I had thought of taking off before the troops arrived so I wouldn't get caught up in whatever had happened, but the Greenbelt police car was still blocking me in. In addition, the female cop had already radioed in my car's license plate. It would have taken no more than a simple phone call to the rental agency for the police to get my name. Besides, the two injured officers needed my help. As much as I wanted to get the hell out of there, I wasn't about to turn my back on them.

The policewoman was standing now, directing medical personnel to her partner. I backed off and let them do their job. Several fire trucks were tending to the safe house building, and uniformed and plain clothes police were pouring in from everywhere. The medical people checked me as well, and other than a few scratches I was fine.

As a helicopter circled overhead, I noticed a line of ambulances on the other side of the trees. They were staged on Ivy Lane in a sort of mass casualty exercise, only this was no drill. Then the big boys started arriving in their slick-top, 4-door sedans. Moving in their respective packs, they all wore the same dark suits and ties over starched white shirts, and the same mirrored sunglasses. FBI, CIA, ATF, NSA, you name it.

From that point, it didn't take long before they started sniffing my way. Instead of getting treated, I was getting *the treatment*. It only made sense, I suppose. Without any other suspects, they were forced to focus on the only civilian at the scene.

It did not escape my notice that I was also the only person they could indict right away. Never mind that my heinous crimes consisted of no more than sleeping in a car under a shade tree, in a bank parking lot, on a Saturday afternoon.

"I'd like to see some ID," said one suit.

And as he grabbed it from my hand, two other suits moved to either side of me. "Turn towards the car and place your hands behind your back," said one of them.

So there it was, just like déjà vu, I was their number one, *and only*, suspect.

CHAPTER 19

They took my phone and car keys, then searched me for weapons before loading me into the back of a plain white minivan.

The driver's compartment was walled off, and there were no windows in the rear section. A single chair, set between two welded steel support beams, was all the interior held. Each of my hands were cuffed separately to them, and my feet in ankle cuffs to eyebolts in the floor. When they slid the door closed, I was alone and in complete darkness.

I heard the muffled sound of the engine and the vibrating road beneath us, but the compartment was obviously sound insulated. There was also a fan vent blowing fresh air toward me, which helped camouflage the outside noise. If we had driven over a bridge, or near a train, or through the middle of a KISS concert, I wouldn't have known it.

About an hour later we stopped, and I thought I heard voices before we started moving again—this time much slower. Imagining a security checkpoint, I guessed we were entering the grounds of the CIA headquarters in Langley or the FBI complex in Quantico, or perhaps some other super-secret government interrogation facility. My takeaway from all of this was that they weren't playing around.

The texture of the roadway transitioned to a smooth flat surface, and we stopped only seconds later. I had the feeling that we were inside a building—like a parking garage or a carport.

I was taken out and whisked into an elevator that descended from where we had entered. Two male agents were on either side of me, expressionless and facing straight ahead.

"I hope you guys are careful with my car," I said. "It's a rental, and I didn't pay for the extra insurance."

Silence.

The door opened and I was led into a changing room. They removed my handcuffs, then handed me a blue spandex shirt and spandex pants. It looked like something a weekend bicyclist wears.

"Remove all of your clothes, shoes, socks, and all your belongings, and place them in there," said one of the agents, nodding toward a clear plastic bag. "Then put on the stretch pants and shirt."

"What is this all about?" I asked. And when neither answered, I sat down on the bench and folded my arms. "I think I like my own clothes just fine."

They glanced at each other, then one of them put his hand solidly on my shoulder. "There are a couple of different ways we can get this done," he said. "But make no mistake, it's going to get done."

The other agent added his piece. "The sooner you cooperate, the sooner we can rule you out as a suspect and refocus on the person or persons who did this."

At least his logic made more sense than the threat. "And why is it that I have to dress like a ballet dancer in order to be ruled out?"

Again, they didn't answer.

Shaking my head, I went ahead and stripped down to my boxers and put everything into the plastic bag.

"Underwear too." The guy slid the spandex outfit to me. "And your knee brace."

It wasn't my best look. The fabric clung to each fold and pucker, accentuating every extra pound on my body and making me wish I'd skipped the sweet roll at the airport.

They led me into the next room—which was no bigger than an elevator car—and closed the airtight door behind me. The walls were black glass, and the room was brightly lit through a translucent ceiling panel. There was no handle on the inside of the door and no place to sit. So I just stood there, feeling like a zoo animal on display.

"Please stand in the center of the room and turn to your right," said a man's voice over a speaker. "Good. Now, we need you to remain standing, and remain facing in that direction while I ask you some questions."

They began simply enough via the speaker, asking me things that they had obviously gotten out of my wallet: full name, birthdate, height, weight, address, and so on.

I stood there, feeling like a fool, answering each of their questions. The inquiry moved on to more personal things about my marital status, my daughter's name, and my employment history. When he asked if I'd ever been arrested, I sighed.

"Have you ever been arrested," he repeated in a monotone voice over the speaker.

"Twice," I said. "Once in San Francisco, and once in Mexico."

I thought he would want me to explain, but he moved on without a change in tone. I also wondered if this would count as arrest number three.

"Did you take a flight from Oakland, California to Washington D.C. yesterday?" he asked.

"Yes."

"Did you rent a room at the Motel Americana in Arlington?"

"Yes."

"Were you in Greenbelt, Maryland this morning?"

"Yes."

"Did you take photographs of the Marshals Service Police building today?"

"Uh . . ."

"Yes or no?"

"Yes."

"And of the federal courthouse?"

"Yes."

"Did you park your rental car in the parking lot of the Capital Business Park today?"

I noticed that they didn't ask about the photos I'd taken of the safe house, which was only further confirmation that I'd gotten it right. On the other hand, it tended to make me look that much worse.

"Yes."

"Did you handle any explosive device today?"

"No."

"Is your rental car a sub-compact?"

"Yes."

"Do you belong to, or are you affiliated with a subversive group or terrorist organization?"

"No."

"Did you buy a coffee at Dunkin' Coffee Shop in Alexandria this morning?"

"Yes."

"Did you run the name Gerald Shur on your phone's search engine today?"

"Yes."

"Thank you Mr. McKenna," said the speaker voice. "You may step into the next room and dress. Someone will be with you shortly."

The door opened and the same two agents stood by while I shed the spandex and put on my own clothes. Then they led me to a 5X8 jail cell, shouldered me through the door, and closed it behind me. There were no bars, just three concrete walls and a metal sliding door. Inside, there was a single aluminum bunk. An aluminum sink/toilet combination sat in the corner, the latter half of which I made urgent use of. Then I sat on the bed and waited.

I'd lost track of time, but I knew it was late evening. I yelled, pounded on the door, demanded a phone call, claimed to know my rights, and even threatened a lawsuit—all of the things that I'd seen prisoners do when I was a cop. My efforts were just as useless as theirs had been.

In a way, I probably deserved it for breaking my own rule against traveling. It never seems to work out for me.

Finally falling asleep, I dreamed I was in a cage and that my old bosses at the SFPD were outside spectating. I saw Greg Dowd, the former Homicide Captain—now Police Chief. Next to him were duel recliners where Mike Prowse sat with my wife. They were both eating popcorn and laughing. My daughter stood there behind a cake full of candles, only she wasn't laughing. She had a sad look on her face, and when she opened her mouth she was still wearing braces.

I awoke thinking that by now, word of my arrest had probably gotten back to SFPD. Chief Dowd would be alerted, and Prowse would only be an ass sniff away. Surely, he and Doris would be spasmodic with laughter after hearing that I was now being held in the custody of the federal government.

Having missed the night flight back to San Francisco, I realized that there was no way I'd ever make it home in time to see my daughter. I couldn't even use a phone to wish her a happy birthday. Awake for what seemed like hours after that, I just sat at the end of the mattress waiting for someone to tell me what was happening.

It was midmorning of the next day by my estimation, when two men in Army uniforms came to get me. They escorted me down the hall and sat me in a standard looking interrogation room—plain desk, rigid chair, ceiling mounted camera, and two-way wall mirror.

As I sat alone in the room, exhausted and angry, I wondered how they had known what to ask me the previous night. They must have searched through my phone's memory and immediately accessed my credit cards. They had even known about my prior arrests. Probably studied through my entire life history during the time I was being transported from Greenbelt.

I hoped I'd passed their test. But since they'd held me all night, it was looking as if they didn't believe my answers. What worried me even more was the secretive nature of the facility. If they decided I was being untruthful, or was a threat to national security, who on the outside would ever know? I'd be shipped off to Guantanamo, and that would be the last anyone would ever hear about me. Sadly, I had nobody to notify even if they did give me a phone call.

Low voices in the outside hallway drew me out of my mind's scenario. The door suddenly opened and in walked an exotic looking woman wearing a dark business suit. She stepped to the opposite side of the table and set down an accordion file.

"I'm Deputy Soltani, United States Marshals Service," she said. "The person you have to convince not to throw you in prison for the next twenty years."

CHAPTER 20

It was a hot and gritty ride into Bangkok from Suvarnabhumi Airport. Having spent most of her life in Thailand, Mai felt at home in the heat and bustling chaos. But the crowded streets and muggy air only reminded JR of his time standing guard at the embassy. Now that they were back, he wondered if they should have fled somewhere else.

Mai's intuitive smile soothed JR. "We have nowhere else to go," she said. In a faint voice she added, "*Nee seua pa jo ra kay.*"

JR lifted an eyebrow.

"Escape from the tiger to the crocodile," she said. "It means you may get out of one problem, only to find yourself in a worse situation than before."

He frowned and shook his head. "We call it going from the frying pan into the fire."

Mai chuckled.

JR glanced behind them out of habit, making sure they weren't being followed. "Ask the driver to take us to the U.S. Embassy."

Mai relayed the instructions in her native tongue.

The leathery skinned man shrugged, then headed west on Route 7 toward the glistening spires of downtown. He motioned to a group of kids lighting firecrackers along the side of the road and said something to Mai.

She gave a single syllable response, then turned to JR as she pressed her palm to her forehead. "No wonder there are so many people out. It's *Songkran*!"

JR squinted out at the scene. "It's what?"

"Thai New Year celebration."

"Does that mean the embassy is closed today?"

She nodded. "The driver reminded me that everything is closed, and not just today. It's a 3-day national holiday."

JR rolled his head back and exhaled. "We have to find some way to let Shawn know we're here. He's the only one who can help us."

"Unless you have another way to contact him, it will have to wait until Thursday."

"We lost touch after he reenlisted," JR said. "All I know is that he was promoted to staff sergeant, and he's still stationed here at the embassy."

"We should find a place to stay that's close by." She tapped their driver and directed him toward the river.

Passing a large shopping complex, Mai motioned down a narrow lane. They stopped where the road dead ended, and she paid the driver. JR glanced up at the white building pinched between others just like it. At the dead end stood a concrete wall topped with wire mesh. Beyond the wall, JR could see the Chao Phraya River bisecting the metropolis of over eight million people.

The tiny hostel seemed a suitable place to meld into anonymity. Except, JR thought, its position at the end of the street would leave them no escape route in the event of a problem.

JR paid 500 Thai Bhat for a private double—which was about $16 U.S. The room was on the third floor and had a small balcony facing the front of the building.

Opening the French doors, JR and Mai gazed out at the view. Mai was pointing out the 35-story CAT tower across the river—its glass exterior displaying a 100-foot image of the King. But JR was too distracted to appreciate the building or the exotic charm of their surroundings. "What do we do now?"

"We wait," she said, setting her meager collection of clothing in a dresser drawer. "We wait for three days."

JR smirked. "Unless somebody from Willoughby-Klehs finds me first. Or your uncle finds you."

"First of all, that's why we need to stay put inside. Secondly, I have concerns about us just showing up at the embassy. And third, he's not my uncle."

"Then why do you call him that?"

"It's how the Thai people refer to older men of stature. The man I call *Uncle* is a colonel, very powerful, but he's also a very bad man."

"All this time I thought he was actually your uncle."

"My point is that he is dangerous." Mai's fear was evident in her troubled expression. "And anyone looking for us would probably expect us to show up at the U.S. Embassy. If Uncle already knows we're in Bangkok, which he might, it will not end well for either of us."

CHAPTER 21

It's a good thing this deputy, marshal, whatever, didn't see me last night in the skintight suit, or she would have put me in the electric chair right then and there.

The woman sat back, crossed one leg over the other, and folded her arms. Then she just stared across the table at me.

Deputy Soltani was a very attractive woman. Probably in her early 30s, her dark hair and eyes gave her a seductive look that could have been straight out of the Arabian Nights. Her build was fit and shapely, and she was close enough to my age that it wouldn't raise eyebrows. Her ring finger, I also noticed, was unadorned.

Gazing across the table into a face that was all business, it seemed that the woman's soft almond eyes only mildly cushioned her harsh bearing. Not that I gave a damn, because I was mad as hell at that point.

"Where am I?" I demanded. "I have a right to know what I'm being charged with!"

"How about I ask the questions?" She flipped a lock of hair back over her shoulder and opened the file. "Let's start with why you came to D.C."

I hesitated, wondering if I should even be talking to her without a lawyer. But since I was innocent, I decided to give cooperation a shot. "I'm a private detective, and I'm following leads on a missing person case."

"You're a PI from the Bay Area, and your missing person is in Greenbelt, Maryland?"

"I don't know where my missing person is," I said. "Like I just told you, I'm only following a lead."

"And you're alone?"

I gave an exaggerated glance around. "Yes, I'm alone."

"I mean, are you traveling alone?"

"Yes," I answered.

"Care to tell me why you were taking photos of our Greenbelt police substation and the federal courthouse yesterday morning?"

My reason wasn't the best, but I answered her anyway. "I didn't have a pen in the car and I wanted to keep a record of where I went and what I found."

She tilted her head slightly. "And what was that?"

"I found that the courthouse is right across the street from the Marshals' building, which is right around the corner from the building that someone tried to blow up."

"You mean the realtors' offices?" Her expression stayed deadpan.

"Uh, yeah, right. The *realtors' offices*." I debated whether to add to it, then finally caved to my irritation. "The building that I also took photos of, but that nobody wants to talk about."

"We'll circle back to that later," she said. "First, I'd like to know a little more about your case. Who is the missing person, and who hired you?"

I shook my head. "Maybe we'll circle back to *that* later. First, I'd like to know where in the hell I am."

We locked eyes, and neither budged for several seconds. I could see her weighing how far she should or could push me. She also had to factor in that I had been held incommunicado all night, and that I'd been completely cooperative up to that point. Also, probably, the fact that I was the one who radioed for help and tended to the two Greenbelt cops after the explosion.

"I'll be honest, McKenna. I don't like guys like you." She leaned forward on her elbows. "Arrogant as hell. Always trying to run the show."

"What *show* am I trying to run?" I asked. "I've cooperated with everyone since yesterday when my ass was nearly blown off. And all I want to know is where I am."

"Fort Meade, Maryland," she said.

If it was true, I'd been way off in my time and distance calculation. Perhaps that was part of the transport van's disorienting effect, or maybe they intentionally drove all over hell and back just to confuse me. They had probably used the extra time to background check me.

"How did I do on the spandex test?" I asked.

The tiniest smile broke the line of her lips. "You passed."

"Yet here I am. Still being held against my will."

"Last night's examination was to determine if you were involved in the explosives incident, and if you are affiliated with any terrorist organizations," she said.

"That was a lie detector test?"

She nodded. "It's all accomplished using biometrics now. Retinal and pupillary scans. Voice analyses. And digital monitoring of a host of other physical reactions. We also swabbed your clothing for explosives while you were in the examination cube."

"What was with the tight outfit?"

"Makes it easier to observe fine muscle contractions, involuntary movements, and variations in stance and posture."

"Nothing like the polygraph I had to take back in the day."

The deputy shook her head. "The cube also measures rate of oxygen exchange, respirations, heartbeat, blood pressure." She pulled a sheet from her file. "Since you've been cleared by the NSA, this investigation is now solely the jurisdiction of the Marshals Service."

I nodded.

"Which is why I need to know the name of your missing person," she said.

Closing my tired eyes, I sat there caressing them with my thumb and forefinger. "I think you already know who he is," I finally said. "Since your people have gone through all my things, I'm sure you've seen his personal papers in my overnight bag and his photograph on my cell phone."

"Fair enough." She reached into her accordion file and set Johnny's papers on the table. "Is this him?" she asked, flipping open the passport I'd taken from his safe deposit box back in Oakland. "Jonathan Roy Teagan?"

"Yeah," I said, playing along. "Also known as JR Travis."

She didn't have to be wearing spandex for me to spot the tell. Her flinching jaw was all the confirmation I needed."

"Look," I said. "I was hired by a concerned relative. Johnny hasn't been heard from since his parents' funeral, and they just want to know that he's all right. Can you at least tell me that?"

"No." Her sober eyes stared back at me.

"No, you can't tell me?"

"No," she said. "He's not all right."

Soltani swept the hair up off the back of her neck, as if the room was suddenly too hot. Then she let out a long sigh.

"Was he inside the building that blew up?" I asked.

"No, he had already fled from his protective detail, but I'm certain that the attack was meant for him."

I thought for a minute. "I still haven't figured out what he did to warrant that level of protection in the first place."

She shook her head. "Not at liberty to say."

"Is that the first line they teach you guys in the academy?" I said. "Because it's not going to get things done out here in the real world. I'm willing to help you any way I can, but I've got to know what I'm dealing with. I already know it has something to do with him killing people."

"Why in the world would you think that?" Her stunned expression slowly relaxed into an amused grin. "Nothing in JR's file has ever suggested violence. He was an accountant for goodness sakes. It was all about the position he held in a company the FBI wanted to take down."

"What did he do?" I asked. "Testify against them or something?"

Soltani had a pained expression. "Look, I really can't give you this information. Like I said, it was an FBI case, and the Department of Justice worked out a deal with him. Anything else you need to know, you can probably find through open sources. All you have to do is look up *Willoughby-Klehs*, they were all over the news out here on the East Coast."

"I will." Stretching my aching back and neck, I asked. "Were you part of his protection detail?"

She nodded. "I've been JR's primary handler since he entered the program. And I'm the one now responsible for finding him."

CHAPTER 22

An envelope containing my personal effects was waiting. After signing for them, I was set free. Deputy Soltani was kind enough to give me a lift across the base to an evidence processing warehouse where my rental car was also released to me.

Traffic on the freeway crawled through D.C., even though it was Sunday. Inching over the bridge into Arlington, I was both hungry and exhausted from the past two days.

Soltani had recommended the Doubletree as a better lodging option, so I checked in there when I finally arrived. It was three blocks from the Marshals Service main headquarters, which is where Soltani said she worked. I had the feeling she still wanted to keep an eye on me, though I didn't think her interest was romantic in nature. In any case, it was too late for me to catch a flight back to the Bay Area, and all I wanted to do was eat something and go to sleep.

After checking in, I took the elevator up to the 15th floor where a revolving restaurant-bar looks out over the freeway and the Potomac. I ordered a Wagyu burger and a martini, and wolfed them down while the Washington Monument passed by me, again and again and again.

I mindlessly checked my phone, then noticed that the feds had returned it to me in the *silent mode*. There was a missed call from Shanay, and my call back went to her voicemail. I left a message telling her where I was and that I'd be returning the following day.

There were also several voicemail messages from Elaina, all of them asking me if I was making headway on her brother's case. Tired, beaten, and without any good news to share, I went to bed without calling her back.

Monday morning was clear and sunny, and I felt better after having slept solidly through the night. In fact, I'd fallen asleep so early that I woke at 6 a.m. with an abundance of energy.

Sitting in bed squinting into my phone screen, I searched the name that Deputy Soltani had given me. She was right, there was a lot of news about Willoughby-Klehs. But it was a legal firm, not a person. Based in Providence, Rhode Island, the company had apparently been investigated for SEC violations, as well as federal money laundering and conspiracy charges. The details were difficult to see on the tiny screen, especially without my readers—which I had forgotten to bring.

The key witness in the government's case was described in the media only as "a 28-year-old accountant" who worked for the firm. I surmised that the *accountant* was Johnny Teagan. What wasn't clear from the news articles, was whether or not the witness had actually testified. At that point, none of it really mattered. The whole thing was way above my paygrade, and I had diligently taken the case about as far as I was able.

I showered, then realized I'd have to put on the same clothes I'd been wearing—which kind of defeated the purpose of the shower. But it wasn't as if I'd be staying longer, as my plan was to return my rental car at the airport and catch the first flight home.

As I sat at the bottom of the bed towel drying my hair, someone knocked on my door.

"Just a sec." I grabbed the complementary robe from the closet.

Through the peep-hole, I saw that it was Deputy Soltani. Partially opening the door, I leaned around it. "Hey," I said. "Don't tell me you found Johnny already."

She shook her head. "I come at a bad time?"

"No, I was just... it's fine."

"I've just come from the office," she said, which I assumed meant Marshals Headquarters. "There's been a development."

"Did you want to come in?" I asked.

Eyeing what she could see of me, she only smirked. "I have to get back. But I'll need to meet with you before you leave. I assume you're going back today..."

"I was planning to."

"Can you come by my office first?" she asked. "It's on the 4th floor, room 418. It would be helpful if you could get there before 10 a.m., because I have a meeting after that. Actually, the sooner the better."

"Okay, sure." As she left, I leaned into the hallway and watched until she got to the end. A woman got off the elevator on my floor as Soltani was stepping in, and I saw them give each other the once over the way women do. I then realized who the other woman was.

"Elaina?" I teetered into the hall, not realizing that in the robe and with the towel around my neck I probably looked like Hugh Hefner. "What are you doing here?"

"A better question might be what are *you* doing here?" She glanced back at the elevator, the doors of which had already closed. "I hope you're not out here getting happy pants on my dime."

"Huh? No, of course not."

She walked past me into the room. "I've left five messages, none of which you've returned. The last I heard from you was two days ago when you said you were following a lead."

"I was, but then--"

"I'm paying you good money to find my brother," she interrupted. "And I don't think it's too much to ask that you keep me informed about what's going on." Her eyes began to tear up. "I thought you had found him."

Extending my palms, I motioned for calm. Then, I closed the door. "Why don't you take a seat, and I'll explain everything. How did you know where to find me, by the way?"

"Your Executive Assistant."

I chuckled at the title, but then frowned as I made a mental note to admonish Shanay for giving out information of my whereabouts to a client.

The woman had flown all the way across the country because she thought I had located her brother. I couldn't very well tell her the truth about my incarceration at Fort Meade.

"Well," I said, pacing toward the window. "The reason I didn't call you back is... and I really shouldn't be sharing this... but I've been working with the National Security Agency relative to your brother's whereabouts."

Elaina's eyes widened. "Was that a federal agent who just left?"

I nodded. "Yes, she's one of them."

"Do they know where Johnny is?"

"No, not yet," I said. "But let's just say that I've persuaded the federal government to help us in the investigation. The U.S. Marshals Service has joined in to assist me in Johnny's case, at no extra cost to you, of course."

She covered her mouth with her hand. "This all sounds so serious. Do you think he's okay?"

"I hope so." I shrugged. "But he may be in a lot of danger. In fact, it probably isn't safe for you to be here either."

"I'm so sorry," she said as her shoulders dropped. "I really didn't mean to speak to you the way I did. I flew here because I thought you were getting close to finding Johnny. I guess I thought I could help." Then she buried her face in her hands and began to cry. "I just don't know what else to do."

The right thing would have probably been to give her a hug and tell her that everything would be okay. But the whole terrycloth robe thing might have creeped her out, so I went for the *glass-is-half-full* approach without the physical contact.

Clapping my hands together, I said, "Look, it's a beautiful day out." I motioned out the window. "Why don't you take the morning to relax, see a couple of sites, and get a good meal before flying back?"

"You think so?"

"Absolutely."

I couldn't very well tell Elaina that if not for her showing up in D.C., I would have already been home. It was becoming all too clear that she expected me to see this thing through—which meant that minimally, I would have to buy myself a change of clothes. On the bright side, another couple of days would also mean that she'd be paying for my time, food, lodging, and expenses.

Elaina slowly stood and I walked her to the door. "And you think it's best if I don't stay?" she asked. "I mean, what if you find him? Wouldn't it be better if I waited nearby, just in case?"

"Too dangerous," I said. "Besides, I'll be busy meeting with the feds. But I promise that from now on, I'll let you know what's happening. And when I'm getting close to finding him, you'll be the first person I call."

Elaina looked a little better than when she'd first come in. I figured I'd calmed her down enough to keep her out from under foot. But her visit had taken a bite out of my morning, and I had to hustle if I was going to meet Soltani by 10 o'clock.

CHAPTER 23

They checked my ID and scanned me with a wand before letting me in. Getting off of the elevator on the 4th floor, I found Soltani's office at the end of the hall.

She looked up from her desk, which was covered in 8x10 crime scene prints. "Close the door," she said. Then she slid one of them toward me. "Recognize either of these men?"

I studied the black & white photograph—an enlarged video frame from a security camera. It had been taken from an elevated angle showing a parking lot, a green pick-up truck, and two men standing at the open tailgate.

"Landscapers," I said. "They were walking around, blowing the leaves off of the parking lot before the explosion. Why? Do you think they were involved?"

"We believe the explosive materials were in this vehicle." She pulled out another photo showing the same landscaping truck from another angle. "The debris recovered from the blast site contained parts of a drive shaft belonging to a 2009 Chevrolet Silverado. A ¾ ton service utility truck, just like the one in this photo. The blast crater in the lot tells us that detonation—or ground zero—was right where the truck was parked."

"The two guys I saw were at the far end of the parking lot." I closed my eyes, trying to think back. Shaking my head in frustration, I said, "Couldn't really see their faces because of the distance. Just two average sized men, both wearing work overalls and operating leaf blowers."

"CCTV cameras got a shot of a third man," she said, pushing another photo across the desk. "Looks like he drove the work truck to the scene. He left the area first, and the two you saw slowly followed him out toward Kenilworth Avenue. Did you notice what time they disappeared from the area?"

I shook my head.

"They either had another vehicle stashed outside the blast zone, or a fourth person was waiting to pick them up. You must have heard the noise from their blowers stop at some point."

"I hadn't gotten much sleep the night before." Lowering my head, I said, "They probably left around the time I nodded off."

"Did you see anyone else?"

I thought for a second, and my mind drifted. "I had knocked on the door of the building before the bomb went off," I said. "Talked to a guy through the building's window, pretended to be interested in buying some real estate."

"We know." She pursed her lips. "You were also on the security cam footage. And we interviewed the two deputies who were working in the lobby at the time."

"Then they're okay?"

Soltani nodded. "They were shaken up, for sure. But the blast wall did its job."

It was a huge relief to me; I'd wondered about them ever since the explosion. And if they had endured it without injury, then anyone else in the building—especially on the higher floors—would have certainly survived.

"Well, that pretty much clears you completely." She gathered her photos into a pile and slid them back in the file. "What are your plans now?"

"Although I'd like to go home and forget that this ever happened, my client is paying me to see the case through."

She stared at me as if weighing something inside her head, but said nothing.

"Is there more?" I stared back.

"His passport was used to leave the States."

"Johnny's passport?" I said. "Impossible. I still have it."

"Not that one. He used the passport we made for him under the name JR. Once a protectee enters the program, we never use or refer to them by their former name. Anyway, he was ticketed on a flight from Washington's Dulles, to Istanbul International in Turkey."

"Turkey?" My mind raced in reverse to remember anything at his house or on his paperwork that hinted of Turkey. "How does that even figure in?"

"It doesn't," said Soltani. "Not as far as his background file goes."

"So, what does the Marshals Service do now?" I asked. "Follow him to Istanbul?"

She shook her head. "They won't do that, for a couple of reasons. First, once a protectee leaves the program—and especially if they leave the country—the Marshals are absolved of all responsibility."

"And the other reason?"

Soltani motioned toward a world map on her office wall. "JR never left the Istanbul Airport, at least not on foot or by vehicle. Back-channeling through a friend in their security service, I learned there was no Turkish visa application made by JR."

Trying my best to follow the bouncing ball, I could only picture the Tom Hanks movie where he lives inside an airport terminal.

"The place is an international hub," said Soltani, "and my guess is that it was only a stopover for JR. He probably bought another ticket once he got there, which means he could be anywhere in the world by now."

I thought for a moment. "There's an NSA computer thing called STILLS. It might be able to tell you how he purchased his tickets and what other flights he paid for."

Soltani looked surprised. "How do you know about that system? It's highly classified."

I smiled. "I'm pretty well connected within the intelligence community back in the Bay Area. In fact, I just recently closed out an international drug smuggling case from Mexico."

"Well, STILLS won't work anyway," she said. "It's a proprietary system that is only in use in the United States. I did check with both U.S. and allied countries' airlines, and none had any record of him leaving Istanbul. Anyway, I'm going to be late for my meeting. Here's my card. If you happen to come up with anything, give me a call." Then she bum-rushed me out of her office.

As I walked back to my hotel, I began to wonder about something Soltani said. She wanted me to give her a call, *if I came up with anything*. Why would my coming up with anything matter if her agency had already backed away from the case? Unless she was planning to continue looking for her protectee, off the books. Or, maybe it was just her way of asking me to call her.

Taking her card from my pocket, I held it at arm's length so I could read it. *Aafreen Soltani – Witness Security Program.*

Gathering my things back at the hotel, I mulled over my options. There really weren't any good ones, except to tell Elaina that her brother had fled the country. It was a dead end for me and for the Marshals, so there was no need for me to stay any longer and there was no need to buy a change of clothes, after all.

It was noon when I checked out of my room. I sat in the lobby trying to arrange my flight home over the phone. It seemed that the only thing available was a redeye later that night. About to purchase the ticket, a thought whisked across my mind. It made me stop what I was doing. I disconnected from the airline and sat there trying to pull the pieces together in my head.

In a flash of awareness that slapped me across the face, I dug Johnny's paperwork out of my duffel bag. Then I hit my cell phone's photos icon, and thumbed through them until I found what I was looking for.

Pulling the card from my wallet, I dialed her number. The formal-sounding recording ended with a beep, and I left my message:

"Deputy Soltani, it's Danny McKenna. I'm pretty sure that I know where Johnny, I mean JR, has gone. Call me back if you can. If I don't hear from you, I'll be upstairs in the spinning restaurant at six o'clock. Meet me there and I'll explain everything."

CHAPTER 24

I had made a reservation for two on the off chance that Deputy Soltani didn't call back, and by 6 p.m. she still hadn't.

Sitting alone at my table by the window, I began to feel a little foolish. The deputy could have been too busy with work to return my call. Maybe she hadn't even gotten my message, or maybe she didn't really care what I'd found out.

Then I spotted her standing near the entrance. But it wasn't the *her* I expected. Instead, it was my client, Elaina Teagan.

Son-of-a-bitch!

She took a seat at the bar, thankfully with her back to me. When Elaina had come to my room earlier, I had assumed she was staying somewhere else. Had I known we were at the same hotel, I never would have encouraged her to stay and see the sights. Not that I had anything to hide by meeting with a Deputy U.S. Marshal, but I didn't want or need the distraction of an over-involved client.

"Hi."

I peered over the top of my menu to see Soltani's soft brown eyes. Apparently, she had come into the restaurant while I was focused on Elaina. The deputy wore a rust colored sweater, tight fitting jeans and high black boots that came almost to her knees. Definitely not the disciplined ensemble from earlier.

Debating whether or not to jump to my feet and pull out her chair, I was relieved when the maître d' stepped over and did it for me. Standing just the same, I shook Soltani's hand. "You look nice," I said.

Another smirk. "I'm meeting someone after," she said, nudging her sweater up to cover an exposed shoulder. "Your message said you have information?"

Suddenly, I felt really foolish, like I'd been busted trying to set a romantic trap. "I was in my room, packing my things to leave," I said, "when something occurred to me."

The waiter interrupted. "Can I bring a couple of drinks to get you two started?"

I looked at Soltani.

"Uh, scotch rocks," she said.

"Any particular scotch?"

She glanced at the menu. "How about the Macallan?"

I knew then that I liked her. "I'll have the same," I said, stealing a glance across the room at Elaina. She was alone, still at the bar with her back to me.

"Expecting someone?" asked Soltani.

"Uh, no." I played it off by taking out my phone. Then I scrolled through my photos, clicking on a picture I'd taken in Johnny's room.

Soltani tilted her head to get a better view. "A lapel ribbon?"

I nodded. "Marine Corps. I found this in a box containing your protectee's personal papers. It didn't mean anything to me at the time, but I looked it up this afternoon to see what is signified."

Our drinks came and it crossed my mind to make some sort of lighthearted toast. I didn't, but instead I said, "Oh, I think I got your drink by mistake."

Soltani only frowned at my little ice-breaker.

"Anyway," I said, "I looked up this particular ribbon—single red vertical stripe surrounded by two white and two blue stripes—and it's unique, only awarded to members of the Embassy Security Group."

"I'm not following," she said. "JR's military service ended a few years ago."

"Right, but you have to be stationed at an overseas embassy for a minimum of 24 months to be awarded this particular ribbon. Which means he spent at least two years in another country, and it would only make sense that he might be comfortable enough to return there. Especially if he didn't want to be found. Hell, he may even have a network of friends still over there."

"Where is *over there*?" she asked. "Our background didn't go that deep."

"It prompted me to check through his military papers again." I set them on the table between us. "I found this notation on one of them: *October 28, 2014: PCS approved – Detachment 23.*"

Soltani gazed back at me, still in the dark.

"Permanent Change of Station," I said, flipping the form to the other side. "I looked it up; Detachment 23 is our embassy in Bangkok, Thailand."

Deputy Soltani immediately pulled out her phone and furiously thumbed the keys. While she was occupied, I took another look over at Elaina. The bar seat next to her had opened up and a young man quickly took it. Probably some married guy here on business, I thought, wondering what pick-up line to try out on her.

"Ukraine International Air," said Soltani, shaking me out of my voyeurism. "They had a flight that left Istanbul the same night that JR arrived there. It had a scheduled plane change in Kiev, which would have gotten into Bangkok at 9:45 a.m. this morning."

I stared out the window. Istanbul, Kiev, Bangkok... what the hell? I was so far out of my depth it wasn't even funny. Glancing across the restaurant at Elaina again, I considered inviting her over to our table so she could hear the latest bizarre turn of events. Then I'd terminate my contract with her and be done with the whole mess.

Turning back to Soltani, I asked, "So, I guess that's that then. We're done."

"What do you mean?"

I shrugged. "Well, you said your agency is through with the guy, right? And there's certainly no way that I'm going overseas..."

"Look," she swigged the last of her scotch. "My boss doesn't like women and he really doesn't like me. There's no way he would ever authorize an international road trip. Not on this case."

"So, you're finished with it then."

"I never said that. I also told you that I was responsible for his safety." She glanced around for the waiter.

"So, what can you do about it at this point?" I asked.

She waved the waiter over. "I can order myself another drink, and then I'm going to book a flight to Thailand."

CHAPTER 25

I thought she was joking, or maybe the scotch had gone to her head. But it was clear that she meant it. Soltani was intent on taking the earliest possible flight to Bangkok.

A few minutes later, she had purchased a ticket.

"Cathay Pacific flight 869," she said. "Departs Dulles at 1:40 a.m."

"Tonight?" My face twisted into a knot. "God, do I hate foreign travel."

Soltani shrugged. "So, who even invited you?"

I unconsciously glanced at Elaina, who was now talking with the guy next to her. I wondered how far she really expected me to take this case.

Soltani followed my gaze and rolled her eyes. "It's probably better for you to stay here, anyway. I'm the type of person who prefers to work alone."

When I looked back at Elaina, her admirer was gone and she was sitting by herself again.

"You just told me that your bosses wouldn't let you just up and fly across the globe?" I said.

Soltani shook her head. "It's one guy. ACD Kingsbury—the Assistant Chief Deputy, and he's a real prick. Besides, I've got plenty of unused time on the books. I'll just call it an impromptu vacation. The Service doesn't have to know where I am or what I'm doing."

I asked if she'd be in trouble if they found out.

"This whole mess is solely my responsibility," she said, not really answering the question. "Everything was going smoothly with the protectee, until it wasn't. I have no idea why JR fled or who is after him, and I'm not going to rest until I find out."

With that, she knocked back the rest of her drink and stood to leave. She started to unsnap her small clutch purse, and I raised a hand to stop her.

"I've got this," I said. "It's the least I can do to thank you for your help." She didn't have to know that I already planned on submitting the receipt to Elaina as a business expense.

Soltani smiled. "I guess I'll catch you up on *your case* when I get back." Then she walked out, passing within a foot of Elaina—who had turned around on her barstool and had watched the exchange between the two of us.

The "your case" crack had been a low blow. I wanted to go after Soltani and let her know that it wasn't as if I was afraid to travel. Hell, I bounced all over the world when my dad was in the Navy. It's just that as an adult, I'm more comfortable staying put.

Elaina waited until Soltani got on the elevator, then came directly over to my table and sat down. "Quite an attractive woman," she said. "Isn't she the same one I saw leaving your room?"

I nodded. "She's a Deputy U.S. Marshal, and she was assigned to your brother."

"Well, she must have done a piss-poor job of it." Elaina sat back, eyeing the empty tumblers. "Does she know where Johnny is yet?"

"No, but we've been working on it."

Elaina was about to deliver another smart comment, so I spoke before she could. "Why are you here, anyway? I thought you were heading back."

She raised a shoulder. "Couldn't get a flight until tomorrow."

"Well," I said. "The update is; it's looking like your brother may have left the country. So we're at kind of a dead end."

It took a few seconds to compute, then Elaina rolled her head back and let out a sigh. "Do you have any idea where?"

Several thoughts wrestled for position in my mind. For one, I knew that Elaina would try to pressure me into following the clues, no matter where they led. Not that my nearly comatose private eye business couldn't use the money, but even if Elaina could entice me to go to Bangkok, I wouldn't have the slightest idea where to start. Besides, I didn't trust that Elaina wouldn't show up there like she had here.

My client also seemed a tad jealous about my relationship with Soltani, which was a little concerning. On the other hand, I hadn't had that kind of attention in a really long time and it actually felt pretty good. I tried to keep that out of the decision-making process, but the fantasy of two woman fighting for my attention had wormed its way into my head along with the rest of the factors—though to be honest, it really was only a fantasy.

Finally, I realized that working overseas with Soltani—a stunning woman in her own right—might make foreign travel at least a little more bearable. That, and the money, convinced me to throw Elaina off the scent while I continued investigating the case.

"No," I said to Elaina. "We have no idea where he's gone." I felt guilty for lying, especially when I saw her crushed expression. "But I'm going to stay on it a few more days to see what I can come up with. What about you?" I asked. "Are you headed back for sure this time?"

"In the morning," she said, without looking up. "Please call me if you find out anything." Defeated, she got up and left without another word.

My waiter gave me the bill, along with an envious grin about the two women who had taken turns at my table. It was a slight ego boost, though it mattered little since both women were now long gone.

We were three hours ahead of the West Coast, and I realized that Shanay might still be in the office. She answered the phone, leading with her new title.

"Shanay, it's me. I'm still in D.C."

"I know it's you, your name's on my caller ID."

"Anyway," I said, "I wanted to let you know that I'll be out for a few more days."

"Uh-huh."

"And I think I'm going to book a flight to Bangkok."

"Uh-huh."

"Thailand," I added.

"I know where Bangkok is at. Hey, can you pick me up one of them silk kimonos?"

"What?"

"I'll pay you back, McKenna."

I shook my head. "Look, just don't give out information or tell anybody else where I am."

"I ain't told nobody where you at."

"Okay, whatever. I'll check back in a couple of days."

I hung up before she could respond.

Having already fronted the money for my trip out to Washington, I was now going to buy a ticket to Thailand. My credit card limit was hovering over my head, and I could only hope that Elaina would compensate me sooner than later for my out-of-pocket costs.

My next call was to Cathay Pacific Airlines.

CHAPTER 26

The flight was horrific. I was sandwiched in the middle seat between two women who talked across me in a language that I couldn't understand. Our row was at the back of the plane, flush against the bathroom bulkhead. So, aside from the foot traffic and a sundry of obnoxious odors, the seat couldn't recline. With my legs crammed against the seatback in front of me, my bad knee throbbed something awful. I blamed Elaina for hiring me, and I blamed Deputy Soltani even more for losing the kid in the first place.

Finally able to get up and stretch, I walked around the aircraft until I found Soltani. She was in the first class section, asleep next to an empty wine glass and a half eaten meal. I could have kicked myself for not spending the extra money for a top-shelf seat, since Elaina was paying the tab.

I stood there for a minute, full of envy and wanting to wake her out of spite, then settled for snatching the desert cup off of her tray before walking back to the economy section.

The two women had moved next to one another, which left me the aisle seat flush up against the line of people waiting to use the bathroom. I could extend one leg into the aisle now and then, but otherwise it wasn't much of an improvement. The ladies stopped talking only long enough to watch me wolf down the stolen apple crisp.

About the time I was ready to ask the flight attendant for a rope to hang myself, the pilot announced our arrival at Hong Kong International Airport. We were to deplane there, go through another security check, and then board the final 2½ hour flight to Bangkok.

Being one of the last people to leave the plane, I didn't see Soltani again until we landed the next morning in Thailand. Feeling as if I'd been mailed across the ocean in a FedEx box, I was also hungry and tired.

When I finally caught up with Soltani at baggage claim, she gave me a wry grin as if she'd known all along that I'd join her on the trip.

"Decided to come," I said.

"I see that."

"What time is it here?"

"Three o'clock in the morning," she plucked a purple hard-sided spinner off of the carousel. "So, where do we start?"

My carryon duffel bag was already slung over my shoulder. "How about with breakfast and maybe a nap?"

"He's already a day ahead of us," she said.

"Exactly. That's why another couple of hours won't make any difference."

The deputy rolled her eyes, an indicator that she already regretted my coming with her.

"Look," I said in a conciliatory tone. "It's nighttime. Johnny, I mean JR, is probably asleep anyway, right?"

She nodded.

"And at some point he'll probably reach out to whoever he knows in Bangkok." I tapped the side of my head. "I'm thinking that means the embassy where he used to be assigned."

"Makes sense."

"So, what do you say we start there in the morning? Like, after some rest and after I get something in my stomach."

We took a tuk-tuk through a maze of streets—still sweltering and still crowded, even at that time of night. We had the driver take us by the embassy which we knew would be closed. The place was tucked safely behind a high wall that surrounded the entire complex. The perimeter was well lit and guarded by a solitary Thai policeman.

Directly across the street stood the Monet House. I made a mental note to check it out more thoroughly after we ate.

I asked the driver to drop us off at the closest 24-hour restaurant. It only took him a few blocks to find a Lebanese eatery called Bamboo. When we stepped off in front of the place, I realized that we hadn't purchased any Thai currency at the airport. The driver reluctantly accepted a U.S. $20 bill, which I figured would probably make him a millionaire once he exchanged it. The bigger problem was that now I'd have to wait until the banks opened before I had money to buy some breakfast. At least the place was air conditioned.

Over Soltani's objection, we sat ourselves at the only open table in the packed restaurant. It was way in the back, and I assured her that we wouldn't be noticed.

"We'll be fine. It's just for an hour or two." I glanced around the place, watching a waiter serve a customer at another table. It was a big dish of what looked like golf balls made of sawdust. "You probably love this stuff," I told Soltani.

"What? What stuff?"

"You know, like eggplant and falafels, and, what's that other stuff? Baba ghanoush?"

Her expression was skeptical. "Yeah, it's okay. Why?"

"Well, you know, being from there and all..."

"Being from where?"

"Uh, Lebanon?" I thought I had impressed her by nailing it, but apparently not.

"I'm from Long Island."

"Oh, I mean, what about your parents?"

"Do they like this food?"

"No. I meant, where are they from?"

Soltani's lips grew tight. "They're from Iran. We refer to ourselves as Persian."

"Uh-huh." I slunk back into the booth. "Yeah, I really like it... the food... stuff from that area... I mean, I can eat just about anything."

A subtle shake of her head and Soltani leaned back and closed her eyes. She kept them shut and did not speak again.

I knew right away that watching other people eat would make for a torturous wait until the sun came up. So, I focused my attention on Deputy Soltani who had apparently fallen asleep next to me.

She had really nice skin—coppery colored and perfectly smooth. And she smelled good too, even after the long flight. I couldn't say the same for myself, however.

After a while, I closed my eyes and rested my head against the booth back.

The next thing I knew, Soltani was rubbing my arm. I was in sort of a dream state, and I imagined her snuggling against me. With my eyes still closed, I stretched and positioned myself so she could more easily tuck her head against my shoulder. But when I opened my eyes, I saw it wasn't her pressing against me.

A uniformed police officer stood to my side, his nightstick driving firmly into my arm.

CHAPTER 27

I thought I was having a flashback, only this guy wasn't a Greenbelt cop. Thankfully, the officer only wanted our seats.

He stood there devoid of expression while we gathered our things and slunk out of the restaurant—still hot, still hungry and still tired.

The sun had come up, and we decided to make another pass by the embassy. It was quiet and the entire complex appeared to have been abandoned—save for a single Thai policeman who kept watch outside. From the narrow street, the only thing visible was the high wall of white brick surrounding it. We walked by, slowing to peer past the guarded gate to a green courtyard behind it.

Two blocks down, we found a currency exchange with a heavily tinted window facing the street. The Happy Money Exchange was happy to gouge me their flat fee for anything under $500, which amounted to about 25% right off the top. The woman behind the glass was kind enough to let me know that most businesses and restaurants will accept American credit cards as well.

I turned in time to see Soltani rolling her eyes.

Cringing, I asked Soltani, "How would I know we could have charged breakfast?"

Slipping the exchange receipt into my pocket for eventual reimbursement, I longed to get out of the blistering heat and inside a modern, air conditioned building.

As we headed back in the general direction of the embassy, I noticed we had strayed into a circular cluster of fancy hotels, business offices, and indoor malls. I assumed these were well positioned to take advantage of dignitaries visiting the embassy—Thailand being the most stable country for Southeast Asian interests. In fact, as we walked around getting the lay of the land, I spotted the embassies of the Russia, Kazakhstan, Vietnam, Qatar, Ukraine, and Latvia, all within a few blocks of one another.

I also spotted a woman seated behind a two-wheeled food cart on the corner, a colorful patio umbrella shading her smoldering grill. Though not the steak and eggs I had hoped for, I ended up with a half dozen *moo ping*—barbecued pork skewers—for about a buck.

I made quick work of them, washing it all down with a cherry soda served in a plastic bag. Soltani watched with disgusted amazement as I licked the garlicky *moo ping* marinade from my fingers.

Heading back to the embassy, I now noticed a police car parked across the street from it with two policemen inside. A little further down were two men in a black Suzuki Swift. It was obvious to me that they were undercover detectives. Interesting level of security, I thought to myself.

"What do you make of that?" asked Soltani, who had found it odd as well.

By then, the strap of my bag was digging into my sweaty neck and all I could do was shrug. "We need to find a place to stow our luggage and get out of this heat."

"Monet House," said Soltani. "Says they're serviced apartments. Kind of like a hotel, but I think they're for longer term tenants."

"I don't really care about the cost to my client at this point." We turned into the driveway. "I just want to find this kid and get the hell out of here."

The building manager rented us a two-bedroom unit, but required that we pay in advance for the minimum stay of 30 days. I charged the entire bill on my own credit card, the thorny reality of which was soothed only by the fact that Soltani hadn't balked at the shared quarters. *She's finally warming to me.*

It was a tidy little apartment that came fully furnished, including washer/dryer combination—which would definitely get some use, since I'd only brought enough clothes for a two-day trip to D.C.

The small kitchen looked to be well-stocked, and it included a miniature fridge. The living room was pretty plain, with only one framed print—a tree with gold leaves in sort of a Buddhist style. There was a flat screen TV, a compact stereo CD player, and on the coffee table was a glossy magazine featuring the major tourist attractions in Bangkok.

Soltani claimed one of the rooms, then hoisted her suitcase onto the bed. I sat in the living room while she showered and changed. Meanwhile, my mind played different amorous scenarios in which she beckoned me to her room—clad in only a towel. Unfortunately, there was no beckoning.

Also unfortunate, was that our apartment's windows faced the wrong direction—southward across Ruam Rudi 5 Alley, toward the Holy Redeemer Church. On the opposite corner sat a 7-Eleven. I wanted to get myself the biggest Slurpee they had, but the A/C felt too good to leave the building.

I had just reclined on the sterile white couch when Soltani came in. Her clothes consisted of a sleeveless denim blouse, shapely white capri pants, and sandals. Her figure just kept looking better with each outfit I saw her in.

"We need to get up on the roof," she said.

I grunted, tossing the magazine back on the coffee table. "Hey, did you know that all males in Thailand were required at one time to be Buddhist monks?"

"When was that?" she asked, halfheartedly.

"A while ago, I guess."

Soltani huffed. "Anyway, we need to see if JR makes contact at the embassy."

She was right, but the roof was going to be scorching. Even worse than the street, it was closer to the spiteful sun. And I still hadn't slept in more than a day.

As I willed myself up from the couch, I said, "Another fun fact: Bangkok was just named the world's hottest city."

Trudging onto the rooftop deck, I knew why. Again, I cursed the blistering heat.

A portion of the roof was covered by a pergola, and a smattering of potted saplings decorated the perimeter. I slid a couple of deckchairs to the building's rim, which stood about waist high, and gazed down at the street from there. We watched the police cars and the guard in front of the embassy, until 4 o'clock came and they closed the gate to the public. There had been no sign of Elaina's brother.

"This is really a shot in the dark," said Soltani. "JR could have made contact with his embassy friends before we arrived, or he could have other connections in Bangkok that we don't even know about. Or, maybe he simply called them on a phone."

"Unfortunately, this is all we have to go on right now." I thought for a minute, wondering if there was a less passive way to move this surveillance along. It was cooling off just a bit and soft lights had come on beneath the pergola. We watched the last of the sun disappear beneath the rust colored smog.

I'd spotted a steakhouse around the corner, and after a quick shower I dressed in the same clothes again. *Note to self: Buy some new underwear, a couple of pants, and a couple of shirts.*

Soltani seemed deep in thought as we walked to the restaurant. She raised an eyebrow as she looked at the sign, seemingly surprised that I'd found such a nice place.

We slid into a booth and I ordered us a couple of scotches.

"I know what you're doing," she said.

"What am I doing?"

"I see your eyes, scrolling over me when I come into the room."

"I scrolled over you?" I shrugged. "Like what, my emails?"

"Humph! This romantic restaurant, the drinks . . ."

"Uh, I thought you might be hungry," I said. "And I remembered you liked a good scotch."

"Maybe your law enforcement groupies get all worked up because you're an ex-jock and an ex-cop, but I'm not one of them."

I leaned back in my seat, my face twisting into a knot. "Huh?"

"We're not sleeping together," she said. "Never. Plain and simple, it ain't gonna happen."

Stunned, I sat there staring at my silverware. Other than my brief fantasy while waiting for her to shower, I hadn't really thought that far down the road. I guess I was kind of hurt by what she said, but more so by the vehemence with which she had said it. However I had come across to her, that window was definitely closed now—locked and barricaded.

"Feel better?" I asked. "Now that you got that off your chest, why don't you pick out an appetizer?"

Her declaration had totally taken the buoyancy out of the night. When our drinks arrived, I wanted to tell the waiter to keep them coming. I was afraid to look up at her for fear that my eyes might inadvertently "scroll" over her, so I kept them aimed toward the tiny table candle.

"Look, McKenna..." Soltani's shoulders dropped a bit. "I didn't mean to--"

I cut her off with a palm in the air. "No worries. You said what you wanted to say, now let's just find this guy and wrap up the case."

We ordered dinner. Soltani had pan seared scallops and I got a New York steak. With another drink it went down easily, though the conversation was almost nil. It gave me time to think about how best to proceed—with the case, that is.

"Let's give the embassy surveillance one more day," I finally said after the waiter brought the check. "If our boy still hasn't shown, we'll take the next step."

"We have a 'next step'?"

I nodded. "I have a plan to flush JR out of hiding."

CHAPTER 28

They had waited patiently for three days, until the end of the new year celebration. Venturing out of their room only for meals, JR and Mai had taken advantage of the ICONSIAM Shopping Center's close proximity. The massive venue with 500 stores and 100 restaurants was literally next door.

JR had found a way to scale the fence between the hostel and the shopping mall, so they wouldn't risk being seen on the street.

At 6:50 a.m. on Thursday—the first day after the holiday—they left the hostel. Hailing a tuk-tuk at the end of the alley, JR planned to be at the embassy when they opened at 7 o'clock. He and Mai had heard the rain come during the night, and hoped it would afford them some measure of concealment

The three-wheeled taxi turned and made its way past the front of the embassy, which was blocked off to vehicle and pedestrian traffic. Two policeman in orange slickers stood on either side of the driveway behind traffic cones of the same color.

"That's weird," said JR. "Tell the driver to go around to the back entrance."

"I understand English," said the grinning man.

JR was too preoccupied to return the smile.

As the tuk-tuk turned onto Sol Ruam Ruedi, JR saw the Thai police cars, both marked and undercover, positioned around the public gate leading into the embassy complex. He then realized what his gut had been trying to tell him.

"Keep going," he shouted to the driver. "Something isn't right."

Mai instinctively sunk into her seat and turned her head away.

"What is it?" she asked.

"All the cops around here." Once they were a safe distance away, JR glanced back over his shoulder. "I worked security at the embassy for over two years, and I can sense when something is wrong."

"He knows." Mai's moist dark eyes widened with dread. "Uncle knows we're here."

JR's face turned ashen. "I used a fictitious name on a phony passport. We went straight from the airport to the hostel, and we paid cash for everything. We've barely left our room. How could anyone have figured out that we're here?"

"All I know is that those are *his* men back there. They wouldn't be parked around the embassy unless they were watching for us."

"What do you mean, '*his* men'?"

Mai's narrow eyebrows wrinkled. "I thought I told you... Uncle is a colonel in the Thai Royal Police. He runs the Central Investigation Bureau."

"Uh, no," said JR. "You neglected to mention that. I thought you meant a military colonel. All you said was that he wasn't really your uncle, and that he was a very powerful man. I had no idea he was a bigwig cop."

"Well, that's what I meant by *very powerful.*" She lowered her eyes. "He must have connections with the immigration people at the airport, too."

"Hence, his cops watching for us at the embassy."

Mai shrugged. "Uncle probably assumes we will try to contact your friends there."

"*Friend,*" he said. "Singular. Everyone else I've worked with has moved on. But Shawn was my best friend, and if there's anyone who can help us it's him."

The driver had pulled to a stop in an alley where a massage parlor butted up against a small motel. Waiting there, he kept his eyes respectfully on the roadway ahead.

JR leaned up and tapped the man's shoulder. "Hey, what's your name?"

"It's Panit, sir."

JR feathered a handful of bills like a game of Old Maid. "Panit, I'd like you to do a favor for us."

CHAPTER 29

The new morning brought rain. It seemed to be suspended in the air, cooling nothing, and adding only steamy haze to the already stifling day. We took turns staring over the parapet, down at the steady flow of visitors to the embassy—none of whom matched JR's description.

The rain stopped around midday, and the sun sizzled its way through the remaining clouds to find us. As I melted in my chair, I began to see my idea of staking out the embassy as ludicrous.

Soltani stood abruptly, her chair nearly tipping over backwards.

"Did you spot him?" I asked, jumping to my feet.

"No, a damn bird just shat on me!" She palmed the shoulder of her blouse. "I'm done with this watching and waiting thing. Let's hear your *next step* plan."

"You go inside the embassy," I said. "Flash your credentials, make noise, let everyone know you're looking for Jonathan Teagan. And be sure that the Marine guards all hear you."

"What about you?" she asked.

"I'll hang around outside. Since JR doesn't know what I look like, it would be better if you and I aren't seen together."

At 3 p.m., an hour before closing, we kicked the plan into gear. Separating as if we were strangers, we started down the block toward the embassy—Soltani on one side of the street and me on the other.

I hung back, sauntering around the unmarked police car as Soltani approached the security gate. The two men inside the Suzuki glared at me, and I gave them a lame grin. "How do you like the Swift?" I asked. "Does she get good gas mileage?"

The detectives waved me off, clearly trying to remain incognito.

I shrugged and continued to where the uniformed cops sat in their tiny patrol car. Not that I was trying to bother anybody, but I wanted to sniff the air for tension, reaction, or interest in Soltani as she accessed the embassy grounds.

"Hey fellas," I said. "Mind if I take a selfie with you guys?"

"No," said the driver, putting a hand in my face. "No picture."

Another disarming grin. "Yeah, sure, I get it, but can I ask another question?" I continued the dense American tourist routine. "How do I get to Khao San Road?" I'd read in a travel magazine that the area was good for foreigners—*backpacking hub of Southeast Asia*, it said.

The cop in the passenger seat took a map from the glovebox and rattled off directions, none of which I understood or cared about.

While standing at their car door, I noticed a 5x7 photograph propped on their dashboard. I leaned down, almost through the open window, to better view the picture. But it wasn't of JR, as I had hoped.

Thanking them for the directions, I ambled off to wait for Soltani at the end of the block. When there was still no sign of her after 15 minutes, I began to wonder if she had struck pay dirt. Maybe she had bumped into JR inside, or maybe someone in the embassy had information about him. Worse case, Soltani had run into trouble and was being detained. My past experience in that area had left me with a bad taste, and I hoped it was paranoia rather than premonition.

I took my mind off of the wait by window shopping at a small clothing store near the corner. A stack of colorful shirts were fanned out across a folding table, and I ducked inside for a closer look. Only two were large enough to fit me, so I grabbed them both. But none of their pants were long enough to even reach my ankles. Finally locating a rack of shorts, I bought the only pair they had in my size. Kind of a cat-puke mauve color, which didn't go with the shirts but at least they would fit.

Beneath a 2-for-1 advertisement sat a basket of reading glasses, and I grabbed a couple of those as well before leaving the store.

Soltani still hadn't come out, so I loitered at the end of the block wondering what I'd do if she never returned. Then I realized that I should have bought some underwear while I was in the store. About to go back, I finally spotted Soltani stepping through the embassy gate onto the street.

I let out a long breath as I hustled over to her. "What happened?" I asked. "You were inside for an hour. I was about to go in after you."

"There was a line." We turned the corner and crossed the street to the 7-Eleven. "But I created a scene," she said. "And by the time I left, everyone within a quarter mile knew I was a United States Federal Agent looking for Jonathan Teagan—AKA JR Travis."

I stood in front of the market, stunned; she'd never used his real name before.

"I know," she said. "But the Marines he worked with knew him as Teagan, and the passport he's using says Travis. Figured for your plan to work, I had to lay it all out there."

We went inside the 7-Eleven. No A/C, but a portable fan. I bought a map of the city and a large watermelon Slurpee.

"What now?" she asked.

"Now we wait." Sipping my drink as we headed back to the apartment, I said, "The embassy closes in half an hour. You watch from the roof and I'll watch from down on the street."

“What are we watching for?”

“A Marine,” I said as we walked into our building’s lobby. “These guys stick together like glue. If JR’s going to contact anyone over here, it’ll be one of his fellow jarheads. Call me on my cell phone as soon as you see anything.”

CHAPTER 30

Panit's hungry eyes were tinged with uncertainty.

"We need you to contact a Marine guard inside the embassy for us. His name is Shawn Foster. All you have to do is make sure he gets this note, and then you come back here to pick us up."

Panit thought for a minute, then bowed awkwardly in his seat. "Which note, sir?"

"Well, I haven't written it yet," said JR. "Wait here a sec."

JR bolted into the alley, with a raised arm shielding himself from the rain. Several minutes later he returned with a message scribbled on Jim's Lodge stationary.

"What does it say?" Mai asked JR as he climbed back into the shelter of the tuk-tuk.

She cocked her head to read it.

> *Shawn –*
>
> *In town and need money. Sending Mai to meet you at Wongwian Yai Market today when you get off work.*
>
> *John*

Then he folded the note and handed it to Panit. "You got it?"

Panit nodded. "John Foster."

"No," said JR. "I'm John. It's Shawn Foster. Shawn!"

Panit nodded again. "Zhawn Foster."

The man's accented pronunciation still sounded wrong. JR rolled his eyes as their driver rattled away with the message.

"Do you think we can trust him?" asked Mai as they ducked under a covered doorway to wait.

"Who, Shawn?"

"No, the driver."

JR shrugged. "I can't think of any other way to let Shawn know that we're in Bangkok. If anyone can help us, Shawn will."

She lifted an eyebrow.

"What?" JR frowned back.

"You have that much confidence in your friend?"

A customer inched past them on his way out of the massage spa.

"Shawn never had it easy," said JR.

"I remember you telling me that he was some sort of troublemaker when he was young."

JR nodded. "His mother died when he was a kid, and his father was pretty much out of the picture. Shawn told me he was sent to live with an aunt in Baltimore, then she kicked him out when he was sixteen."

"Why?" Mai studied JR with penetrating eyes.

"He got arrested for pulling a robbery."

Her expression was now even more doubtful.

JR shrugged. "I guess he spent the next few years in and out of jail."

"Then I can see why you trust him so much."

"Hey, he was still just a kid. Anyway, he must have figured it out, because he dropped out of the gangs and joined the Corps."

Mai heard the passion in JR's voice. It always happened when he talked about his time as a Marine. "Was that when you met him?" she asked.

"No, it was a few years later during his second deployment in Afghanistan. My first. Shawn kind of took me under his wing. Then, at the end of 2014, we both decided to reenlist. Our commander recommended us for MSG duty and--"

"MSG?"

"Marine Corps Embassy Security Group," he said. "It's actually MCESG. Anyway, we were both approved for *change of station* to our embassy in Bangkok."

Mai stared back at him, trying to feel a brotherhood that JR knew she couldn't. It was impossible for anyone who has never served, especially someone from another country and another culture.

"Shawn is a good man," JR finally said. "And yes, I trust him with both of our lives."

"Well, just in case..."

"In case what?"

Mai motioned toward the street. "In case your note to Shawn falls into the wrong hands or gets intercepted by Uncle's men, we might want to think about getting out of here quickly."

JR frowned. "Speaking of which, is there anything else I should know about this uncle who isn't really an uncle?"

"Yes," she said. "Besides being with the police, he's also connected with Red Wa—a Thai criminal organization. Which is how he came to own me."

"Wait a minute. What?"

CHAPTER 31

Soltani said nothing in response to my plan, only stared at me as she stepped onto the elevator and punched the button to the roof.

I left the building, hailed a tuk-tuk, and told the driver to pull around to the side of the church and park. He didn't seem to relish the idea of us idling there while we waited, so I cajoled him with a promise of double his normal rate. Happier now, he shook my hand and introduced himself as Panit. "I like to drive Americans," he said.

Thirty minutes and 300 Baht later, my cell phone buzzed.

"I don't know exactly what we're looking for," said Soltani, "but I'm watching the Marine guard who was right there when I put on my performance."

"What's he doing?"

"He just came out of the gate on a motorcycle, and now he's stopped, talking with another guard out front."

"Okay, good," I said. "Come down to the church parking lot and we'll follow him."

I had Panit pull forward a bit, so I could get a better view of the embassy. The black Yamaha was still on the sidewalk, driven by a young, dark-skinned man with short cropped hair. He was wearing a blue windbreaker over what looked like his service uniform.

Soltani joined me in the tuk-tuk, just as the motorcycle pulled onto the street. The Marine was coming right toward us, and Soltani had to shield her face to keep from being recognized. As the motorcycle passed, I told Panit to follow it.

We were headed west on a main thoroughfare with several lanes—not that Panit or any of the other drivers stayed within them. The guy on the bike snaked through traffic at a pretty good clip, and our driver did his best to stay with him. Soltani's focused expression was set like steel while we jockeyed around pedestrians and bicycles. I noticed, however, that her hands were gripped tightly to the undercarriage of the seat just like mine were.

The Marine veered to the right as the road split, and Panit quickly maneuvered the rattling tuk-tuk across traffic to follow. Crossing a concrete bridge, which I jerkily followed on the map with my finger, we emerged in a district called Khlong San. It wasn't long before the streets narrowed, traffic slowed, and we were able to sidle up behind the motorcycle without being noticed.

The Marine was now glancing around as he drove, but not as if he was worried about a tail. He was clearly looking for someone in the crowd of shoppers. Slowing abruptly at a large outdoor market, the motorcyclist drove onto the sidewalk and parked.

I motioned for Panit to continue to the corner, at which time Soltani and I got out on foot. Having no time to count out the foreign change, I just stuffed another wad of Bhat into the driver's eagerly awaiting palms. Gathering from his bowing and prayer-clasped hands, the payment was more than enough to cover the ride.

"The Marine may recognize me," said Soltani. "I should probably hang back a little."

"Okay, but call me on the phone if we get separated." I moved quickly through the crowd, trying to get back to where we last saw him. As I careened through carts overflowing with vegetables, I passed by tubs and boxes with both live and dead animals. There were also turtles, eels, frogs, and all manner of sea life, along with their attendant odors.

I finally spotted the motorcycle, upright on its kickstand, but with no one around it. About 50 feet behind me, Soltani cautiously worked her way through the crowd. I waved my hand in a forward pointing motion to let her know that the bike was still there. A minute later I saw the Marine, standing with his back to me, next to a huge box of green bananas.

Stopping short of him, I loitered at the front of the tent-like structure. A moment later I felt Soltani's breath on my neck as she whispered, "Who's he talking to?"

I couldn't tell because the Marine's stalwart frame blocked my view of the other person. The terse conversation seemed secretive though, intentionally set in a busy location that would be difficult for anyone to follow or hear. That only meant one thing to me: they were worried about being seen.

"It looks like a covert meeting," I said.

As Soltani stepped around to get a better view, she said, "It's a woman."

Disappointment struck as I realized the clandestine meeting was most likely an illicit affair that had nothing to do with JR. "They're both probably married," I said.

Then, the Marine moved a bit and I did a double take.

"What?" Soltani looked from me to the woman and back to me.

"I recognize her," I said. "The cops who were parked outside the embassy had her photo in their car."

We stood among the clamoring shoppers and unrefrigerated food, wondering what it meant. Had we found a runaway, or perhaps one of Bangkok's most wanted?

The detective in me wanted to follow the girl, or call in a tip to the Bangkok police. But to what end? It would be like watching someone find twenty dollars on the street—good for them, but of no benefit to me.

I looked again at the young woman. Something about her seemed familiar, and it wasn't just the photograph of her in the cop car. I had actually seen her before... but where?

CHAPTER 32

The Thai woman motioned to the street behind her, as if giving directions. Then the Marine handed something to her, and she bowed slightly. It looked like an envelope, but I couldn't be certain from that distance.

They parted suddenly, and walked off in opposite directions. Unsure of which one to follow, I wondered if it was worth watching either of them. This whole idea of the Marine guard leading us to JR was kind of a needle in a haystack anyway.

"He's heading back to his motorcycle," said Soltani. "Let's see where he goes."

But something about the young woman pestered me. "Why don't you go after him," I said. "And I'll follow her."

Soltani rolled her eyes before stepping into the street to wave down a tuk-tuk.

I, on the other hand, gave my best effort to blend in with the local shoppers as I walked behind the girl. But as hard as I tried, I couldn't look like a five-foot-five Asian man. Because of that, I had to drop back quite a bit.

Luckily, the woman continued out of the market on foot, making it easier for me to tail her.

She emerged onto a wide, heavily traveled street, and I saw that her speed had picked up. She was now nervously looking around. That's when the identical image popped into my mind—same girl, nervously scanning the crowd. I had seen her back in D.C., getting off the shuttle in front of the airport. And the guy with her, the guy that looked like JR, had eyed me as we passed one another. *I knew it!*

The girl turned south, hustling along the uneven sidewalk, adeptly maneuvering past pedestrians, construction cones, and motorcycles parked like LEGOs dumped from a box.

My cell phone rang and I saw that it was Elaina. Her bad timing was remarkable, but then I wondered if holding the phone to my ear might help me blend in. Just another tourist talking on his cell. And to be honest, I was feeling pretty good about having made the connection between the girl and Elaina's brother.

"McKenna," I answered.

"Any news?"

"I was just about to call you," I said, trying to sound believable. "I'm almost certain that I've located him." Hesitating a beat for dramatic effect, I said, "In Bangkok, Thailand."

"Yeah, that's super. You're sure it's him?"

"Pretty sure," I said. "I'm following his girlfriend as we speak, and I think she may be leading me right to him."

Somewhat disappointed in Elaina's underreaction, I continued my surveillance narration. "Looks like she's crossing the street now, heading into a narrow alleyway. She's looking around a lot, but I'm experienced in this kind of thing, so..."

At that moment, the young woman turned all the way around and looked right at me. I hoped that my funky shorts and sappy look might be misleading enough to keep me invisible, but few people were in the alley and her eyes registered alarm as soon as they met mine.

"Son-of-a-bitch."

"What?" asked Elaina. "What's wrong?"

"Nothing. I... she... Never mind."

The girl dashed ahead down the alley. It was scattered with parked cars, bicycles, and motorcycles, but still very few people. Both sides were lined with narrow apartment buildings, crammed together like corn stalks in a field. Most had wide awnings that extended out across the pavement, casting shadows that looked like night against the blazing reflection.

The alley dead ended at a cement wall topped with metal fencing. The whole thing was about 12 feet tall. Beyond it was the river and then the towering buildings of downtown.

She was trapped. There was nowhere to run and no way out.

"McKenna?"

Elaina was still on the line, bothersome as ever.

"Just a sec," I said.

Maneuvering around a parked airport van, I half expected to find the young girl cowering against the building. But she was gone.

"McKenna? Are you still there?"

I slowed my pace, my head on a swivel, scanning into each doorway and shadowed alcove. But the woman was nowhere in sight. She'd literally disappeared.

Then I caught a glint of light, reflected on a closing glass door. Above it was a sign. "Petite Hostel," I read aloud. "I'll call you right back, Elaina."

I disconnected before JR's sister could get another word out, then continued past a rack of bicycles toward the door which had now swung shut. It was the entrance into the last building on the left side of the alley—a narrow, white, non-descript structure with balconies littered with clothes and towels drying in the midday sun.

The tiny lobby was empty, except for the man behind the counter.

"Welcome," he said.

I nodded to him as I sized up the setting. There were a couple of red, faux leather couches, a shelf with some tourism books, and a few well-worn local maps tacked to the wall. Craning my neck, I looked past a stairwell into what seemed to be a small internet room tucked in the back. It also appeared to be empty.

"The young woman that just came in," I said to the clerk. "Can you tell me which room she's in?"

He smiled politely. "Are you a relative?"

I tried to calm my breathing. "No, no. I recognized her out on the street and I tried to catch up to her before she came inside. I'm a very close friend of her boyfriend, JR."

He smiled again. "You may take a seat, and I'll call to announce you. Your name, sir?"

This wasn't going to work. First off, JR wouldn't know Danny McKenna from Adam. And secondly, he would assume I'd been sent to kill him. Getting a call from the clerk would only cause JR to run.

Then an idea came to me. With buildings crammed on either side of the hostel, JR's only escape would be out the back toward the river. I gazed through the window toward a jungle-like lot set between the rear of the hostel and the water.

"Please, yes," I said. "Tell him that a federal agent from the U.S. is waiting."

The man's eyes widened.

I forced a laugh. "It's a joke we used to play on each other. He'll know it's me."

As he placed the call to JR's room, I listened to the clerk's side of the conversation. "Mr. JR?" he said into the phone. "Your friend is here from the federal department in America."

The clerk had sort of airballed it, and the words hadn't come out exactly as I'd told him—though I hoped they were close enough.

With a conspiratorial grin as he hung up the phone, the clerk turned to me. But I was already rushing past him toward the rear of the lobby. I startled a young man who was sitting in front of a desktop computer, and then startled myself when I stumbled over the backpack on the floor next to him.

Through a side door I went, finding myself in an outdoor laundry room surrounded by low concrete walls. I used a washing machine to boost myself up and over, but the ground on the other side of the wall was a foot or two lower than on my side. I felt my bad knee pop as I hit the ground, and I let loose a string of profanities that made no sense.

Hearing a door open and then slam shut, I hobbled around the side of the building toward the source of the sound.

It was them. JR had the girl by the hand and was helping her onto a garbage bin next to the fence.

"Wait!" I yelled. "I've been hired by your sister."

But as I stumbled toward them, I could see they had already made it to the top of the fence. Instead of slowing them down, my plea had only incited them to move faster.

"Please," I said. "I'm not here to hurt you."

They were now on the other side of the chain link fence, standing on the loading dock of what looked like a massive shopping mall. And although we were now face-to-face, the fence stood between us. As long as it would take me to climb the damn thing, it might as well have been the Great Wall of China.

We stood there for a second, eyeing each other without a word. My hands rested on my knees as I struggled to catch my breath. "Your sister...she...just wants...to know that...you're alright."

His piercing blue eyes stared into mine. "That's funny," he said. "Because I don't even have a sister."

"What do you mean you don't have a sister?"

My question had sputtered out as if there was no air behind it. Sure, I knew what his words meant. But my brain was having trouble absorbing them.

"Of course you have a sister," I said, hoping to convince him of his obvious mistake. "She showed me your bedroom. Told me about your drum set and your mountain bike."

"Sorry buddy." He gave me a pitiful look. "Never had a drum set, and mine was a road bike, not a mountain bike."

My mouth hung open while my eyes stared into the nothingness behind them, still just trying to comprehend the consequences of it. *No sister* meant there was no Elaina Teagan. And no Elaina Teagan meant that she had tricked me. That she was actually somebody else. So, why would somebody else want me to find Jonathan Teagan for them?

A clamoring sound above me helped the final piece of the puzzle find its place in my brain. Three figures burst through the French doors and onto the balcony two floors up.

Suddenly, the air exploded in gunfire.

CHAPTER 33

Who the hell is going to pay me?

All I could think as bullets flew around me was the amount of money I'd spent on this investigation, charged on my personal credit card, and how in the world I was ever going to get reimbursed.

I stumbled backwards toward the building and out of the line of fire, the whole time trying to get a look at the shooters. Bullets ricocheted off of the fence and the concrete loading dock beyond it, sending sparks and shards of rock into the air. Meanwhile, JR and his girlfriend dove for cover out of my line of sight. I hoped they were still alive, as the gunfire seemed to be focused in their direction rather than mine. I wasn't taking any chances, though.

Moving as fast as possible, I hobbled back through the laundry room into the hostel. The computer kid was up now, crouching at the window, aiming his cell phone camera toward the action.

I made my way through the lobby toward the front door. Off to my left, the clerk cowered behind the counter where I assumed by this time he had called the police. The gunshots trailed off, which told me that the shooters would be making their way off the balcony soon. I didn't want to be around when they came downstairs, nor did I want to be in the area when the cops arrived.

But with my bum knee worse than ever, I was moving like an old man in line for the early bird dinner. With heavy footfalls descending the stairway behind me, I knew I was about to become a sitting duck.

I rumbled out the front door, looking around like a trapped animal. Then I saw the bicycles, lined up in a rack against the front of the building. Probably complimentary for their guests, I jumped on the first one I came to and launched it into a wobbly trajectory out of the alley. Instead of turning left at the main road, I went right along the face of the shopping mall.

Several tiny, silver colored police cars raced past me with their lights and sirens going. There were also motorcycle cops and others in small white cars—some of them slowing near the mall.

Pedaling like a madman, I raced past the row of stores then cut diagonally across the main thoroughfare behind the cops who had just passed. Horns blared and motorcycles swerved around me as I recklessly made it across all six lanes to the far side of the street. Stopping behind a food booth, I stayed hunkered down while I tried to catch my breath.

I waited until the last of the responding cops turned toward the hostel before finally straightening up again. I then noticed JR and the girl running from the area of the mall. They scanned frantically up and down the street as they weaved their way through pedestrians, and then ducked into some sort of outdoor plaza across the roadway. This being possibly my only opportunity to try another approach with JR, I headed back across the street.

This time I would lead with the Marshals Service angle, which I hoped would lend more credibility. But as I zigzagged across the busy street on the bicycle, I asked myself why I was risking my life. Essentially, there was no client paying me to find the kid. Aside from maxing out my credit card and missing my daughter's birthday, I had already been shot at twice. What did I care if Soltani's protectee didn't want to testify? He probably brought all this on himself anyway by getting involved with mobsters.

I made it to the other side and then stopped in front of the plaza. There were food booths, textiles and trinkets under a canopy of tents that only served to keep the sun out and the sweltering heat in. I'd lost sight of the couple, who had descended into the dark recesses of the place.

Then I thought about the wanted poster of the girl JR was with. Maybe there was a bounty on her head—some kind of reward for turning her in. And what about JR's confession in his farewell letter? Maybe he really was some kind of killer. The idea of a payout and associated fame was bait enough for me to stay in the hunt.

Taking up a position in front of the marketplace, I knew JR and the girl would have to come back out sooner or later. With the river behind them and buildings crammed on either side, it would be only a matter of time and patience.

"Excuse me, sir." The voice came from behind me.

I turned to find two uniformed men, their little white car stopped on the sidewalk a few yards away.

"Hi." It wasn't one of my more stellar responses, and it probably made me sound like an idiot. *Hi.*

"We are the Bangkok Tourist Police," he said. "May we see your identification?"

"Tourist Police? Is that even a thing?"

"Your ID, sir."

I patted the empty pockets of my mauve shorts and shrugged. "I must have left it at my apartment. Is there a problem?"

People were starting to gather around, and I envisioned JR and his girlfriend watching the goings on from behind a rack of monkey hides.

These guys didn't really seem like cops, and I doubted that Tourist Police would have law enforcement powers anyway. The fact that they carried only a radio, confirmed my hunch. Weighing their diminutive frames against my bad knee, I wondered if I could break away and outrun them. Probably break away, but not outrun.

Another car pulled to the curb—this one silver colored and packed with three more officers. These guys had guns.

One of the new arrivals, a dark and intense looking guy with a red sash over his shoulder, stepped up to me. "Turn away and place your hands behind your back. You are under arrest."

"You've got to be kidding me," I said.

Two of the others moved up on either side of me. "You are now in the custody of the Royal Thai Police."

I closed my eyes and tilted my head back.

Son-of-a-bitch!

CHAPTER 34

"How do you think they found me?" JR had hold of Mai's arm as they dashed through the shopping mall's food court.

"Did they find *you* or did they find *me*?" she said between gasping breaths. "We don't know for sure which one of us they were after."

"I got a look at them," said JR. "It was a woman and a couple of men, and they weren't Asian. Trust me, it isn't you *these* people are gunning for."

JR and Mai were both breathing hard, partly from the climbing and running but mostly from the shock of the shooting.

"You're hurt," said Mai. "There's blood on your shirt."

He didn't stop to look. "It's nothing." They slowed to a brisk walk in the mall's main rotunda, so as not to draw attention.

Two police officers—a man and a woman—suddenly appeared, walking toward them from the opposite direction.

"In here," said JR, tugging Mai into a store with a pink and white façade and a sign that read: For Cat Lovers.

When the cops had passed, they headed out toward the front, bursting onto the street like drowning victims coming up for air. They continued along the main roadway, slowing momentarily as more police raced past them enroute to the shooting scene.

"We need to get off the street," said JR.

"Up ahead on the right." Mai now took the lead, pulling JR by the hand. "Klongsan Plaza. Shops...under...tents," she gasped. "We'll be safe there. I can check your wound."

They ducked in, moving quickly past a row of green and yellow tuk-tuks queued up at the entrance.

"Wait," yelled JR as he stopped just inside the plaza. "Over there." He pointed to the other side of the street. "The white guy on the bicycle. He's the same one that thought I had a sister."

"He's following us," said Mai.

"The bastard led those people with guns right to us. He must be one of them."

JR took Mai by the hand again and rushed her deep into the recesses of the marketplace. It was narrow and long—a quarter mile end-to-end. The far side opened to the massive river. A wooden pier ran lengthways along the waterfront where a large red and white pontoon was tethered. They fell in line with other passengers lining up to board.

It was only then that JR felt the searing rip on the side of his abdomen. He pressed into it with his hand, feeling the sappy heat of his own blood.

Mai hesitated at the foot of the gangway. "We need to get you to a doctor."

"No hospital," he said. "It's just a scratch."

JR ushered Mai onto the water taxi, turning the bloodstain toward her so that nobody would notice. They were the last to board before the boat pulled onto the busy waterway.

"I didn't have time to grab my bag from the hostel," she said. "We need to find another place to stay, and we'll need some clothes."

"Did Shawn ever show up?" JR said. "I didn't even get a chance to ask you."

"Yes, he gave me this." She handed a plain envelope to JR.

Opening it, he thumbed the stack of bills inside. "There must be 3,000 Bhat in here. That's, like, a hundred bucks."

Mai nodded, then handed JR a business card. "Shawn also gave me this. He wrote his mobile number on it."

JR's eyes widened as he took the card. "I need to call him."

"And tell him what? We don't even know where we're going to be staying. Besides, he was already kind enough to give us money."

JR shook his head. "It's what a brother does when another Marine is in trouble. I'll wait 'til we figure out where we're staying, and then I'm going to reach out to Shawn."

Mai glanced down at JR's shirt. "We had better find a safe place soon, or you won't be able to hide that *'scratch'* much longer."

They took the water taxi directly across the river to the pier at the foot of Si Phraya Road. Police were everywhere, patrolling in groups on foot and in cars. Shootings like these were anomalous to Thai police, and it had obviously shaken them.

JR groaned under his breath, "We need to get off the street, now."

"Hotels on this side of the river are way too expensive," she said. "We'll have to take the Skytrain to the--"

"There's no way. Cops will be swarming all over the BTS stations." JR stopped to steady himself against the concrete balustrade that ran along the pier. "Besides, I'm not feeling too good."

Mai glanced around, saw the spired steeple, and reached around JR's waist. "C'mon, this way."

CHAPTER 35

"I didn't do anything wrong," I said to the officer next to me in the back seat. "What am I being charged with? Where are you taking me?"

He wore dark glasses and spoke without ever turning his head. "Have you heard of the Big Tiger?"

Feeling slightly relieved, I let out a long breath. It was a case of mistaken identity; they think I'm someone else.

The officer in the front passenger seat looked over his shoulder. "Theft of a bicycle will not be tolerated in Thailand. The penalty is three years in prison and a fine of 60,000 Baht."

"That was a mistake," I said. "And I was on my way to return it when you stopped me. I'm sure we can straighten this whole thing out if you take me back to my apartment. I'll get my passport and show you that I'm not this Tony the Tiger guy."

A chuckle worked its way through the car, stopping at me. We pulled up to a yellow building with maroon trim. The two-story edifice could have been a school, except it had state flags and concrete buttresses shaped like elephants on either side of the doors.

"What is this place?" I asked.

The cop sitting next to me finally removed his sunglasses. "They call it Big Tiger."

Above the front doors, a sign read: Bang Kwang Central Prison. Suddenly, I felt as if I was going to be sick. My head spun and I could barely breathe.

Immediately, I launched into panic mode. "I want to talk to a lawyer. I demand a phone call to the embassy. I know my rights. I'm an American citizen!"

They yanked me out of the car. "Maybe you didn't notice," one of them said. "You're not in America."

The guards at the door saluted my escorts as if they'd brought in Lee Harvey Oswald. Roughly ushering me through the golden bars of the prison's entry, I felt my legs shuddering like a marionette on a string. My knee didn't concern me anymore. The problems I faced were much worse than that.

Inside was dark, quiet, and extremely clean. We walked down a long corridor with offices on either side. It was maybe 75 yards long. At the end was another set of double doors, which we walked through. It led to a small, open air space in front of a barred gate. Once we were in the space, the doors closed behind us.

I had begun to think this might not be so bad, and then the cop with the red sash patted me down. He took my cell phone and then ordered me to strip off all of my clothes. Having been through this a couple of times before, I knew it was futile to argue.

My perky new t-shirt came off first, and then my mauve shorts. I had tossed my underpants in the trash back at the hotel, intending to buy a few new ones. The reaction of the two cops made me wish I hadn't gotten rid of them. One officer spoke to the other, who then took out a pen and scribbled something on a small notepad.

They confiscated my t-shirt, my shoes, and my cell phone, then told me to put my shorts back on.

As soon as I did, the gate in front of me swung open revealing a gigantic interior courtyard. It was a zoo, packed full of humanity in its lowest forms. I felt as if I'd stumbled onto the set of The Falcon and the Snowman. Assaulted by the disgusting odors of crap, piss, and cooking food, I was afraid to take another breath. Prisoners of every size, color, and nationality mingled about in the sweltering heat, some in groups, some alone talking to themselves, and others doing push-ups or taking swings at imaginary opponents.

Where were the guards? I glanced toward a gun tower high above me. Two men sat lazily behind rifles pointed downward. Other than the crow's nest, security inside the compound was nearly nonexistent. It seemed like 1,000 prisoners to 1 guard.

We continued through the yard, passing a line of gas stoves and charcoal cooking grates where the inmates were preparing their own meal—if you could call it food.

A man sprawled against the wall lay there motionless, his film-covered eyes fixed in a distant stare. The guy looked dead to me. Another man with a stump for a leg sat on the dirt, sobbing. His oozing wound appeared infected, and I supposed he would soon join the dead guy. A little further, a group of women stood in a corner applying makeup to each other's faces.

"*Ladyboys*," said one of my police escorts. "Be careful or the Nigerians will make you into one, too."

My stomach lurched as I quickly glanced around. Several hulking men with ink black skin huddled together smoking cigarettes. They were twice as big as anyone else in the place. I also saw some white Europeans, though most of the prisoners were Asian.

A guard approached and spoke in Thai to the cops who had brought me in, then motioned with his hand. We all moved off in an easterly direction toward what resembled apartment houses.

They took me through another gate with signage in several languages. The one in English read: COMPOUND #5.

No one in the world knew I was here, not Soltani and not my family. Not even the U.S. Embassy. The farther we walked, the more I felt as if I was sinking deeper and deeper into a bottomless chasm. More panicked with each step, I finally stopped and demanded that the embassy be notified of my arrest.

Unimpressed, one of them roughly prodded me onward with the end of his nightstick. They walked me up a stairway to a second floor landing and stopped in front of a heavy door secured by a padlock.

My heart raced as they unlocked it and opened the door. Inside were 40 or 50 men laying shoulder to shoulder on thin blankets spread across the floor. The far side of the room had a large opening—like a window without glass—which was covered with bars and then louvers so you couldn't see out. Above me were a couple of ceiling fans and a single hanging fluorescent light.

And I thought the Mexican jail was bad.

The prisoners grumbled at the sight of a newcomer who would need more space in a room that had none to offer. The smells hit me like a baseball bat across the nose, making my stomach suddenly seesaw. I began gagging uncontrollably, causing my captors to break into laughter.

It was the straw that broke me. Wheeling around to face them, I yelled, "Wait! I need to talk to someone!"

They smirked as they turned toward the door, about to abandon me inside this hell.

"No!" I yelled. "I'm serious! I know where to find someone you guys are looking for. The police officers outside the U.S. Embassy had a girl's picture in their car. She's wanted for something, and only I know where she is."

It was a huge bastardization of the truth. Since the shooting at the hostel, there was little chance the girl and JR would return there. In essence, I really had no idea where she was—not to mention, what she was wanted for.

The cop with the sash turned and stared curiously at me before saying something in Thai to the others. It seemed to have struck a chord. At least, that's what I tried to convince myself as they walked out and closed the door. I heard the big padlock clamp shut on the outside, which to my ears might as well have been nails hammered into my coffin.

I was suddenly so dizzy that my legs nearly crumpled beneath me. Taking in a deep breath, thick with sweaty despair, I turned back toward my new roommates.

Fifty angry men glared back at me.

CHAPTER 36

The Holy Rosary Church was tucked along the eastern bank of the Chao Phraya River. Built in the 1890s, the ornate building offered sanctuary to the Roman Catholic residents of the Samphanthawong District. On this April evening, it would also serve as a hiding place for Jonathan Teagan and Mai Nakhon.

Kneeling in the empty sanctuary, Mai said a prayer for their continued safety while JR reclined on the wooden pew next to her. Neither of them had a plan, but for the time being they rested in the silence of the church, away from the crowds and the heat.

The bleeding from JR's injury had coagulated some, but his shirt had turned into a sticky mess that threatened to fuse to the wound. Mai wanted to get a better look, but JR wouldn't let her remove his shirt to examine or clean the injured area.

"You are a big baby, do you know that?" Mai gave him a playful swat.

JR closed his eyes as a smile crept onto his face.

"We can't stay here," said Mai.

"Why not?" JR's eyes were still closed. "It's Friday. There aren't any services on Fridays."

"Maybe in America," she said, "but churches in Thailand have lots of masses." Mai got up and walked to the rear of the church where a schedule was posted behind a glass case. When she slid back into the pew, she said, "The bad news is, yes, they have a 5:30 p.m. service tonight."

One of JR's eyes inched open. "What's the good news?"

"The mass is in English," she said. "You'll be able to understand every word of it."

He started to laugh, but grimaced at the pain it caused.

"Do you think you can make it up to the choir loft?"

JR squinted over the back of the pew, then swung his legs down without answering. His feet dropped to the floor and Mai lifted one of his arms over her shoulder to help him stand.

"We need to get you to a doctor," she said again.

JR shook his head. "No doctor."

It took the better part of 30 minutes for JR to climb the stairs to the loft, at the conclusion of which he was exhausted and collapsed onto the floor.

The balcony was a dusty space, obviously used for storage instead of singing. It would have been the perfect place to hide, except that the railing balusters were several inches apart. Parishioners seated in the nave, and the priest giving mass from the sanctuary, would see them simply by glancing up. The best Mai was able to do was move some boxes against the railing to create a sort of bunker. Even with the evening service quickly approaching, they both agreed that this would be as safe a place as any to spend the night.

The evening mass was full, and to JR it seemed to go on for hours. Mai listened intently to the homily, during which the priest made several references to the need for world leaders to be righteous and just. He ended the sermon with a call for the parishioners to protect the innocent and those facing oppression.

After Holy Communion, an invitation to the church fundraiser, and one more hymn, the mass finally came to an end.

JR and Mai waited quietly in their lair for the congregation to leave and the clergy to shut off the lights and lock up for the night.

Suddenly, footsteps in the stairway froze them in place—neither dared to take so much as a breath.

"What is going on here?"

A short, round man stood before them. His cream colored cassock and purple stole left no doubt of who he was. And his facial expression left no doubt that his surprise at finding them was greater than theirs at being found.

"My name is Mai and this is John." Mai offered a gentle bow. "We took refuge here from the heat."

JR squinted through one eye as if her story sounded fishy, even to him.

"From the heat," repeated the priest as he stared at the tacky stain on JR's t-shirt—a mottled crimson likeness of the Asian continent. "I'm quite sure you need to go to the hospital. I can call--"

"Thanks, but don't bother." JR started to sit up. "We were just about to leave."

"I think that would be a good idea." The priest stood beside the stairway opening. "We don't need trouble here."

JR struggled to his feet and started for the door. He stopped and turned toward Mai, who had not moved from where she sat on the dusty floor.

She said, "Your homily tonight was very inspiring, Father."

He nodded his thanks.

"I particularly enjoyed your reading from the Book of Jeremiah, 22:3, I believe it was..."

The priest cautiously nodded again.

Mai continued, "About offering help to those in need. To those who have been oppressed and persecuted. I think the words were, 'Do no wrong or violence to the foreigner...'"

"...and shed no blood in this place," he said, completing the verse.

JR stood at the doorway with his elbow tucked against his wound, looking back and forth between Mai and the priest. What had just happened? Had Mai managed to beat him at his own game?

"Anyway," she continued. "Thank you again for the fine sermon."

The father paused for several seconds before speaking again. "There are others that might see you." He rubbed a hand through his matted black hair. "And we have some policemen in our congregation as well."

"All the more reason to keep us hidden," said Mai.

The clergyman grimaced. Then in their native tongue, he asked Mai, "And you did nothing wrong? Nothing illegal?"

"No Father, nothing."

He regarded JR, his eyes again dropping to the bloodstain. "Will he need medical help?"

She answered in Thai. "He's a stubborn one, Father. But I think he'll be okay."

They both smiled and JR wondered if they were talking about him. In any case, the dialogue had turned pleasant and JR sensed that Mai's subtle retort had made the difference.

"I am Su Suk Chaimongkhon," he said, extending his hand to JR. "Most people just call me Father Su."

They shook hands.

"I'll bring you something to eat. In the meantime, you may both stay the night here in the balcony."

CHAPTER 37

It was the worst night of my entire life.

All I could do was wedge myself into a space half my size, close my eyes, and try to imagine that I was reclining on a secluded beach. A very hot, noisy, and smelly beach.

It didn't work very well, and I didn't sleep a wink. But I managed to survive the horrendous experience until eventually, tiny rays of morning sun crept though the louvered windows. I had made it through one night, but I was pretty sure I could not endure another.

It was about that time that the sound of locks turning compelled the rest of the men to stand and face the door. I followed suit.

A pair of guards stood one behind the other, calling out in thickly accented words—none of which I caught. The men around me began mumbling and nodding toward me with their heads. One prisoner, a Thai man who apparently knew some English, spoke to me. "Guard says you must go with them."

I had to step gingerly around several prisoners to get to the guards. Once I was out of the room, they closed and locked the door before spinning me into the wall. Having me pinned there, they secured rusted metal manacles around both my ankles and wrists. These were tethered together in the front by a heavy chain. Feeling like Hannibal Lecter, I hobbled behind them through the complex.

When we reached a low concrete building that looked like a WWII bomb bunker, they pushed me inside and onto one of several metal seats in a long row. The place was some kind of visitor room, but there were no other prisoners. Through the chain link fencing, I saw an empty 5-foot gap separating me from the fence on the visitor side. The space between was strewn with trash and cigarette butts.

"Hello," shouted a woman sitting opposite me. "I'm Ruth Billings from the Embassy of the United States, and I'm here to help you."

Best words I'd ever heard. "I'm innocent," I said. "You've gotta get me out of here."

The woman reminded me of my third grade teacher, Sister Mary Benita. Frosted hair lacquered into place for the next millennium. She smirked as she lit a cigarette and blew a plume of gray smoke into the air—her ruby pucker print remaining around the filter.

"We don't do that," she said, as if it was an answer she'd given a hundred times before. "We can't testify on your behalf, can't provide legal advice, and can't serve as a translator at your court hearing."

"Swell." I pressed my face into the fence. "Mind if I ask what it is you do do?"

The woman winced at my clumsy wording. "We can ensure you receive adequate medical care while you're incarcerated. We can issue emergency passports if yours are lost or stolen. We'll contact family, friends, or employers back home. And we can provide a list of local attorneys who speak English."

I felt my head drop onto my chest. "Yeah, I guess that will help."

"Where are you staying?"

"I *was* staying at a place called the Monet House, it's over by--"

"I know where it is." Ms. Billings blew another sideways smoke stream. "Your charges don't appear too serious—by our standards, anyway. At least they're not death penalty offenses."

"What, exactly am I charged with?"

Billings glanced at a slip of paper. "Bicycle theft, and not wear--"

"That's a bunch of BS," I said. "The bike was parked in front of a hostel, and I told the cops I only borrowed it. Not to mention, I know about some girl they're trying to find. I'd be willing to make a trade: The girl for my freedom."

The woman stubbed out her cigarette. "You told them that?"

"Yep."

"Well," she paused. "I'd go with that then. It'll probably be your best chance to get out of here before you're sentenced to an inflexible term."

I had a few more questions for Ms. Billings, but she glanced at her phone, gathered her papers, and stood. "I have other detainees to see. Best of luck to you, Mr. McKenna."

No sooner did the embassy woman leave when the cops who had arrested me the day before showed up. Without a word, they signed me out of the jail and stuffed me back into their tiny police car.

I wanted to kiss Billings for arranging my release so quickly. I mean, who else could have gotten me sprung?

Glancing out the window, I saw we were heading south toward the downtown district. I breathed a sigh of relief when we exited the highway and I recognized some of the sites around my hotel.

But I continued to be vexed by their failure to remove my shackles or mention my release. When the little Suzuki Swift sped past the street where my hotel and the embassy were located, I began to fear the worst.

Within a few blocks, the car turned abruptly and pulled though a guarded gate. We were in a compound of official looking buildings, all of which were adorned with flags and giant yellow ribbons. The one in front bore a life-size mural of who I assumed was their king.

Having no idea what the place was, I spoke for the first time during the 45-minute ride. “I’d like to know where you’re taking me.”

The car pulled to a stop at a rollup door on one of the buildings. As the passenger got out to show the guard my paperwork, the driver turned slightly.

“Central Investigation Bureau,” he said.

I stooped in my seat to gaze up the side of the 4-story building. “It was a freak’n bicycle, for Chrissake!”

The other cop got back into the car and we proceeded to an underground garage.

By this time, it had become pretty clear that my transfer here had nothing to do with the Billings woman. Suspecting that I was just one of many American screw-ups on her caseload, I doubted that she’d even given me and my situation another thought.

It remained to be seen whether this new *situation*—whatever it was—would be better or worse than Bang Kwang Prison.

CHAPTER 38

It was a rough night for both JR and Mai. One tossed and turned with the discomforting injury, and the other was restless from worry.

An early morning mass put an end to what little respite the night had afforded them.

"The bleeding is worse," Mai whispered. "How is the pain?"

JR only shook his head.

After the service, Father Su brought breakfast to the loft. Holding two bowls, he paused at the doorway as he assessed JR's obvious decline.

The father spoke to Mai in their native tongue. "John does not look well. I really think he needs medical help."

"Yes Father, I agree." She accepted the bowls from him and knelt on the floor, next to JR.

"It's khao tom," Father Su said to JR. "You need nourishment."

JR's eyes went from the breakfast to Mai.

"Rice porridge," she said. "Eat."

JR tasted it and then slid the bowl back toward her. Under other circumstances, he might have enjoyed it. But he felt like he had taken a cannonball to the abdomen, and the pain had sapped his energy and quashed his appetite.

"I guess we need to do something about this," JR said. "It doesn't seem to be going away."

Mai and Father Su both looked relieved. Mai handed the priest some bills from the envelope Shawn had given her, and though he wouldn't accept any of it he prayed a blessing over JR.

As Mai stuffed the money back into the envelope, she noticed Shawn's business card sandwiched between the bills.

"I forgot," she said. "We have your friend's mobile number."

JR looked at Mai with dread. "But what good does that do us? We ditched our phones before leaving the States."

Mai turned to Father Su. "As you have probably guessed by now, there are people, bad people, who are trying to find us. We worried that they may track our cell phones to find our location, so we discarded them.

"Father Su," said JR. "Is there a phone here that we could use?"

The priest nodded. "But you're not going anywhere. We'll be right back."

Leaving JR in the loft, Father Su led Mai to a small office in the rectory. "I'll give you some privacy," he said, stepping out.

Mai dialed the number on the card and Shawn answered.

"Hello Mr. Shawn. I am John's friend, Mai. We met yesterday at Wongwian Yai Market."

"I remember," he said. "How are you two getting along? I hope the money helped."

"Yes, thank you, very much so." Mai hesitated. "Is it safe to talk?"

"Yeah, no problem. It's my personal cell. Is everything all right?"

"Not really," she said. "John's been shot."

"Uh-huh. Where?"

"Just off Charoen Nakhon Road near the--"

He interrupted her. "No Mai, I mean where on his body was John hit?"

"Oh, yes, of course. It is his abdomen. On the right side, just below his ribs."

"Uh-huh. How long ago?"

"Yesterday. It happened shortly after I met with you."

"Uh-huh. Describe the wound itself. Single projectile? How wide is the entry hole? Does it look like through-and-through?"

"I don't know," she answered. "He won't let me look at it."

Mai thought she heard Shawn chuckle.

"That answers my next question," he said. "So he's conscious. No sign of shock?"

"No, but he's weak and the injury is still bleeding." She hesitated again. "I think he needs a doctor."

"Uh-huh." Try to keep him quiet and immobile until I can get there. Lay him flat on his side with the injury facing down. We don't want the blood pooling in his chest cavity. Is he in a safe place?"

"Yes," said Mai. "The Holy Rosary Church. We're upstairs in the choir loft."

"Uh-huh. I'm on a detail right now, so it'll take me a few hours before I can get someone to cover for me. I'll pick up some medical supplies on my way. Let John know that I'll be there as soon as I can."

"Okay, thank you." Mai hesitated again. "I don't mean to be impertinent, Mr. Shawn. But are you bringing a doctor with you?"

"Not yet," he said. "I'll take a look at the wound first and see what I can do. After John left the Marines, they trained some of us in the Security Group as EMTs."

"I see." Mai wasn't sure if she should be more or less anxious.

"We're like corpsmen or medics," Shawn continued, "but without the battlefield experience. Anyway, no, I won't have a doctor with me, but if I can't fix John I'll definitely get someone who can. Again, it probably won't be 'til this afternoon."

Mai walked through the sanctuary with a somewhat lighter load. She hoped JR would receive the medical attention he needed, and that his trusted friend might also help them find safer shelter.

"John," Mai called out as she started up the steps to the choir loft. "I got in touch with Shawn, and he..."

She stopped abruptly at the top of the stairs. Their breakfast bowls sat untouched on the floor where she had left them, but JR was not there. Mai had been on the phone for only a minute or two, gone not more than ten minutes in total. She could not imagine where he had disappeared to.

The click of a door echoed throughout the hallow sanctuary, and Mai went to the railing to see if it was him. Father Su stepped out of the sacristy onto the alter, closing the door behind him.

"Father," she called over the railing. "John is gone."

CHAPTER 39

The police colonel got up and came around his desk, stopping only inches from the wooden chair I was chained to. He was a tall man, probably my height, and he seemed like a giant compared to the other officers—all of whom stood no more than chest high.

The brown skin on his face was heavily pocked, and only puffy slits on either side of his broad nose were visible. Somewhere inside them were his eyes, which I knew were sizing me up without a word. A knuckled smack from one of his meaty hands would have hurt like hell, but to my good fortune they were still resting at his sides. He turned away suddenly, and went back to his seat behind the desk.

Finally, after what seemed like several minutes of silence, the man nodded to one of the other officers—the one who had driven the car.

"The colonel would like to know why you are here."

I started to shrug, thinking that they should know; it was *them,* after all, who had brought me here. But I realized it wasn't the time for smart ass answers. All they would have to do is return me to Bang Kwang, toss me back into Compound #5 and throw away the key. That would be the end of me.

"I was arrested for borrowing a bicycle, and--"

"Stop!" said the officer. "The colonel is a busy man and he is not interested in your excuses. "Where is the woman that you believe is wanted by the police?"

A couple of things occurred to me at that moment. First, that the colonel must not speak English. Either that, or he is too high and mighty to talk directly to me, himself. The other thing I realized was that I'd overstated my knowledge of the wanted woman. I had no idea who she was, where she was, or if she was actually wanted. All I knew was that I'd seen her photo in a police car outside the embassy, and then saw her later in the company of my missing person.

"She came with you from Washington D.C., America." The driver took a bladed stance, as if he now meant business. But then he looked back at the colonel for approval.

The colonel nodded again.

"You are the boyfriend," said the driver.

"No, that's not correct." I had addressed my response to the colonel, but the little driver stepped between us.

"You speak to me," he said, raising his voice. "The manager at the hostel identified you. We know you were with her when she paid for the room."

They don't even know who they're talking to, I realized. The man at the check-in counter had mixed us up, had misidentified me as the woman's companion. We probably all look alike to him.

"Jonathan Teagan!" he demanded. "You are the ex-embassy guard who took her to the United States against her will."

"I don't even know this girl," I said, thinking that now they'll probably charge me with accessory to whatever it is that she's done. "Until yesterday, I'd never even seen..."

I stopped myself before digging my grave too deep. The only reason I was here instead of rotting in Bang Kwang was because I'd said I know where she is. If I backpedal too far, they'll have no use for me and they'll send me back. On the other hand, if they think I'm mixed up in whatever the girl's done, I'll probably end up back there anyway.

Son-of-a bitch!

The second escort officer stepped forward, joining his partner in front of me. They weren't big men, but they were fit—a couple of martial artists about to throw a spinning hook kick into my head.

The colonel stood abruptly and waved them off. The two officers quickly backed their way out of the room, leaving me and the big boss alone together.

"I have no time for these games," said the colonel using perfect English. "You Americans are too much trouble, and I have enough problems already with all of your drug trafficking. I can't be bothered with minor mischief. You may go."

I wasn't sure if *go* meant back to the prison, or freedom. When the two officers returned and unlocked my shackles, I realized that I was free to actually leave. Why? I had no idea. But I wasn't about to argue the point.

The one who had driven the car walked me back downstairs.

"I guess I'm okay to take off?" I asked as we got to a wide reception area at the front of the building.

He nodded and handed my phone back.

"One question," I said. "The colonel mentioned other crimes that I'd been charged with. What was there besides the bicycle thing?"

"Violation of underwear law."

I laughed. The little guy had a sense of humor. "No, seriously."

His sober expression did not crack. "Thai law prohibits being in public place without underwear."

He pushed open the heavy front door then stood to the side while I exited.

"Illegal to go commando in Thailand," I said aloud to myself. "Who would have known?"

Once outside, I turned on my phone. If I didn't already feel shitty enough, I was greeted by several missed calls from Doris and one from Deputy Soltani. I decided to call her first.

"Soltani," she answered right away.

"Hey, it's me."

"Where the hell have you been, McKenna? Why didn't you call?"

She stopped herself just as I noted the tinge of Doris in her voice. Soltani must have recognized the proprietary tone, too. Then again, we were partners, and we had agreed to work together on this. Be upfront with each other. Transparency, and all that. But what could I say to her? That I hadn't vetted my client, who claimed to be JR's sister, and who had used me to find him, probably twice now, nearly killing him in Greenbelt, and now in Bangkok? Soltani would think I was even more of an idiot than she already did.

"I was following JR," I said. "Watching him and his girlfriend. But then my phone got wet and I think the battery shorted out. I knew how important this case was to you, so I didn't want to just pull off of the surveillance. And, well, it took me awhile to find a phone store that carried the same cell battery."

"You watched them all night?" There was a hint of doubt in her voice. "So then you know where he is, right?"

"Uh, well, they were staying at this hostel over next to some huge shopping mall, but I'm pretty sure they checked out. Then I followed them to this outdoor market..." I wasn't sounding too convincing, so I changed course. "That guy from the embassy, the Marine on the motorcycle. He's their contact. We need to set up on him, and I'm pretty sure he'll lead us right to our guy."

Soltani groaned. "Kind of sounds like we're back to where we were yesterday."

"I wouldn't say that."

"No? What would you say?"

I thought for a minute. "Well, we know he has a girlfriend..." Nothing else came to mind, since 99% my story was a lie anyway.

Just then my phone vibrated with an incoming call. The screen flashed DORIS.

"I've got another call," I said. "We'll talk when I get back. I need to take this."

CHAPTER 40

Father Su ignored Mai, looking away as if he hadn't heard her. Maybe he hadn't. Or perhaps the father didn't care that her injured boyfriend had suddenly disappeared.

She was about to yell to the priest again, but stopped when she heard voices in the vestibule directly below the choir loft. Father Su's eyes held panic, though they never gazed upward toward her.

"What can I do for you, *officers*?" asked Father Su in their native tongue.

It was at that moment that Mai saw the backs of two tan uniforms walking down the main aisle toward the priest. They were the reason he hadn't responded to her. Mai immediately ducked back behind the stack of boxes.

"An issue of some urgency has come to our attention, Father." said one of the police officers.

Their voices lost volume as they drew nearer to the priest, and Mai could only hear the officious tenor of the exchange. She waited a few minutes before daring a peek over the parapet, where she saw Father Su doing his best to keep their backs to her. He appeared engaged and even interested as one of them pointed with gusto to a sheet of paper he held.

Not knowing why the officers were there, Mai assumed the worst: the police knew where she and JR were hiding, and had come to search for them. Maybe they had already found JR while she was making the phone call to Shawn.

Her heart pounded in her chest as she ran back down the steps. Mai had to get to their car and somehow free JR, if he had indeed been arrested. At any moment the door behind her would open and the police officers would emerge from the church, but she continued to the curb outside where their car was parked. Reaching for the door, Mai stopped when she saw the empty police car.

Mai felt the uneven street beneath her feet as she raced across the intersection to a bookstore on the opposite corner. There, she took a position in the shaded entryway where she had a clear vantage point of the church. But panic struck Mai again when she saw her own photograph staring back at her through the shop's window.

Gasping, then glancing around out of fear of being recognized, Mai read the caption above the photo: MAI NAKHON WANTED FOR CRIMES AGAINST THE KINGDOM OF THAILAND.

"What crimes?" she heard herself whisper. "I did nothing."

When the officers came out of the church, Mai waited until they drove away before crossing the street and going back inside. She found Father Su seated in the sanctuary, shaking his head as he read the bulletin they had left him. It looked similar to the one Mai had seen in the shop window.

"Why are the police looking in this area of Bangkok?" she asked. "Do they know I am here?"

The priest brought a hand to his forehead. "The officers said a passenger on a water taxi reported seeing a wounded Caucasian man getting off the boat at the Si Phraya Pier. Apparently there was a shooting on the other side of the river."

Mai was about to explain to the priest, when a door suddenly opened behind her. Spinning around, she sensed Father Su jumping to his feet—both of them thinking that the police had returned.

"Easy," said JR, stepping from the confessional. "It's just me. I saw the cops as I was returning from the restroom, and had to hide quickly. I didn't think I could make it up the stairs in time."

Mai let out a sigh emptying the last of her energy as she fell onto the seat next to the priest. "I thought they took you," she said. I didn't know what to think."

JR joined them on the wooden pew, and they both saw that JR's skin tone had faded to a chalky pallor.

With a slack hand, he picked up the flier that Father Su had just set down. "What's this?" he asked. "Wanted? Wanted for what?"

"It doesn't give any other information," said Mai. "But they are posted in all the shops around here."

"Your uncle's men?"

"Yes, I'm sure they are. And, again, he's not my uncle."

"Who is this man you call Uncle?" asked the priest.

"Somchai Boontam," said Mai. "He is Colonel in charge of Central Investigations Bureau."

"Yes, I know of him. A prominent figure in the Royal Thai Police Force, very influential. Very powerful."

"And very bad," added Mai.

Father Su nodded. "Yes, I know that too."

Mai glanced at JR, then back to the father with a curious frown. "How would a Catholic priest know that?"

"You must remember," he said. "I hear confessions."

It was as close to violating the Seal of the Confessional as Mai had ever heard a priest get. But she was relieved that Father Su didn't know him personally or as a friend. Still, their brush with the police and the fact that she was now wanted worried her immensely.

Father Su's eyes held the same concern. "I want this place to serve as a safe shelter for you both," he said. "And I know your friend is coming to provide medical care for John. But in order for me to feel comfortable allowing you to stay, I'll need to know exactly what you two are involved in and why the police are looking for you."

Mai nodded her agreement. After all, it was not an unreasonable request. Just by being there, they had put the church, Father Su, and his congregation at risk.

JR was slumped cockeyed against the seatback, resting on an elbow. He knew very well why he was wanted, and by whom. But his understanding of Mai's situation was still a little murky, and he was just as interested in her story as the priest was.

"Why don't you start," JR said to her.

Mai gazed upward as if to find the words or maybe the courage to begin.

As she opened her mouth to speak, the loud creak of an opening door interrupted. The sudden sound echoed through the sanctuary, freezing all three of them in place.

A bright wedge of light shot through the doorway and the silhouetted figure of a man seemed to take up the entire opening. A sheet of paper was gripped in his hand, and on it Mai saw her photo beneath a wanted banner.

CHAPTER 41

"Doris, I already know what you're going to say." I switched the phone to my other hand so I could pay the tuk-tuk driver. "Had there been any possible way to make it to Bridget's party, I would have been there. But it just wasn't possible."

"I suppose you're going to tell me that you were on a *big* case."

"As a matter of fact, that's exactly what happened." I paused just inside the lobby of our place, letting the refrigerated air blow though my hot, sticky shirt.

"So, tell me about it." Doris had a fair amount of condescension in her voice, and I knew this may be my only shot to make her feel foolish for questioning me.

"Well, it's a missing person case," I said. "And the person who's missing was in the witness protection program. I'm sorry that I can't tell you everything, because it overlaps with a federal government investigation."

"Oh, is that so?"

There it was in her voice again. "Yes, that's so, Doris. In fact, I've been working hand-in-hand with the U.S. Marshals Service."

"Really... Where?"

I didn't want to go into the whole overseas thing. Besides, our nation's capital would undoubtedly carry more clout.

"Washington, D.C." The sound of my own words felt authoritative and weighty. "And like I said, I'm working with the feds to find--"

"Find what?" Doris interrupted. "Your missing underpants?"

My throat suddenly squeezed shut, and nothing could get in or out. How could she possibly know about that?

Realizing she couldn't, I figured, *In for a penny, in for a pound.* "What in the hell are you talking about, Doris?"

"I received a strange call in the middle of the night from the State Department," she said. "Mrs. Billings, I believe her name was, from the embassy in Bangkok."

Son-of-a-bitch!

Doris continued, "She told me that you were arrested in Thailand of all places, for stealing a bicycle in your underwear, or something like that."

"No, no. Now, that's not accurate at all," I said.

"And this Billings woman never mentioned anything about you investigating a 'big case' or about the Marshals Service."

"I was about to tell you that my case led to Bangkok, and we followed this Marine guard from the U.S. Embassy. Then there was a shooting at a hostel. Thankfully I wasn't hit, but in order to escape from the assassins... I borrowed a bike."

It didn't sound that believable, even to me. Especially, now that Ms. Billings had already thrown me under the bus and turned my wife against me.

"I'm sorry, Danny. I can't listen to any more of this crap. Bridget was brokenhearted that you didn't make it to her party, and I'm tired of running interference. I won't make excuses for you anymore."

"Can I talk to Bridge? I know I can fix this."

"No, Danny. You can't."

"Which one? Can't fix it or can't talk to her?

"Both!"

The phone abruptly disconnected. I felt like shit as I took the elevator up to our serviced apartment, and I still had the lie I'd told Soltani hanging out there.

"You're back." Soltani seemed somewhat happy to see me, which made me glad I'd gone with the story about the new phone battery, instead of the truth.

"Yeah," I said, holding up my phone. "All good."

"Well, while you were following JR and his girlfriend, I stayed on that Marine Corps friend of his. Guy's name is Shawn Foster. Staff Sergeant in charge of the embassy protection people. He drives a 2020 Yamaha V Star 250, license plate has three squiggly Thai letters followed by the numbers 787. He shares an apartment with two other Marines from the embassy. And here's the kicker: They live on the third floor of *this* building."

"The guy is our neighbor?" I walked to the window. "Then they're one level below us."

"Right. We have no view of his unit from here," said Soltani. "But the garage is over there." She pointed downward to the right. "And, we can see when he drives out."

I nodded. "Except that by the time we get downstairs and flag over a tuk-tuk, he'll be long gone."

"Now that you're back, we can set up on the garage properly." Soltani was already grabbing her purse. "Or, one of us can watch the garage while the other keeps an eye on the embassy."

It didn't take long before we were at street level, watching for Staff Sergeant Foster. This time, we knew what he looked like and what he drove. Having followed Foster before, this time we were prepared and would be ready for him.

It was just after 2 o'clock in the afternoon when Soltani spotted Foster exiting the embassy's back gate. He crossed the street, and a few minutes later pulled out of the parking garage on his Yamaha.

I had already waved down a tuk-tuk and had the driver standing by. So when Soltani hurried around the corner of the building, we were ready to roll.

It was almost the same as the time before; Foster had on a light windbreaker over his uniform. He never looked back, so we were easily able to keep him on a short visual leash.

He headed south around the park, and then turned right, onto Rama IV Road—a semi-elevated highway with several lanes. After a couple of miles, Foster turned off and stopped his motorcycle in front of Sawang Pharmacy. It was a tiny storefront in a mostly pedestrian shopping district.

He emerged carrying a paper bag, which he held between his thighs as he continued driving. Heading in a westerly direction now, Foster was driving toward the river.

Without warning, he stopped abruptly in front of a Catholic church. It reminded me of St. Paul's, our parish when I was a kid in San Francisco. Same Gothic Revival style; steepled rooflines, pointed arches, and the same religious statues. Except this chapel had a serene view of the river instead of the noisy J-Church streetcar line.

We waited for a minute before paying our driver and sending him on his way.

"Did you see where he went?" I asked Soltani.

"Not exactly. But it looks like the only place he could have gone is into the church."

We cautiously followed the route he had taken, which led to a small courtyard. Soltani stood to the side with a hand on the door handle. "After you," she said.

"On three." My heart pumped hard as she counted.

"One, two..."

The door flew open and I stepped through. Knowing that I was backlit by the ambient light outside, I immediately moved to my right. Soltani filed inside behind me and took a position to the left. As our eyes quickly acclimated to the dim interior, we both straightened up from our quasi-crouched stances.

The Marine, who was about ten steps ahead, turned to face us. A bit further, about the middle of the sanctuary, sat JR Travis—formerly Jonathan Roy Teagan—and his wanted girlfriend. Next to them, now standing between pews, was a Catholic priest.

For a second or two, we all stared back and forth at each other without a word. The silence was as thick as the tension.

CHAPTER 42

Suddenly, several of us spoke at once. It was a loud, overlapping mush of words that only served to further confuse the situation.

I'd pointed at JR and said, "Don't move!"

The Marine sergeant asked JR something about being shot. Having recognized my partner, JR yelled out, "Deputy Soltani?" And the priest, flummoxed by the sudden squall of activity, simply crossed himself in prayer.

The Thai girlfriend was the only one who never said a word, but glared with eyes that wanted to slice and dice me with a meat cleaver.

A few things became clear to me at that moment: One, the girlfriend probably blamed me for leading JR's fake sister and crew of assassins right to them. Two, she probably blamed me for getting her boyfriend shot—which I just now deduced after seeing the amount of blood on his shirt. And three, I was going to be pretty screwed if she or JR mentioned anything about it in front of Soltani. It seemed highly probable that it would come up, so I decided to get in front of it.

Turning abruptly toward Soltani, I asked, "Can I have a private word with you?"

"Right now?" She lifted an eyebrow. "Uh, sort of in the middle of something at the moment."

"I know, but--"

"This guy nearly got us killed," said the girl, pointing me out like a witness at a police lineup.

JR turned to Soltani. "You know this guy?"

"He's a private eye," said Soltani.

I held out my palms to calm them. "A person hired me to find you. It's kind of a mixed up story, but none of that matters now."

JR rolled his eyes. "Yeah, he told us his client was my sister."

The girlfriend's arms dropped to her sides in exasperation, "But JR doesn't have a sister!"

Soltani's brow became a deep furrow as she turned toward me.

I said, "That's what I wanted to talk to you about."

The Marine gave us all the once over and shook his head. "I don't know what the hell's going on with any of you, but my friend's been shot and I'm here to fix him up." With that, he walked over, crouched down next to JR, and began pulling first aid supplies from the paper bag he'd brought.

I started toward them to help, but felt my shirt being tugged from behind.

"Not so fast," said Soltani. "Was there something you forgot to tell me about your *client*?"

I tried my best to explain that I had been duped, while at the same time trying to keep from looking like a chump. Soltani just stood there shaking her head.

"I knew JR was an only child," said Soltani. "Had you told me at the beginning that the woman claimed to be his sister, none of this would have happened."

I reminded the deputy that, unlike her, I didn't have the resources to do an in-depth vetting of my client or her supposed missing brother. "The entire federal government is at your disposal," I said.

Soltani didn't respond, but looked at me as if I were something she'd have to scrape off the bottom of her shoe.

My phone vibrated in my pocket, and it was Doris. "Hello," I whispered, turning away from the group. "What is it, Doris?"

"Bridget has been very worried. Where are you, and why are you whispering?"

"I'm in church, if you must know. But it's not a good time to talk. Tell Bridge that I'm fine, and I got her a nice birthday present."

Disconnecting the phone, I turned back to the rest of them. They had begun talking among themselves, but Soltani was still there staring at me.

I moved closer and continued my defense. "We are both trained professionals," I said, "and it's important that we maintain an air of competency in order to gain JR's cooperation."

"What do you care about his cooperation?" she asked. "It's not like *you* actually have a missing person case to solve, now that there is no client. Why don't you just catch a flight home?"

I had no logical comeback for either of her questions. She was essentially right; I didn't have any investment in the outcome, which made me about as useless as a pork chop at a vegan dinner.

"Is there anything else you didn't tell me?" Soltani asked.

JR leaned over the back of the pew. "How did you get out of jail?" he asked. "We saw the police arrest you in front of the food plaza."

I turned to Soltani, "...and there was that."

Hands loudly slapping together hushed the sidebar conversations that had erupted in the church. The priest stood in the center aisle, clapping above his head. "Excuse me... I'm Father Su, and I would like to have everybody's attention for a moment."

It was perfect timing for a distraction. Giving Soltani a nod toward the priest, I implied that we needed to follow the father's commands. Soltani rolled her eyes as I turned to listen.

"This place is not a conference room, nor is it a hotel or a hospital. This is a house of God, and though it is a place of peace and safety, it is also a place of reverence and prayer." The priest took a breath while letting that sink in. "Now, once again, if you want to take shelter here at Church of the Holy Rosary, you must tell me what is going on."

The staff sergeant spoke up first. "What's going on is that my buddy is slowly bleeding out. The bullet may have nicked a blood vessel, which means that the wound needs to be cauterized."

That took the wind out of the father's little speech, and it provided yet another distraction for me.

The sergeant then slid a flier across the pew to JR's girlfriend. "Oh yeah, and this thing was taped to the window of the pharmacy down the road."

That seemed to rekindle the priest's interest in the girl's situation: why she was wanted by the police and how her boyfriend got himself shot. As the Marine sergeant went about cleaning JR's wound, the girl began telling her story to the father.

"I was orphaned as an infant and was cared for at a home for girls near Chiang Rai. On my 14th birthday, I was sold to a man named Somchai Boontam. He is the colonel in charge of police investigations in all of Bangkok."

JR struggled to lift his head. "What do you mean, you were 'sold'?"

The young woman shrugged. "There were three of us," she said. "All young girls. We were sold to this man under the pretext of a legal adoption."

I supposed that all of us silently wondered if she had been a victim of sexual exploitation. Forced prostitution was suddenly the elephant in the middle of the church, although I figured it was a subject more appropriately broached by JR—who was now being prepped for what could only be a very painful procedure. I felt for the guy, knowing that the answer to the human trafficking question could make the pain of his cauterization pale in comparison.

"We were not sexually assaulted," volunteered the girl. "The three of us have been held there as household servants ever since. We were neglected, beaten at times, and kept in a dirty basement."

Father Su had a forlorn expression. "May I ask what crime you have committed."

"No crime, Father." She gestured with hands apart. "After I met John, I finally worked up the courage to run away."

Holding the wanted flier, he asked, "Why would this policeman..." Then, the priest's voice trailed off as he realized the bulletin was only further evidence of the colonel's depravity.

"It's a matter of pride," said the girl. "He'll make an example out of me in order to save face with his other servants. In the colonel's mind, John took property that belonged to him and now John will be made an example of as well."

I tilted my head. "That doesn't add up for me."

They all turned.

"While I was in jail, the cops took me to their headquarters building. This colonel guy had me in his office, because he thought I was JR, John, whatever. If what you say is true, wouldn't he have made an example of me then? He could have left me to rot in prison forever. Instead, he just let me go free."

Mai was already shaking her head. "Not possible. If he let you out, it was only so you could lead them to me. Once he has me, you will be arrested and thrown back in Bang Kwang."

I'd already led assassins to JR. If I've now allowed the colonel to follow me here, I'm toast. None of them will ever trust me, and Soltani will have every right to treat me like shit. Of course, it won't really matter because the colonel will have Mai back under his control and I will be spending the rest of my life in that sweaty prison.

"Could they have tailed us?" asked Soltani. "We were so focused on following the Marine sergeant that we might not have--"

My eyes darted toward the doors. "Uh, no, that's impossible. I'm pretty sure we weren't followed."

"Pretty sure?" asked the Marine.

"Like, about 99% certain, maybe 97%," I said. "I mean, how would we not have seen them?"

Now we were all glancing toward the front doors.

CHAPTER 43

"Quickly!" said the priest. "Everyone into the sacristy."

Me and the Marine helped JR up by propping his arms over our shoulders. He was growing weaker by the minute, and I could see that he didn't have much time.

The sacristy room was not unfamiliar to me. I'd spent my share of Sunday mornings preparing for my altar boy duties at St. Paul's in The City.

The wailing sounds began as we made our way across the altar. I'd thought they were car alarms, but then it donned on me that the odd, hi-lo pitches were Bangkok police sirens.

"They're here," the priest said as we funneled into the small room.

The obvious problem with the father's *hide-in-the-sacristy* plan was that it only had one other way out. The back door led directly outside to an alley behind the rectory. If these cops had any brains at all, they would throw a perimeter around the building in case we tried to flee, in which case we were trapped. I guessed that's why Father Su was a priest and not a police tactician.

"Now what?" asked the Marine.

The father walked past a long row of tall wooden closets where the vestments were kept, stopping next to a heavy wooden counter with an ornate faucet and sink. "This is called a *piscina*," he said.

I sighed loudly. "And the drain is called a *sacrarium*." Yes, I know all about these things, but, chop-chop, can't the history lesson wait 'til another time?"

"This is an old church," he continued, ignoring my point. "Built in 1891 on the site of two other church structures. Back then, water for the sacrarium used to come from a well, which still sits beneath us."

I shook my head in frustration. Soltani leaned in and asked me, "What's he getting at?"

"Not sure," I whispered. "This thing is for dumping holy water, washing chalices, stuff like that. It has no bearing on our situation, and it certainly isn't going to help us escape."

"This doesn't drain into the sewer like the rest of the plumbing," said the priest. "And back when the church was built, the sink drained down into the well. The architects had to have a way to access the--"

I interrupted again. "Seriously Father, we're running out of time here."

Suddenly tugging on the counter top next to the sink, the entire six-foot section swung away from the wall exposing a subterranean stairway. "This is what I was getting at," he said. "It's a hidden room beneath the sacristy—roughly the same dimensions as this room, but undetectable from anywhere outside of it."

The Marine leaned over the opening to look down.

Soltani asked, "Are there spiders?"

It's called *Passagem de Kalawar*," said Father Su. "It was used to shelter Portuguese priests during religious clashes with the French."

"I'll need a paper and pencil in case there's a quiz later," I said. When nobody laughed, I took a more serious tone. "Okay," I said with a sweeping hand motion. "Everybody inside."

"Wait," said the Marine. "What I'm going to do requires candles, matches, and a thick piece of fabric."

It sounded like Sergeant Foster was planning on saying mass himself. Nonetheless, I helped to gather the items and carry them down the secret staircase. Foster assisted JR down ahead of me, and I was the last to descend. Father Su waited above in the sacristy.

"I will close you in," he said. "And then I'll deal with the police."

As the last of the lambent light from above disappeared, I fumbled in the dark to light a candle. It was a cool, dank space that probably hadn't been seen by human eyes in a hundred years. The ancient rock walls were supported by hand hewn beams disappearing into the blackness above us. The only sounds were occasional drops of water into a manhole sized shaft that I imagined was the well.

"Anyone find King Tut's sarcophagus yet?" I asked. Then, holding the candle out, I saw only expressions of annoyance staring back.

"Shit," said the Marine. "I didn't think to grab a knife or scissors."

"What do you need them for?" asked Mai.

"For the cauterization itself. It needs to be a hard metal, about the same size as a pinky finger."

"I'll clean the wound and try my best to close it up," he said. "But if bacteria has gotten in there, John could get peritonitis, which could lead to sepsis. Cauterization is really the only way we can be sure to stop the bleeding."

"I have a hair brush," said Soltani.

"Plastic will melt," he said.

"What about a metal key?" asked Mai.

"Too small."

I asked, "Would brass work?"

Sergeant Foster started to shake his head. "Brass is softer than iron or steel. It conducts heat, which makes it difficult to hold. I'd have to work fast, before it cools down. But if brass is all we can get our hands on..."

"The processional crucifixes are all made of brass. The poles are about the right diameter, but they're kept upstairs in the sacristy."

The sergeant glanced upward as he thought. "Aren't they the long poles they carry?"

"Yeah, but they come apart," I said. "The pieces are only about 16-inches in length."

There was a round of shrugs and nods, which I took to mean that mine was the accepted plan. Also, that I had been elected to sneak up to the sacristy and grab the damn thing.

With very little light, I climbed the rock steps not knowing if the secret doorway/countertop could even be opened from inside. More concerning was that I had no way to tell if anyone was in the sacristy at the time. It was quite possible that I'd pop out right into the arms of Colonel Asshole and his mini-cops.

At the top of the stairs, I stopped to listen. The place was too well insulated. Several layers of old stones, bricks, and thick wood lay between me and the room I was about to enter.

Wedging my shoulder against the cover above me, I gave it a push. I felt like a plow horse as the cabinetry began to give way and separate from the wall. One last heave and...

I felt the pop, and immediately a burning pain shot through my knee. It wasn't the first time this had happened, but in terms of timing—it was certainly one of the worst.

I flopped onto the floor of the sacristy, holding my knee like a carton of eggs as I writhed in pain. On the good side, the room was empty. On the bad side, it wasn't going to be for long. Stern voices outside grew louder. As the men approached, I heard their malevolent footsteps storming across the marble floor.

In a matter of seconds, the altar door would swing open and I'd be tantamount to a beached whale surrounded by harpoon-carrying Eskimos.

Rolling onto my back, I used my good leg to shove the cabinet back into place. Frantically, I scanned the room for the processional crucifix. Nothing.

I awkwardly got to my feet, putting all of my weight on my good leg. Knowing that the crucifix had to be close by, I began checking the taller cabinets around the room. Finally, I located two of them inside a closet—one mounted on a stand and another affixed to a telescoping pole. That was the one I needed.

But it was too late.

An assertive voice from the altar side of the door made several gruff commands, too muffled to understand. It was undoubtedly the colonel wanting to know what was behind the door.

I momentarily imagined Father Su's fright as he tried to fend off the cops. In my mind, I saw him ratting us out—folding his hand, laying down his cards and cashing in his chips. After all, our ragtag group seemed a poor bet against losing his position in the church and possibly going to jail.

Suddenly, the knob began to turn, and a second later the door to the sacristy swung open.

CHAPTER 44

I held my breath inside the closet, trying not to move my throbbing knee. Multiple footsteps confirmed that the colonel had brought at least one of his men to help search for us.

Of course, it was the wrong us. The colonel still believed I was the ex-embassy guard who had run off with his housekeeper. Which, if there was any upside, it's that I must have appeared fit and trim enough to have been a Marine, and to have attracted such a youthful beauty as Mai. I hoped Soltani might also put those pieces together and maybe feel a little guilty for her *'we're never sleeping together'* comment.

Anyway, as I heard voices nearing my hiding place, I gripped the crucifix like a baseball bat. I'd made up my mind that I would knock the colonel's head out of the park when he opened the closet door. And why not? The jerk was planning on throwing me back in prison anyway, and then forcing *my girlfriend* into indentured servitude.

Their voices got closer and closer, until they were directly in front of the closet. My mind was a flurry of last minute thoughts. Would God be angry with me for bashing someone in the head with a holy crucifix? Probably. But I hoped He would be on my side, since my only real sin was trying to help those among us who could not help themselves.

Suddenly, divine intervention. The colonel's phone rang and he stopped what he was doing to answer it. The caller must not have been Thai, because the conversation was in English. At first, I listened only to get a feel for if and when he would leave the room. But then I heard them mentioning Mai and JR—who he probably still thought was me. If I had any doubts about the colonel's disdain for JR, they were gone now. His side of the conversation went something like this:

"No, I haven't located him yet."

"Yes, we believe he is still with her."

"Don't worry Leo, we'll send the woman back and we'll kill him."

"Okay, I'll let you know when it's done."

Now I was really pissed. Kill him? Whether God wanted me to or not, this time I truly was going to take the colonel's head off. And whoever this *Leo* guy was, his head too.

For whatever reason, the interruption caused the colonel to give up the search. Maybe the priest had convinced him we weren't there.

The fact that he hadn't found me was the only fortuitous detail in my otherwise worsening situation. The colonel still believed that I was JR, and I had no idea how he knew to search for us in the church. How safe would it be to return to the Monet House? My passport was there. All my money. And my newly purchased clothes, as well. For all I knew, the cops had already searched the place and confiscated my passport.

Once I was certain they'd left the room, I slipped out of the closet and used the crucifix like a walking staff to help me across the floor. For penitence sake, I hoped that using it in that manner was better than as a weapon.

The cabinetry moved easier this time, probably since centuries old rust and grime had been shaken loose. I felt my way downward into what now resembled the depths of hell, only to find the rest of the group huddled around JR. Poor guy was on his back with a rolled up *amice* in his mouth. A prayer candle burned next to him as the Marine cleaned the area of JR's wound with isopropyl alcohol.

Leaning his head up, JR gritted his teeth. "Just pour it in if you need to."

Foster frowned and elbowed JR back down. "It would damage the exposed tissue inside the wound. Besides, the hot metal will take care of any leftover bacteria."

Having seen plenty of gunshot victims during my time with the SFPD, I leaned over the Marine to assess the damage. It's often difficult to tell from the tiny hole outside, what trauma was done on the inside. In JR's case, the injury appeared to be just above his intestines—which was usually a good thing. Almost better to nick an organ than to suffer a perforation along the 25 feet of entrails carrying feces through the abdomen. From what I've seen, that's usually one hell of a cleanup job and a much longer recovery.

Foster took a syringe from the bag and held it to the candlelight. "This will knock you on your ass, so don't worry, you won't feel a thing."

JR couldn't talk because of the cloth in his mouth, but struggled to shake his head no.

The Marine shrugged. "Okay, have it your way."

Then Foster turned to me. "Take the crucifix thing apart. I'll need you to hold the smallest section you can find over the flame until it gets really hot."

I tried to conceal the limp as I made my way over to them, though I saw Soltani eyeing my bum leg. When I tried to kneel down, the gig was pretty much up. I had to sit with my legs outstretched like a girl playing jacks.

Then, as the piece of brass began to warm, I felt the heat radiating up into my hand. Quickly glancing around, I saw that the only cloth in the room was clamped between JR's teeth. So, I took off my t-shirt and used it as an oven mitt.

It was when I gazed down at my stomach that I wished I had kept up with the Lean Cuisine dinners. As painful as it was for me to expose myself that way in front of Soltani, I realized that what JR was going through was probably worse.

When the rod had heated to a whitish glow, I passed it to Foster.

In a quick swirl of movement, JR bit down hard on the fabric and the Marine plunged the hot poker into the wound. A two or three second sizzle, the acrid smell of burning flesh, and the whole thing was suddenly over.

I had expected to hear a Michael Jackson style high-pitched yelp, but JR grinded it out in silence.

His Marine Corps buddy held the candle up to check his work, and the bleeding had indeed stopped. Sergeant Foster applied what he called an occlusive dressing, which he said would seal the wound—air and water tight.

We all let out a collective breath. And though I was happy for JR and Mai, I selfishly hoped that my calm assistance had redeemed me, at least a little bit, in front of Soltani.

Quickly putting my shirt back on, we waited silently in the light of the flickering candle for Father Su to return with the *all-clear*.

It was the Marine sergeant who kicked off the next round of truth or dare.

"So John..." he said. "Why in the hell did somebody want to shoot you in the first place?"

CHAPTER 45

"Are you sure that fireplace poker you stuck me with worked?" JR asked Foster, avoiding the question. "Even though the hole in my gut stopped bleeding, it still hurts like hell."

"Does it feel like a bad burn?" Foster asked.

"Yeah."

"Good. That's how it's supposed to feel." The Marine gathered his first-aid supplies, then sat facing JR. "Now back to my question. Why did someone shoot you?"

JR glanced around the room, taking in our curious expressions. All of us seemed to know bits of JR's background, though I probably knew the least.

He let out a sigh, then started. "I met Mai while serving at the embassy a couple of years ago, and we hit it off pretty quickly. But I was nearing the end of my tour in Bangkok, and she couldn't join me in the U.S. without a passport. So I returned to the States alone, hoping to find work and save enough to fly her over."

"Aren't your parents wealthy?" I asked. "Couldn't they help?" It was kind of clumsy timing, but I didn't want to listen if it was all just a BS story.

"First of all, yes, my parents *were* wealthy. But I wasn't about to show up after four years in the Marines, only to slip into my cowboy jammies, and ask Daddy for money while Mommy makes me a cup of hot cocoa."

It wasn't a subtle point he'd made, and I decided not to interrupt him anymore after that.

"Long story short, Mai finally got her passport and I finally got a job. At the time, of course, I had no idea that Mai was trying to get away from some lunatic police commander. She never told me."

Mai shrugged. "It's a Thai thing. People here don't wear their shame for everybody to look at. Saving face is a really big deal here."

Her excuse made enough sense that everybody turned back to JR for the next chapter.

"I got a job as an accountant for a firm in Rhode Island. Paid so well that it was almost too good to be true. They seemed kind of shady, which should have been a red flag, but I figured, why look a gift horse in the mouth?"

Mai frowned at him.

"Hey," he said. "It's an American thing. Making money is a really big deal over there."

I laughed and Soltani nudged me hard. It was clear that we were already choosing sides.

"So, turns out this place handled the books for an international money laundering network. Seventeen different countries. Everyone from drug cartels and illegal arms, to corrupt politicians and human trafficking. It went against everything that we'd fought for over in the sandbox, and it was eating me up inside."

JR winced, and I wasn't sure if it was his painful gut or his painful memories. In any case, Soltani jumped in at that point.

"He had enough information to sink the whole operation," she said. "Everybody from the FBI to the State Department wanted in. They offered him immunity from prosecution, which was a moot point since it could be argued that JR's roll was only as an unwitting, low-level bookkeeper. And they offered him a change of identity, relocation, and witness protection—all in exchange for his sworn testimony."

"As we waited for the U.S. Attorney to get the indictments going, the people I was to testify against figured they could draw me out by going after my parents. Killed both of them in a hit-and-run out near Pacifica. They made it look like an accident, so it didn't signal any warning bells at first. The Marshals even let me leave the program temporarily, to attend the funeral. But a hit squad was waiting for me there. When they came after me, I ran. That's about it."

"Why didn't you come back into the program?" asked Soltani.

"A couple of reasons," he said. "For one thing, I couldn't get to the evidence that I'd hidden. When I tried to sneak into my parents' house to retrieve it, the same people—the assassins—were waiting for me again. Shot the hell out of the place."

"You should have told us," said Soltani. "We would have sent a protection detail right away."

JR kind of shrugged and shook his head. "Without the evidence, I was no good as a witness. Besides, I wasn't going into hiding without Mai."

"It's a simple process to add a family member or significant other into the program." Soltani turned to Mai, "You should have submitted a request."

"We did," said Mai.

Soltani's face slowly morphed into a mixture of angry confusion. Then she spun back toward JR. "Wait, what?"

Now JR looked confused. "Yeah, I put in the formal request and you denied it."

"I never saw it," she said. "Are you sure it wasn't lost in the mail?"

JR smiled. "I wouldn't mail something that important. You were out of the office and your boss said he'd get it to you right away. Two days later he called to tell me that you denied the request."

Soltani's face looked like the red hot poker. "What was the guy's name? Do you remember?"

JR squinted into the darkness above him. "Kingsland, Kingsford, something like that."

"Kingsbury?"

"Yeah, that's him."

"Deputy Director Kingsbury." Her eyes were on fire.

CHAPTER 46

I suppose I understood why the money launderers wanted to put JR in a casket, but other than that nothing was adding up for me. For starters, how did this colonel guy figure into the equation? He obviously wanted to get Mai back to cleaning his house and making his curry and rice, but why did he also want to kill JR—vis-à-vis me? And who was this Leo the colonel was talking to on the phone?

Father Su still hadn't returned, and our little group in the Secret Annex were quickly burning our way through the last candle.

"I think we need to talk," I said to Soltani, leading her away from the others. "I have a couple of questions."

Her expression was rife with irritation, like I was that sappy kid following her around the playground—too dense to get the clue. "What is it, now?"

I looked at her appraisingly, wondering why I had let her demean me as she did. Sure, she was beautiful and intelligent and witty and successful. And what did I bring to the table? I was an ex-cop, ex-football player, almost ex-husband, whose private eye business was barely staying afloat. But Soltani's aversion to me couldn't all be a class distinction thing. There had to be something more behind her sizzling anger, distrust, and condescension.

Clearly, she thought of me as an arrogant ass—some part of which I probably had to own. After getting the heave-ho from SFPD, I'd possibly overcompensated a bit for my humiliation. The fact that my marriage was falling apart and my wife was dating the Internal Affairs lieutenant who got me fired, hadn't helped my attitude either.

"Look Soltani... Aafreen..." I had used her first name to show my sincerity. Then, ushering her over to the darkest corner of the cellar, I said, "Have you ever been to a bullfight?"

"That's what you wanted to ask me?"

I fanned my hands between us in frustration. "No. Yes. Just, have you ever been to one?"

"No." Soltani rolled her eyes. "Have you?"

"Well, no, not exactly. But I had a case in Mexico a few months ago and there was a poster advertising one. They had just built a new bullfighting arena in Ensenada, and I remember thinking that I would never want to watch a bullfight."

"Okay," said Soltani. "Good talk." She turned and headed back toward the group.

"I wasn't finished." The words came out a tad louder than I'd intended, and they stopped her in her tracks. "That's what I'm feeling like here, the bull in a bullfight."

Soltani inched back into the shadows until she stood facing me.

"It's not really a fair fight," I said. "It's an ambush. It's a setup. It's a suicide mission for the bull. Not for anyone else, just the bull. And everyone in the whole stadium knows what's happening, except the stupid bull. He thinks he's fighting the good fight, doing what comes naturally to him, doing the only thing he knows how to do. All the while, everybody is cheering him on. Until a sword is thrust into his heart and he starts bleeding to death. That's when the bull realizes that he's been tricked. He was the last one to be let in on the joke."

Soltani stared directly into my eyes for a minute, then gazed into the shadows beyond me. "And you're feeling like you're the bull."

"Yep."

"You think that everybody knows something that you don't.

"Yep."

Her eyes came back to mine. "Okay, what do you want to know?"

I took a breath and let it out. "A couple of questions... For one, I'd like to know what the deal is with your boss. That Kingsbury guy."

Soltani's eyes narrowed. "How is my personal life any of your business?"

Her defensive response was a huge *tell*. "Who said anything about your personal life? My question has to do with your protectee, and why your boss backdoored you. Unless you really did deny JR's request to take Mai with him into the program."

Soltani's face reddened. "Of course I didn't. I would never have rejected their request, and I would never have lied to them if I had."

"Then explain it to me."

Soltani's expression began to soften. Her eyes grew glassy and she started fanning them as she shook her head.

I'd seen women do that before, and it was usually when Doris was so frustrated with me that she couldn't speak without crying. But this time it wasn't about me.

Turning away to wipe her nose, Soltani said, "Just move on to another question."

"Well," I said, "If you didn't like that one, you sure ain't gonna like the next one."

Her shoulders dropped as she turned back.

"You and Kingsbury..." I paused, giving her time to gather herself. Also, to give me time to figure it out in my own head. I was still putting the pieces together as I spoke.

"What about us?"

"An affair, right? A relationship, romance, whatever you want to call it. Messy break-up, lots of hard feelings, compounded by the fact that you still have to work for the guy. Your raw nerve hasn't really been about you bucking up against the glass ceiling or working for a man who doesn't like you, has it? And it hasn't really been about me, either."

The tears were coming too fast to fan now, and they told me that I was right on the money. Furtive glances came from the others in our group, but they had the sense to stay out of it.

"Which one of those is your second question?" she asked.

"None of them. I'm still playing catch up here—trying to make this an even match." I lowered my voice. "So, could this Kingsbury guy be so bitter that he would actually sabotage your case?"

Soltani's hand covered her mouth. Then she frowned and shook her head. "I don't see it. Leo Kingsbury can be jealous and vindictive, but he's also the Assistant Chief Deputy. I can't imagine how derailing my case would even benefit him."

Her answer satisfied me for a fraction of a second, until the name permeated into my tired brain. "Did you just say *Leo*?"

CHAPTER 47

My mind spun like tires in the mud, splattering fragmented thoughts in every direction. Instead of answering a question, Soltani's words had only generated more of them. Instead of fitting the pieces into matching slots, she had warped the entire puzzle.

The odds of logic were against there being two different *Leos*. But I decided, for the moment, not to tell Soltani about the phone call I had just overheard. More time was needed to wrap my head around all of this. As probable as it seemed that Soltani's boss was the one who had called the colonel, it still didn't explain how he would even know that JR—and Soltani for that matter—were here in Thailand. Unless...

"I reached out to him," she said, her voice weak and cracking. "Last night when you didn't come back. I didn't know what happened to you, and I started thinking about the danger of working this case alone, without anyone back home even knowing I was in Bangkok." She dabbed her eyes. "So I called Leo and admitted that I was tracking JR on my own time."

I chewed on that for a second or two. "And I'll bet he was friendly. Compassionate. Forgiving, even."

Soltani slowly nodded.

I figured either we were followed to the church by the colonel's men, or Kingsbury had a fix on her phone's GPS.

"You didn't happen to mention where we're staying, did you?"

She could only close her eyes.

At least it answered that question. What still wasn't adding up for me was why Kingsbury gave a shit in the first place, and how in the world he and the corrupt Thai colonel even knew each other.

Soltani looked crushed enough, so I decided not to drop the bomb about her boss and the colonel working together—which still didn't really make sense to me. At least I was gaining some understanding of the nuances of this investigation. At the same time, I now had some insight into where Soltani's anger and distrust came from.

Hopefully, she and I were now on level turf.

"It happens," I said. "Don't beat yourself up over someone else's character flaws."

She looked almost amused for a second, then gave me a warm smile. For once, it seemed as though I'd said the right thing.

Light crept in from above us as Father Su slid open the secret entrance and made his way down the old staircase.

"It's okay, they've gone."

Everyone got up and headed for the stairs—JR with Foster's help.

Stopping suddenly, I stared off into the dark recesses of my mind. This whole thing still didn't feel right to me. Either that, or my brain wasn't seeing it for what it was. In either case, I clearly hadn't asked the right questions.

"Wait... hold the phone," I said, motioning everyone back. "We're not done yet. How many people are after you guys, anyway?"

"What are you talking about?" asked JR, as he and the Marine stopped at the foot of the stairs.

"You were about to give testimony against a money laundering operation, right? But it had nothing to do with this Thai Colonel?"

"Not as far as I know." He shuffled himself around to face me. "Like I said, there were shell corporations in several countries, but I'm sure Thailand was not one of them."

Turning to Soltani, I said, "Okay, so we've got that group--"

"Willoughby-Klehs," she interjected. "Which includes the woman who claimed to be JR's sister."

"Right, so they're presumably responsible for blowing up the safe house in Maryland. And they're the ones who shot JR at the hostel."

JR and Soltani both nodded their agreement.

"Next, we have Mai's former employer. He's responsible for the wanted posters and searching for us in the church today."

"Searching the church for *me*," Mai added.

Father Su started to interrupt, but I was on a roll. Holding my hand up to forestall him, I continued, "And now, this colonel is supposedly trying to kill JR, too?"

They nodded again, but Mai shook her head no.

"I have to agree with Mai on this," I said. "It doesn't make sense."

JR asked, "Why doesn't it make sense?"

"When I was hiding upstairs, I heard the Colonel talking on the phone about JR and Mai. He said that he would send *her* back, and then he would kill *him*." I turned to Mai. "Send you back where? That doesn't add up. Especially, if he's gone to all the trouble to find you so he can make his point with the other girls. And why kill JR?"

The priest, who'd been fidgeting like he'd had too much coffee, finally spoke up. "I've been trying to tell you," he said. "Those weren't police, and that wasn't the Colonel."

With puzzled expressions, we all turned toward Father Su.

"They were not looking for John and Mai." Then sweeping a hand toward me and Soltani, he said, "They were looking for you two."

CHAPTER 48

I had violated the most basic rule of any criminal investigation: *Question everything, but assume nothing.*

By wrongly presuming that the Thai policemen had searched the church, I compounded the mistake by concluding it was the colonel I'd heard talking on the phone. As the errant dominoes continued falling, I then mistakenly believed that JR was the one whose life was in danger when it was apparently mine.

A voice in my head admonished me like a car's navigation system: *"Route recalculation..."*

As the colonel began to fade from the equation, he was replaced by Leo Kingsbury. *But why would this guy want me dead? And who did he send to look for us at the church?*

"Well, who were they?" asked Soltani, beating me to the draw.

The priest shook his head. "They didn't say. But there were two of them. Both big, both tough-looking, and both wearing all black."

I turned to Soltani. "Does that sound like anybody you know?"

The warmth left her eyes. "Why would I know them?"

"Because they were on the phone with your pal, Leo. I overheard them receiving orders to kill me and bring you back."

Closing her eyes, she palmed the bridge of her nose. "Now I feel like the bull in the arena."

Father Su led the rest of the group up the steps, while Soltani stood with me in the darkness. I was at a slight disadvantage without the ability to gauge the sincerity in her eyes, but I heard it in her voice.

"I have no idea what's going on," she said. "If it's true what you said about Leo, then the man's wheels have completely come off the tracks. I mean, yes, he's jealous. But having you killed?"

"Hey," I said with a pliant shrug. "I've never even met the guy. He's your..."

Even in the dark, I sensed her expression warning me not to complete that thought.

"Okay," I said, wiping the invisible slate. "Let's work backwards from the presumption that Kingsbury wants to harm me. How would he or could he accomplish that?"

Soltani stood in silence. "Well, two things immediately occur to me," she finally said. "He would definitely try to protect his career by insulating himself from the situation. And he would need to have connections that reached all the way to Bangkok."

"Good. I agree." I unconsciously rubbed my hands together. "So, knowing the man's background, does anything jump out at you? Any way he could accomplish those two things?"

She thought for a minute before shaking her head. "Nothing."

After gathering the crucifix pole, candle holder, matches, and medical supplies, Soltani and I followed the wedge of light back up to the sacristy.

The priest had gone to heat a pot of tea, and Sergeant Foster was rechecking JR's injury under better light. Even from across the room, I could see improvement in JR's color.

As the two men reminisced about their military tours together, the conversation evolved into present day—Foster bringing JR up to speed on changes in training since he'd left the service.

Something Foster touched on caught Soltani's attention, and her bearing suddenly hardened like Super Glue.

"What is it?" I moved toward her.

"SOG." Soltani ran her hands back through her hair. "I don't know why it didn't occur to me. Leo used to be commander of the Tactical Operations Division."

"Okay." I waited for the rest.

"SOG is under Tactical." Her eyes bore the intensity of a bobcat. "Special Operations Group."

I could figure out enough from that to know that I was in serious trouble, if it was true.

"The Marshals are a domestic agency," I said. "You even told me yourself that you don't have overseas operations."

"Well, yes, that's mostly true," Soltani said. "But the Special Ops guys have been known to work at the behest of the State Department, offering support abroad. In any case, there are a good number of ex-SOG members who are now on contract."

"Meaning what?"

"Meaning they're like mercenaries," said Soltani. "They're loyal to whoever pays them. Kingsbury ran the unit just after 9/11, which means that some of the guys who were under him have likely moved on by now. But they're a devoted bunch, and I'm sure a few of his men are still operational and loyal to him."

"Now give me the good news," I said.

I saw the Marine and JR in my periphery, shaking their heads.

"They'll definitely stand out in Thailand," said Soltani. "These guys are known for their toughness and their size. When they come for you, at least you'll be able to spot them."

"Well, that's a load off."

CHAPTER 49

I tried to pin down the priest about the two men who had intimidated their way into the church, but he wasn't much help other than to say they were Caucasian. It was almost as if the reality of the situation had frightened him into detached indifference.

Father Su couldn't even be sure where they were from, because, as he put it, "To my ear, anybody who's not Thai speaks with an accent. I can't tell a Canadian from an Aussie, or an American from a Brit."

In the end, the priest had abstained from any further involvement in our melodramatics—not that I blamed him. Leaving a wad of Thai Bhat next to his scorched crucifix holder, I led the group out through the back door and down the alley toward the side street.

We flagged down two tuk-tuks, then helped JR and Mai into one. Soltani and me took the second, and Foster led the way back toward Monet House.

Our driver motioned proudly at a tiny gilded cage dangling overhead. A small monkey moved about inside, his tail thrashing this way and that. It took a minute for me to realize that it was a battery operated toy. Realistic in appearance, it was undoubtedly a clever way to generate more tips. The man spoke no English though, so we could only smile and nod our amusement—though my focus was on our surroundings and whether or not we were being followed.

About halfway to our apartment, the alarm bells sounded in my head. Two Caucasian men on motorcycles quickly approached, zig-zagging through traffic behind us. They both wore dark clothing and wraparound sunglasses. With short cropped hair and bodies like Turkish wrestlers, they definitely stood out—just like Soltani had warned.

Nudging her arm, I motioned behind us. "We got trouble."

Color drained from her face as she looked back.

They did not fit the profile of the colonel's men, and I supposed they could have been the money launderers coming after JR. But after the phone conversation I'd overheard, I had to assume that these men were the Special Ops goons Soltani had told me about. And if that was the case, they were here to kill *me*.

Still a few cars sandwiched between us, the motorcycles were moving up quickly and would be on us soon.

"Go!" I yelled to our driver.

The man flashed a confused grin and nodded, but it was clear he didn't know what I meant.

Motioning frantically with my hands, I probably looked like I was signing to the hearing impaired. "Go, go," I repeated.

The man nodded again, then took his hands off of the wheel to bring them together in a prayerful bow.

JR and Mai were in the taxi in front of us, and Foster was in front of them on his motorcycle. None of them had noticed the men or knew what was about to happen.

Running diagonally to our left was a cobbled driveway with an arched sign overhead that read: Lumphini Park.

"That way," I yelled, pointing toward the park entrance.

Thankfully, the driver turned and accelerated. His fearful glances into the rearview mirror affirmed that he had picked up enough from my tone to sense danger.

Two seconds later, a gunshot blasted the tuk-tuk's front window into tiny shards that flew everywhere.

Soltani screamed and our driver squealed a long medley of Thai words that were either prayers or expletives. In any case, his wild eyes and terrified expression made him a question mark in my mind.

Just then, he jerked the steering wheel toward a raised concrete shrine and hit the brakes. Diving over the seat, I grabbed the wheel just as the driver jettisoned himself out of the tuk-tuk.

Soltani glanced behind us and screamed, "Oh my God." Then, wresting the little monkey cage off of the ceiling, she heaved it back at the motorcycles.

I was already climbing around to the driver's seat, but I saw that her aim was pretty good. One of the bikes wobbled badly after the metal cage was momentarily caught up in its front wheel.

Our former driver had cut back across my path toward the shrine, and I nearly ran over him in my effort to gain control of our 3-wheeled taxi. Stomping on the accelerator, I continued into the park with the shooters still hot on our trail.

The crack of another gunshot sounded behind us, but it went wide, striking a metal signpost in a burst of sparks. Then another, and another. The little three-wheeler shook violently as I pushed its speed to the max.

In front of me was a gate closing the roadway to all vehicle traffic. Banking sharply, and nearly rolling the tuk-tuk, I headed for a narrow pedestrian entrance.

It would serve as a choke point for the bikes, and it gave me a sudden flash of inspiration.

"The paper bag," I yelled over the seat to Soltani. "The antiseptic and the matches!"

When I glanced back again, she had emptied the Marine's first-aid kit on her lap. With one hand tightly gripping the seatback, she had already placed the isopropyl alcohol between her legs and was unscrewing the cap.

"Use the gauze as a fuse," I said. "That shit's super flammable, so watch yourself."

Stuffing the gauze into the plastic bottle, Soltani readied the matches we had used only moments before to light church candles. I hoped that her aim was as good with a Molotov cocktail as it was with a monkey cage.

I slowed the tuk-tuk, cocking it sideways about 15 feet inside the gate. "Hit the guy in front, if you can."

They had tucked away their guns to maneuver through the narrow opening. The timing had to be as good as the accuracy, otherwise the device would have no more effect than a Fourth of July sparkler.

Motorcyclist number one was just starting through the opening when Soltani let loose. The bottle sailed on a trajectory that seemed a bit high to me, with its sputtering wick arcing through the air behind it. At the last moment, the contraption dropped like a perfect slider, exploding across the motorbike's fairing.

The fireball splashed like a Rorschach inkblot, with blue flames licking the driver's face, neck and chest. He crumpled to the ground beneath his overturned bike, effectively clogging the path for his partner.

Flipping them off, I continued farther into the park. "Where did that come from?" I called to Soltani in amazement.

"What, my throw?" She grinned at me. "First-team, all-conference softball pitcher my senior year."

I wished I'd had the chance to tackle one of the bastards, and show Soltani what I did in my senior year. "Nicely done," I ended up saying, offering a fist bump over the seatback.

Sweeping around to the right and then back to the left, I could have been in Golden Gate Park. Dozens of people strolled and rode bicycles—many of whom had to dodge us as we serpentined our way on the narrow pedestrian paths. Bouncing over a grassy knoll like an out-of-control lawnmower, I kept the gas pedal to the floor.

My worry over driving a stolen taxi was now eclipsed by whether or not I would live through the rest of the day. The predators who had followed us from the church were clearly out for blood, and I still wasn't 100% sure why. Maybe if I let this Kingsbury guy know that there's nothing going on between me and Soltani...

"You need to call him," I said, veering to the right around a large amphitheater.

"And say what? Sorry for throwing a firebomb at you?"

"Not him," I said. "You need to call Kingsbury and confront him about all this. We have to find out why he sent those thugs after us. Why he wants *me* dead."

Soltani pulled out her phone. "He's been calling me. Already left three messages."

But instead of listening to them or returning his call, she pried off the back and plucked out the battery.

"What are you doing?"

"My phone may be part of the problem," she said.

Police sirens wailed on the streets outside the park, and it occurred to me that our problems were about to get worse. We had been involved in a shooting—my second in as many days—and I had stolen a tuk-tuk to make my getaway. Driving through a public park at breakneck speeds, I had nearly run down several people—including our former driver. The topper, of course, was our use of an incendiary weapon to sear a man like a tuna.

I was already an ex-con as far as Bangkok police were concerned, a two-striker what with the bicycle and the underwear thing. And the top dog cop still blamed *me* for absconding with his housemaid. At this point, I couldn't think of too many scenarios that could end well for me.

Then, as the tuk-tuk rounded a large fountain in the middle of the park, a little white police car came to a jerky stop directly in our path. It blocked the narrow roadway, and there was no way our taxi could fit past it.

Shifting into idle, I pulled up on the parking brake.

Soltani leaned forward. "We're pretty well screwed now."

CHAPTER 50

"I command you to stop!" yelled the officer, stepping from the car with an outstretched palm.

I whispered to Soltani. "Tourist Police."

"What does that mean?" she whispered back.

"He's not real."

"What is he, a hologram? Because he looks pretty real to me."

"No, I mean he doesn't have a gun."

We climbed out of the taxi and stood next to the fountain with our hands over our heads. The officer gesticulated wildly into his walkie-talkie while moving cautiously toward us.

"He's calling for backup," I said. "Radioing his location and our descriptions."

"I'm assuming that means the real cops will be here shortly."

I was about to answer in the affirmative when the officer yelled, "No talking. Turn around. Lift hands higher."

I remembered from last time, the Tourist Police were more like cadets or volunteer officers. No official police powers—hence the lack of weapons.

Sensing the officer moving into my personal space, I saw him from the corner of my eye reaching for one of my hands. This signaled his intent to handcuff me, which I was not going to let happen again.

Lifting my arms even higher, I knew the diminutive cop would have to stand on tiptoes. As soon as I felt his hand come in contact with my arm, I made my move.

Spinning and lowering my elbow at the same time, I caught the officer on the side of the head. The impact knocked him off balance, his hat flying in one direction and him stumbling in the other.

Soltani's gasp was not lost on me, as I momentarily wondered if she approved of my actions or would end up testifying against me.

Recovering quickly, the officer lunged for me—which is what I had counted on. Taking hold of his wrist, I pulled him toward me as I swung my other hand upward under his bicep. With one quick yank, I used the officer's own momentum to send the poor guy into the fountain behind me.

After the huge splash, I saw that Soltani's shocked expression was equal to that of the cop. We jumped back into the tuk-tuk and left the roadway, cutting over a dirt mound in another direction. My prayer was that a park this large had to have multiple exits.

"You said he was radioing our descriptions to his partners," said Soltani once she regained her composure. "They'll be looking for us in this taxi."

She was right. Every cop in Bangkok would now be watching for us, if not for me personally.

A modern three story building emerged through the trees, as we whizzed past a sign that said it was a school. As we got closer, I saw a huge blue arch suspended in the air above an open courtyard.

"There," I said, motioning toward the place.

Camouflaging the tuk-tuk, I wedged it tightly between two parked trucks. Abandoning it there, Soltani and I strolled casually onto the school property. The open area beneath the canopy was lined with bicycles, and luckily none of the students were around.

"Perfect," I said. "Grab one and let's get the hell out of here."

"You don't think the police will spot us on these?"

I shrugged. "What choice do we have. The tuk-tuk is out, and we'll be sitting ducks on foot."

Taking the first two bikes at the end of the row, Soltani's was a sleek blue roadster. Mine on the other hand, was a small, red bike with white trim and a basket on the front.

"Do you want to trade?" I said, my knees repeatedly bumping the handlebars as I tried to catch up to her.

"Nope." Soltani was clearly enjoying the ease with which she stayed ahead of me, and even more that I was on a girl's bicycle.

On the opposite side of the park, the path widened and veered left. Following it proved fruitful, as I could see an opening onto a busy street. The gate was unmanned, as far as I could tell, but I still heard sirens around the park's perimeter.

We slowed and got off our bicycles as we approached the opening. Peeking around a concrete pillar, I saw two police cars—real ones this time—driving up and back on the street. With lights flashing, it was obvious they were patrolling for us. In my mind, the chances of them spotting us on the bikes was better than 50/50.

I heard someone yell my name, and suddenly a motorcycle pulled to the curb in front of me. It was Foster, the Marine, and right behind him was the tuk-tuk carrying JR and Mai.

Turning to Soltani, I said, "These guys aren't kidding when they say, *"no man left behind."*

"Or woman," she said.

Leaving the bicycles, I jumped onto the back of the motorcycle and Soltani joined the other two in their tuk-tuk. Grateful that they had returned to aid our escape, one troubling question still gnawed at me: Is there any safe place for us to go now?

CHAPTER 51

Monet House was only a few blocks from the park, and we took a circuitous route back to make sure we weren't being followed. After seeing no cops and no suspicious motorcyclists, we sent JR's taxi on its way. Foster parked his motorbike and then met us in the alleyway behind the apartment house.

It was nearly dark and there was no traffic, yet standing in the open still felt vulnerable. Scanning our surroundings, I happened to glance up at the window of our unit. I had to count the floors to be sure of what I was seeing.

"The lights in our apartment are on," I said, pointing upward. "Fourth floor, all the way to the right."

"They were off when we left," said Soltani.

"Somebody's in there," I said. "It's just now getting dark, so they would have had to turn on the lights to see."

"The men who just shot at us?"

"I don't think so." I glanced up again. "One of them was injured, and there's no way they could have made it here before us. This is either the police looking for Mai, or it's the people who are after JR."

"You mean your so-called client," said Soltani. Then, realizing the trouble her steamy little dalliance with Kingsbury had caused, she raised her hands in submission. "Sorry, sorry."

"You guys can stay the night in my apartment," said Foster. "It's me and another Marine, but he's away on leave. Plenty of room."

Assuming that JR would be recuperating there with Mai, I tried to imagine all five of us sharing the cozy quarters. Depending on the arrangement, it could either be a good thing or a bad one. In any case, I wasn't going to make the call—lest I give Soltani another reason to reject me.

"Yeah, as long as you don't mind." Soltani shrugged and glanced over at me. "Not much we can do until whoever's up there leaves."

Turns out the Marine's apartment was directly below ours, same exact layout and décor. We tried to listen, hoping to hear upstairs, but apparently the building was well made and well insulated.

Foster heated a couple of frozen pepperoni pizzas, and we all snacked on them while kicking around our options. JR and Mai were exhausted, but Foster, who had guns, was ready to storm our unit and take out whoever was in there.

If we were fighting on only one front, I might have gone along with that plan. But there were too many people coming after too many of us, and I don't like unknowns.

It had been a long day, preceded by a longer night for most of us. We ultimately decided to hold off on any further action until morning. Foster had his own bedroom, and offered the other one to JR and Mai. A foldout sofa bed in the living room would serve as our billet for the evening.

I'd wanted to shower, especially after my night in prison, and a shave would have would have been nice. Soltani, on the other hand, looked like she'd just stepped out of a bubble bath. It was warm, even with the air conditioning, so we just rested on top of the thin mattress, in the clothes we had on.

"What's that?" I asked, motioning to a bandage on her forearm.

"I think a piece of glass cut me during the shooting. It's nothing."

I wanted to take a look, make sure she was alright, but could tell the attention embarrassed her.

Staring upwards and wishing I could see into our apartment, I wondered how I'd managed to get myself into such a predicament. Not only did I have no client to reimburse me for my numerous credit card charges, but there were now people committed to killing me. Listening to Soltani's soft breathing next to me, I wondered what she felt about all of this.

"I'm sorry," she whispered out of the darkness. "It's my fault that you are a target. It's all because of my stupid decisions."

"We don't know that," I said. "And I blame myself more than you, anyway."

"I also feel badly for the way I've treated you. My hostilities were misdirected, and none of this was your fault." Then she added, "Well, maybe a little bit of it was."

We both laughed, and it seemed like the big glacier was finally starting to melt. It felt nice, not having my guard up for a change. After a minute, I turned onto my side and faced her in the dark. Wanting to say something romantic, or sensitive, or something about the two of us, my mind suddenly took a left turn.

"I missed my daughter's birthday," I said.

Soltani stared at me out of the blackness. "Tell me about her."

"Bridge? She's great. Just turning thirteen, which, as I've learned from my wife, ex-wife, almost ex-wife, is a really big deal to a girl."

Silence.

I was left wondering if she thought I was a complete idiot, or maybe she had just fallen asleep.

Then I felt her hand on top of mine. "It is a big deal," she said. "Sorry if I screwed that up for you, too."

"Nah, I own that one."

She was quiet for a long time before she spoke again. "I think I misjudged you. You're not a bad guy, McKenna."

My breathing quickened and I wondered if she could hear it. Her words were like a pain killer to a dying man. They somehow made me feel better about everything that had gone wrong–from missing the birthday party to being imprisoned in a Bangkok jail.

There was a momentary hesitation, and then I felt Soltani's hand pulling me toward her.

"Oh my God," came a voice from the other side of the room. "Turn on the TV!"

CHAPTER 52

My eyes rolled back in my head. It was Mai, darting across the living room toward the big flat-screen in the corner. If we had gone to war with Russia or had put a man on Mars, I couldn't have been less interested at that moment.

The room suddenly lit up with the flickering light of the evening news. It was all in Thai, of course, which made it even less interesting. Then a picture flashed onto the screen of Lumphini Park.

I sat up, eyes glued to the image as Mai translated.

"Two people injured," she said. "And the suspects escaped in a stolen taxi."

The next image on the screen was a black and white frame of me driving the tuk-tuk. Probably taken from a security camera.

"This suspect is wanted for the crime," translated Mai.

I looked pudgy in the shot, and wondered if the TV really did add ten pounds. "That's illegal," I said. "They're supposed to say this man is *a person of interest*. You can't call someone a suspect in the U.S."

Mai said, "You can in Thailand."

The next clip was of a woman lying on the ground near the shrine we had passed, and medical personnel were tending to her.

"Gunshot injury," said Mai. "This woman was an innocent tourist from Australia. They are blaming this on you as well."

Suddenly my extra weight didn't seem as important.

Soltani knew the truth because she was there, but the rest of them eyed me as if I really might be responsible for the shooting.

"Sooner or later we're going to have to get into our apartment, said Soltani. "I've got things in there I need."

I assumed she was referring to her passport and money, but if she was anything like Doris it could mean makeup and a hair brush.

"I'll go upstairs and check it out," I said.

Soltani shook her head. "You're the last one who should go. In addition to the men who just tried to kill you, the woman posing as JR's sister has already used you to lead the assassins to JR. And every cop in Bangkok is looking for you for the shootings."

She had a point. Regardless which of the three groups of bad guys had burgled our apartment, they all knew me. I'd be walking right into a trap if they were still up there or had the place under surveillance.

After hearing the commotion, Foster had come out and stood leaning against the wall. "I'll go up to check on your apartment," he said. "I'm the only one that nobody wants to kill."

The Marine also had a point. Out of all of us, he was the only one not known to any of the killers or the police. Plus, he was well-trained and well-armed.

Foster's offer took me off of the hot seat, but he also had the least to gain from it. I guessed he was doing it solely out of loyalty to one of his Marine brethren.

"I'm going with you anyway," I said. "If they're still inside the apartment, you'll need backup."

Soltani had a worried expression, which made me feel even better about joining the mission.

JR struggled from the bedroom, having also heard the banter. "I'm going with--"

"No!" we all said in unison.

"Try to stop me," he said.

It was like a game of who will blink first. A stubborn and opinionated bunch, we all eyed one another until I finally broke the stalemate. "Forget it, let's just go. Me, Foster, and JR."

Soltani said, "And what? The ladies get to stay home and bake cookies?"

I waved her off like a Neanderthal heading out for the hunt. Foster came with his sidearm, and JR clung to my shoulder as we made our way to the end of the hallway where the elevator waited.

Exiting on the 4th floor, we started toward our apartment door. Foster leaned his ear against it while I watched ahead of us and JR scanned to the rear.

Turning with a shrug, Foster couldn't tell if anybody was inside. The three of us were stacked against the wall on the hinge side of the door. I was in the middle, with Foster in the lead and JR behind me.

I quietly reached over Foster's shoulder to hand him the key.

Without warning, the door suddenly swung open.

CHAPTER 53

"What the hell?"

Soltani leaned out of the doorway and was met with the business end of Foster's pistol.

"How did you get up here before us?" I asked.

"Took the stairs," she said. "Nobody's in the apartment now, but whoever was here totally trashed the place. Anyway, I came up here to warn you guys. As soon as you left, four police cars drove into the alleyway behind the apartment building. I watched them from the window. Saw the cops coming in through the service entrance."

"Was the colonel one of them?" asked JR.

"Too far away and too dark to tell," she said. "But my guess is they know we're here and they're on their way up right now."

We all turned to watch the elevator while my mind worked in reverse, starting with how they knew I was here. It seemed logical that they had also been here earlier to ransack our apartment. But I wasn't about to make any more assumptions.

"The cops are probably looking for me," I said. Then turning to JR, "They may take you as a bonus, but I doubt they know Soltani and Foster."

"Then you two hide in the stairwell," said Foster. "Me and Soltani will take the elevator down to the lobby and check things out. We'll come get you once the cops leave."

It sounded like a plan of sorts, and I reluctantly went along with it. But something didn't feel right to me, and it was more than the fact that I was hiding like a rat in the stairwell. Another possibility was trying to work its way into my head, but my brain was clogged.

Helping JR as much as I could with my bad knee, we hobbled through the doorway into the hollow fourth floor stairwell. I kept the door cracked, while peering out to see if the colonel stepped off of the elevator. The door opened to an empty car, and Soltani and Foster got on.

The cops should have made it up here by now, I thought. Unless...

A mental snap of my fingers came with the realization that I had done it again. I'd made another assumption. A wrong one.

"C'mon," I said to JR. "They didn't come here for me."

Hobbling again, the two of us bumbled down the staircase to the next level. Again, I cracked the door and peered into the hallway.

Foster's apartment was at the far end, the same relative position as mine on the floor above. A slanted rectangle of light emitted into the hallway from the open door, and a police officer stood like a sentry just outside it.

JR tried to see around me. "What's happening?"

Turning to break the bad news, I saw from his expression that he had already figured it out. My new concern was that JR would do something stupid like try to intervene.

I looked back into the hallway and saw no less than six police officers escorting Mai out of the apartment.

"We can't let them take her," JR said, leaning into me as if he was ready to extract her with or without my help.

"These aren't Tourist Police," I whispered back. "They have guns. If we try to free her, they'll have three prisoners instead of just one. Think about it; their boss already has a hard-on for you, and I'm public enemy number one after today's shooting. You won't be any help to Mai if you're in jail."

JR swallowed hard and his eyes teared up. Easing the door closed, I put my hand on his shoulder until they passed by and I heard the elevator kick on.

My next worry was that they would run smack into Soltani and Foster in the lobby. Not that the cops would know them, but Foster was still a loose cannon in my mind. There wasn't much he wouldn't do for his buddy.

After the police left, several minutes passed without any sign of Soltani and Foster. The elevator motor finally came on again, and when the doors opened they were the only people aboard. Their faces told me that they had seen Mai being led away. Soltani seemed emotionally upset, and Foster looked pissed off.

We stepped out of the stairwell to meet them in the hall. Nobody spoke for several seconds, and then Foster leaned close to JR and quietly reassured him.

I whispered to Soltani, "I'm surprised the Marine didn't try to take on all six of them."

"He would have," she whispered back. "But I was able to talk some sense into him. Not sure how long that'll last, though."

"What do you mean?"

Soltani raised an eyebrow. "They're ready for battle. Between the two of these guys, they're going to want to take her back."

Foster and JR had stopped talking, so I broke my little huddle with Soltani. "I wonder how they knew where to find Mai," I said, forging a new direction in the conversation.

"Manager," said Foster.

Soltani turned to me. "We played dumb downstairs and asked the desk clerk about all the police commotion. She told us that a resident had seen a woman entering an apartment on the third floor, then called down to the manager. Apparently the resident had recognized Mai from one of those wanted posters—which, by the way, are also posted at the front desk."

I said, "You know what that means."

"Yea," answered Foster. "It means that after I kill the colonel, I'm coming back to take out that nosy resident and the nosy manager."

Hoping it was just his anger and bravado talking, I said, "Well, actually, I was thinking more about the fact that my picture has already been all over the news and they could recognize me as well."

Perhaps my words had come out sounding a tad self-absorbed. The two men looked at me like I was a deserter, a turncoat, like I'd committed treason. To them I was more concerned about myself than fighting for the greater good.

"I mean, if I get caught again..." I paused, trying to figure out what to say that wouldn't sound narcissistic. "What I'm trying to say is... if I end up in prison, I won't be able to help you guys."

Their expressions eased a bit, but Soltani's face twisted into a big sour question mark.

"Then you'll help us?" JR asked.

"It's the least I can do." Not sure what that meant or why I said it.

Soltani finally spoke. "Help them do what?" She looked at me and I looked at them.

"Take Mai back," said Foster. "We're going to mount a hostage rescue operation."

CHAPTER 54

"What is wrong with you?"

Soltani's question came as soon as we got back to our ransacked apartment.

"They already blame me for leading a hit team to JR," I said. "And also for getting him shot. Didn't you see their faces when I mentioned that I was also wanted? They were pissed. I had to say something."

"So, what now? You're going to storm police headquarters and liberate the damsel in distress?" Soltani shook her head. "I'm telling you McKenna, you get caught this time and you'll never get out of prison. That's if the police don't kill you first."

Having already buried myself up to my neck in this, I could only give her a gallant face. "Whatever it takes to do the right thing," I said. "Sometimes other people are more important than one's self."

She rolled her eyes. "Aren't you suddenly the altruistic one."

This wasn't something I wanted to do, but I was kind of between a rock and a hard place. My sincere hope was that fate would take an unexpected detour and this plan to rescue Mai would be for naught. In the meantime, I had hoped to rewind the tape to last night's foldout couch scene by trying to appear chivalrous.

My efforts didn't seem to faze Soltani, because she immediately began checking the apartment to see what, if anything, was missing. Having taken hundreds of burglary reports during my time with SFPD, I followed her around making my own observations.

The place had literally been turned upside down, but several things struck me as odd. High value items such as stereo and TV hadn't been touched. In fact, nothing seemed to have been taken. Not even money. Our passports had been looked at, and both had been tossed on the floor. Every drawer had been taken out, every piece of clothing removed from closets, and all the toiletries gone through—including Soltani's numerous soaps, shampoos, and powders.

No wonder she smelled so good.

She noticed me noticing her personal things and frowned.

"I'm just wondering," I said. "The police were either looking for Mai or for me."

"Uh-huh."

"So, why pull out drawers and open toiletry bags? It's not like one of us could be hiding in your Tylenol container."

She nodded, looking at her jumble of cosmetics through new eyes. "And since they didn't take anything..."

I stood in her bathroom lost in thought, my eyes gazing into the wall behind Soltani. I knew the answer was here, in front of me, only I couldn't see it. I'd been involved in another case once, and the answer to the whole thing was found on a computer's hard drive. But we had no computers with us, and the places searched were too small for a laptop—or even a cell phone.

"What is it?" asked Soltani.

I held up a finger. "What if it wasn't the police who were in here?"

"You think Kingsbury's men broke in to search for something?"

"No, I think we left *his* guys licking their wounds at the park today. Besides they wanted to kill me, not search through your mascara."

"Then who?"

"What about the Willoughby-Klehs people who JR was going to testify against? They blew up a government safe house, then came all the way to Thailand to shoot him."

"Still, they obviously weren't searching for him in our dresser drawers."

"Right." I tilted my head back and closed my eyes. Then it came to me. "But they could have been looking for evidence."

"What, like photos and documents?"

"Sort of, although *if* he has something it's probably not in that format. JR never mentioned exactly what his evidence was, but I think we need to talk to him about..." I stopped myself abruptly.

With a perplexed expression, Soltani waited for me to finish my sentence. When I didn't, she let out a sigh.

My eyes scanned the bathroom counter, around the room, then back to her.

Soltani started to speak and I reached across the space between us, covering her mouth with my palm. Her eyes grew wide—not angry or scared, but curious. I felt the soft moistness of her lips trembling beneath my hand. Leaning close enough to smell her fragrant hair, I brought my face side-by-side with hers.

CHAPTER 55

"Don't say anything else," I whispered. "I think I've just figured out why they were here."

Taking my hand away, I saw that the whole episode had confused Soltani. Thinking for a second, I reached around her to turn on the faucet. "We've been looking at this the wrong way," I said. "The reason that nothing is missing is because instead of taking something, they left something."

She glanced around. "Drugs?"

"What?"

"Do you think they planted drugs to set us up?"

"No." I eased my face back against hers. "I think they may have bugged the apartment."

Soltani's eyes swept around, more frantic this time. "Where?"

I took her hand and led her out of the bathroom. "I noticed it when we came in," I whispered, "but wasn't sure what it meant at the time."

We paused in front of the living room couch where the cushions were still cockeyed on the floor.

Soltani mouthed the word, *"Where?"*

Stepping around the glass coffee table, I nodded toward the wall. A painting of a gold leafed tree hung there, mounted on a frame of brushed bronze. But unlike everything else in the apartment, it appeared untouched. I had initially wondered why the burglars would search through every space larger than a pinhead, but not look behind a painting.

"That was their mistake," I whispered to Soltani. "Rehanging it perfectly plumb."

Gently lifting the picture off the wall, I found a black transmitter about the size of a matchbook affixed to the back of the canvas. Scrolling back through my mind, I tried to recall what conversation it may have already picked up. Not enough to worry about, I realized. Just speculation about JR's evidence. Nothing they didn't already know.

When I rehung the picture, Soltani gave me a puzzled look. I nodded toward the painting again and rotated my hand in a forward motion.

Winking at me, she leaned over the coffee table. "I'm going down to the lobby to get some trash bags so we can clean up this mess."

I assumed that she wanted to warn JR and Foster about the hidden transmitter. Winking back, I gave her the thumbs-up.

This winking thing was pretty fun. It got me thinking about the scene on the hide-a-bed again, which got me thinking about Soltani's bedroom and what if they'd also put a bug there.

After she left, I checked her room, my room, both bathrooms, and the kitchenette. Nothing. I was certain that only the living room was being monitored.

Carefully removing the framed image again, I examined the bug more thoroughly. I'd seen wireless RF transmitters before and had a general idea how they operated. This one was quite small and set in a plastic housing. There was no hardwired power source, so my assumption was that it operated on a battery—which would probably have to be replaced or recharged at some point. Then again, it could also be set on voice activation, which would reduce dead time and extend the battery life. After inspecting the device, I hung the frame back as it was.

Along with smaller circuitry, I knew that transmitters had become more sophisticated. Their signals could travel a kilometer or more away, and the units themselves can sometimes be set to activate or deactivate remotely. It bothered me that a transmitter like the one in our apartment didn't necessarily have to be monitored from a long distance, and the people who hid it could very well be listening from next door.

I turned on my shower and then tiptoed out of the apartment. Strolling past the neighboring doors, I listened discreetly to see if I could hear anything. As might be expected, it was a waste of time.

Soltani got off the elevator and met me in the hallway. Motioning her well away from our unit, we walked to the opposite end of the hall where a small window looked out at the building next door.

Leaning close to her, I wanted to keep the whispering thing going. "What did they say?"

"Foster wants to find them and... I'm not even going to repeat what he said." Soltani self-consciously swept her hair back. "And JR didn't seem at all surprised. Apparently, this group is technologically savvy and well equipped. Speaking of which, how come you put their transmitter back instead of smashing it into a million pieces?"

"I thought we might be able to use the device to our advantage, especially if they don't know we're on to them."

"How?"

"Not sure yet, but for now we'll just play along. Just be careful not to mention anything more about JR. That's the whole reason they're listening in; they want to find out where he is and snuff him out."

"Are we safe staying in the apartment?"

"I'd say so." Turning together we started back toward the room. "The lock isn't broken, so they must have picked it. We'll just have to wedge a chair or something in front of it." I had decided not to worry her with the possibility that they could be close by, or could return at some point.

Soltani nodded.

"And any conversation we don't want them to hear should be held in one of our bedrooms."

She gave me a sidelong glance.

I paused in front of our door. "It's showtime."

CHAPTER 56

"Why is your shower on?" asked Soltani.

I frowned at my forgetfulness. "I'm steaming the wrinkles out of my trousers."

She laughed. "Who calls them trousers?"

"My dad."

Soltani laughed again. "How old are you anyway?"

"Uh... in my thirties."

She tilted her head. "You're 37. I remember from your paperwork at Fort Meade. You went to Cal on a football scholarship, and were a San Francisco cop for thirteen years."

Quite the memory, I thought. And charitably, she left out the unceremonious end to my career.

It seemed like she was about to say more, and I made an exaggerated motion toward the painting. Apparently, it dawned on Soltani before she recited my address and phone number for them to hear. It hardly mattered though, since the fictitious *Elaina Teagan* already knew all that.

Which got me thinking. JR's bogus sister had to be involved in the Willoughby-Klehs organization, if not actually one of their assassins. Yet, I'd never thought to probe into her background.

Excusing myself, I motioned to my phone and went outside to the hallway.

It was 3 p.m. when I dialed Sha Nay Nay's number.

"I swear, McKenna!" Her hoarse whisper reminded me of the time difference.

"Sorry," I said. "Tell me I didn't wake the baby."

She listened for a few seconds. "Nah, she still asleep. I'll give you a pass this time, since your ass is already in enough trouble."

"Yeah, there are some people trying to kill me... Wait a minute, how did you know?"

"I didn't. But if they don't kill you, your wife will."

"Oh that," I said. "Yeah, I missed my daughter's--"

"I already know, McKenna. I was there."

"You were at my daughter's birthday party?"

"Uh-huh. She called me up and invited me. I been tell'n you that I'm kinda like a big sister to Bridget. Anyway, I made some excuses for you, so that should help out a little."

"Okay... thanks? I guess." Then I imagined the look on Grandma Abrams' face when she met Shanay, and I almost had to laugh.

"So, why you call'n me at 1 o'clock in the morning?"

"The woman who hired me for this job..."

"Uh-huh?"

"I need you to check her out for me."

"Already did," said Shanay. "Had a bad feel'n about that *biatch* from the get. When you flaked on Bridget's party, I decided to call up that weird dude who runs your marina. He checked her paperwork and sort'a gave me the low-down."

"You phoned Cliff?"

"Yup. But it didn't help us much. I'm pretty sure the chick used a BS name. Cliffy told me she paid cash to rent the boat she was in, then beat it out of there the day you left for D.C. Not only that, but the references she put on her application were all *jengas*.

"They were no good?"

"That's what I jus' said."

I stared out the window at the end of the hallway as a couple of thoughts circled my mind. First, the woman masquerading as JR's sister must have been planning this for a while. Long enough to seek me out, pose as my neighbor, and then manipulate me into finding her so-called brother.

And second, Sha Nay Nay Moore had turned into a pretty damn good secretary—or executive assistant, as she now calls herself.

"Good work, Shanay." I started down the hall to the apartment. "For the call to Cliff and for helping me out on the home front."

"So, you're okay then?"

I had stumbled over some hefty obstacles in this case, and a couple of really big hurdles were still ahead of me. Not the least of which was the plan to rescue Mai from police custody. And then there was the fact that I had no client to pay me for any of this. But why worry Shanay? "Yeah, I'm good. I'll try to call with an update in a couple of days."

When I returned to our apartment, water was running in Soltani's bathroom and I assumed she was actually bathing. I waited in the living room, flipping through the TV channels until I found a live soccer match. Then I turned up the volume to portray normalcy for the transmitter.

We had heard nothing from Foster and JR, and my nerves were still on edge about their idea to spring Mai. I hoped their silence didn't mean they'd attempted something crazy on their own. Hopefully, they had realized the plan was a fool's errand and were now having second thoughts.

Stretching out on the couch, I tried a few different positions to best cover my flaws. The water shut off, and I moved around to the other end of the couch so that I'd be facing Soltani's room. At least that way, the first thing she saw wouldn't be the thinning hair on the crown of my head.

A loud rap on the door caused me to jump to my feet. Worrying that it was any number of the people who were after me, I hoped that it was only someone complaining about the TV volume.

Grabbing a steak knife from the kitchenette, just in case, I peered through the peephole.

It was Foster, dressed in a jacket, denim pants, and carrying his motorcycle helmet. When I opened the door, he glanced over at the painting, then down at the knife in my hand. The hint of a grin crossed his face, but he said nothing. He handed me a folded piece of paper, then nodded and headed back toward the elevator.

Soltani came out of the bathroom, fully dressed, hair wrapped in a towel, and smelling like Dove soap. Under the dinette lamp, we read the note together.

She finished reading it before me, and I could feel her eyes boring into me. My slack hand swiped down across my face, as I read the note for the second time.

M & S,
Got called in to pull a late shift at the embassy.
My man is resting—not really up for company.
If you guys get hungry, Cleanfit Delivery 097-236-2306
has good cheap food and they deliver all over Bangkok.
P.S. We make our move tomorrow night.
–Foster

CHAPTER 57

Soltani didn't seem happy about it, and I wasn't either. But I couldn't let her know that, since I had already committed myself to *the cause.*

Reading the note for the third time, I flipped it over and saw that he had left his cell phone number—*In case of emergency.*

"We make our move tomorrow night?" Soltani tilted her head. "What in the hell?"

I raised my palms. "Relax. Something like they're planning can't be pulled off without lots of intelligence. We'll have to surveil the colonel, find out what he drives and where he lives. At this point, we have no idea where Mai actually is. She could be in jail or even back to her housecleaning job by now."

"Or dead," she said.

I grimaced at the thought. "Just don't mention that in front of..." Stopping myself before saying JR's name, I glared at Soltani with my eyes wide. Then, plunging my face into her hair, I said, "We shouldn't be talking about any of this in here."

"My bedroom?" she whispered.

Under different circumstances, those words would have had me dancing like the Lucky Charms leprechaun. But I knew it would lead to nothing, and besides, there wasn't much more to talk about.

"Tell you what," I handed her the note. "Why don't you order us something to eat? I'm in need of a shower and some clean clothes. We can discuss the operational points of their plan later."

That seemed to satisfy Soltani for the time being, though I caught her watching me as I tossed my clothes into the washer. Maybe she was surprised that I did my own laundry—a talent I'd perfected since living on my own. My hope was that I looked much younger in the terry cloth robe I'd found in my closet.

The shower felt amazing. Besides finally scouring off the residue from Bang Kwang, it gave me a little breather to think. By the time I joined Soltani, my clothes were clean and dry, and our dinner had been delivered—along with two cold bottles of beer.

"How about some fresh air?" she said. "It's finally cooling off, and I was thinking we could eat on the rooftop." She winked, which I took to mean she wanted to talk without being monitored.

For such an attractively maintained deck, I was surprised that no one else was up there. I found a small garden table and slid it over to the two chairs we had used during our surveillance.

The colors of Bangkok gleamed all around us, while we sat at a private table on a private veranda beneath flickering white lights. It was so pleasant that I almost forgot how sweltering hot the night was.

"Better?" she asked, clinking her bottle against mine.

"Much."

We sat in silence, eating and sipping, but mostly enjoying the moment without having to fill it with words. Between the long shower and the quiet dinner, I was finally loosening up.

"Is this the real you?" she finally said, catching me deep inside my thoughts.

I smiled but wasn't really sure how to answer.

"You need downtime to figure things out, don't you?"

"I suppose that's true," I said. "Sometimes it takes me a while, but sooner or later I'll usually find my way there."

"Is that how you got yourself out of that mess they had you in back in San Francisco?"

I studied Soltani. There was more insight behind her question than what she could have found in my file back in Maryland.

"Something like that."

"And now? Are you finding your way there?"

"I think so, but you'll have to decide that," I said. "I've been giving it a lot of thought, and this is where I'm at... We've got to help Mai, there's no question about it. And we know we can't go to the police, or to anybody else for that matter."

"So, we're back to you three trying to pull off some kind of rescue." Soltani sipped her beer and then shook her hair back. "Which is ludicrous."

"Well, maybe not." I scooted my chair forward and rested my forearms on the table. "The Marine is a great guy, but he's also a bit of a loose cannon. Would you agree?"

Soltani nodded.

"And JR is still recovering from a serious gunshot wound. Even though he's getting better, the kid lost a lot of blood and he's still barely able to walk on his own. In my mind, he may be more of a hindrance than an asset. Plus, because it's his girlfriend we'd be going after, JR's decisions will more likely be emotional than logical or tactical."

Her brow started to curve downward. "What are you suggesting?"

I paused...

"I'm suggesting you and me do this without them."

CHAPTER 58

Soltani stared into my eyes as if her face had suddenly become stone. "You're kidding, right?"

"No, I'm 100% serious." I slid my chair around the table until I was next to her. Pushing the cardboard dinner containers out of the way, I used our beer bottles as place markers. "Okay," I said. "We're here—at Monet House. The colonel is here, at police headquarters," I set the other bottle down a few inches to the right. "I've been there; It's only a few blocks away."

Soltani shrugged. "Okay..."

"And this..." I plucked a piece of roti bread from her red curry rice and set it on the table about six inches to the left of the beer bottles. "This is the Holy Rosary Church. It's a little farther away —about a half mile from the colonel's office."

"Wait, what?" Soltani flicked my roti church with her finger. "You think Father Su is looking to get into the hostage rescue business?"

I pinched the bridge of my nose. Besides sounding ridiculous, this *idea* of mine had sort of killed the romantic mood.

"Look, the plan is still in the *chalk talk* stage," I said. "There are a lot of moving parts, and I'm still working it all out."

Soltani started to take the last sip of the headquarters building, but left it where it was on the table. "We still don't know where Mai is being held, or even where the colonel lives."

My hand swiped the air as if erasing an imaginary chalkboard. "Admittedly, there is some intelligence work we still need to do. And we will. But I guess, the real question is whether or not you trust me."

"Do I trust you?" her head cocked to the side.

I wanted to remind her that she had trusted Leo Kingsbury, and that son-of-a-bitch was probably the one trying to kill me. Though it was kind of an argument not to make the same mistake again with me, I hoped she'd see it a different way—like I was a better bet. In the end, I decided not to bring him up again.

"Well, my friend seems to trust you."

"Your *friend*?" I said. "What friend?"

Soltani's expression remained austere, except her eyes smiled as if she enjoyed holding the ace card.

Pushing back from the table, I turned to face her. "C'mon, who do you know that could possibly know me?"

"Brooksie," she said.

"You're friends with Sarah Brooks? That's impossible."

"Why is it impossible?"

"Because you're a Deputy Marshal in Washington, D.C., and she's a Customs agent on the other side of the country."

A sly grin emerged. "We went to the academy together."

I frowned.

"It's true," She said. "Federal Law Enforcement Training Center in Glynco, Georgia. And if you think it's hot here, you haven't been to Georgia in July. The humidity is--"

"You're telling me that out of all the federal agencies in the United States, you and Brooks did your academy training together?"

"Well, pretty much. Although, the FBI and DEA have their own training centers. But, yeah, me and Brooksie got to be pretty good friends."

"So, how did you make the connection between me and her?"

Soltani raised an eyebrow. Another ace card. "That day in my office when you told me about working with the feds on a drug bust. I got curious and googled you. Brooksie's name was mentioned in the news story and I called her."

"You've known all this time?"

Soltani shook her head. "She was away on vacation, and didn't get back to me until just yesterday."

No wonder Soltani knew so much about my train wreck of a career at SFPD. She had seemed to know more than the media reports, and now I knew why.

Then I thought back to our sofa bed conversation. She'd put her hand on mine and told me that I was a good guy. At the time, I thought her change of heart had something to do with unburdening herself to me about the tryst with her boss. Now I wondered if Brooks had melted the iceberg for me. Maybe it was a little of both.

Wanting to ask what Brooks had told her, I resisted, figuring that to leave well enough alone was the smarter choice. Instead, I rustled up a self-assured smile—which I didn't really feel. "Then back to my original question..."

"Do I trust you, McKenna?" Soltani leaned back and stared up at the canopy of lights. After a long pause, she nodded.

"You know; you can call me by my first name," I said.

"Yes, *Daniel*."

"Danny." I said.

"Okay, yes, Danny."

"Say the whole thing."

Soltani rolled her eyes. "Yes, *Danny*, I trust you."

CHAPTER 59

We needed to talk this plan through, but we couldn't do it in front of the listening device.

With only one beer under our belts, it was somehow enough to lift the millstone that the past few days had created. We ended up talking in my bedroom, relaxed and still under the genial influence of the rooftop dinner.

"What are you thinking? she said, plopping down on my bed.

It was a trick question. My mind was a jumble of plans for the colonel's takedown and fantasies of another takedown.

Soltani looked amazing—perfect in every way. But the signals weren't clear. She didn't bat her eyelashes, or bite her little finger, and she didn't stretch out on the bed like a cat. In fact, there was no overt flirtation at all.

The deep look in her eyes was what confused me—like I was worth something, and she might actually be able to see us together. It could have been all in my mind; it's played tricks on me like that before. But I didn't think so.

The pen and the message pad in my hand suddenly felt obtuse, and I wanted to drop them on the floor and kick them under the bed. This wasn't the time to be drawing diagrams and talking tactics.

My cell phone rang and I realized I'd forgotten to turn it off after my call to Sha Nay Nay. I guess it didn't matter, since Kingsbury's men already knew where I was staying.

"Hello?"

"Dad?"

"Bridge?" I covered the mouthpiece. "I need to take this," I said to Soltani.

Bridget asked, "Where are you?"

"I'm in Thailand." Wandering out of the room to talk privately, I walked aimlessly around the apartment. "I'm really sorry I missed your birthday."

"It's okay. Shanay told me that you were working hard on one of your big cases."

I wasn't sure how hard I was actually working and it certainly wasn't *my* big case, but I wanted to buoy my daughter's image of me. "Yeah," I said. "But I'm hoping to wrap it up soon and get back there to give you your birthday present."

"I'm not a little girl," she said. "You don't have to get me anything. I'm just calling because I miss you, and I wanted to make sure you were okay."

"I'm fine, sweetheart. Nothing to worry about. I miss you too." Pausing, I asked, "Is your mom there?"

"Uh-huh, she's watching TV with...him. You know, Mike."

"Prowse? Your mom's still seeing that douche, Mike Prowse?"

Bridget was quiet, and I realized that she didn't want or need to hear my sophomoric rantings. And her mom's and my problems had already put her through enough. "Sorry, Bridge. Hey, I really miss you too, and I'll see you as soon as I get back."

Standing in the dark living room, I replayed the phone call. My daughter's words felt like salve on a wound, a healing, then another wound. It made me angry that people were always trying to take something from me. A guy I used to work for is trying to take my wife, and a guy Soltani works for is trying to take my life. Of the two, I couldn't figure out which made me angrier.

Picturing my daughter, it suddenly occurred to me that she was probably the same age as some of the girls forced into servitude with Mai. That made me the angriest.

I was no longer going after the police colonel just for Mai and her friends, and I certainly wasn't doing it for money. I was now going after that son-of-a-bitch for my own daughter as well.

Striding across the living room with a new determination, I felt a tenacious certainty and a power to do anything. Speaking of which, Soltani was still in the bedroom, waiting for me.

Should I or shouldn't I? That was the immutable question. Since my wife was with her boyfriend, and hadn't bothered to come to the phone or even ask how I was doing, the answer would be a simple one.

Throwing open the door with the gusto of Jack Nicholson in The Shining, I found Soltani asleep on my bed. She didn't even flinch when I came in, so I could tell it was real. She was exhausted, and in reality, so was I. But my mind was still in high gear. I was all steamed up and wanted to somehow move the plan forward to get Mai back.

A minute later, I was in Soltani's room, pillaging through her things. I found what I was looking for in her bathroom: Sergeant Foster's bag of first-aid supplies. Minus the isopropyl alcohol, which had been repurposed for an incendiary device.

Locating what I needed, I put on my new readers and held the vial up to the light.

> Ketalar (Ketamine Hydrochloride injection) For acute anxiety. Use before diagnostic and surgical procedures; intramuscular dosage 4-6 mg/lb.

I placed the vile containing the remaining liquid, and the unused syringe into my eyeglass case. The remainder of the bag's contents amounted to a roll of gauze and box of adhesive bandages. Taking the bag and the eyeglass case with me, I returned to my room.

Soltani was into deep REM sleep. Her eyelids flickered and her legs flinched. Wishing I knew what she was dreaming, I settled for lying next to her on the bed and staring at the ceiling with the comfort of her resting soundly next to me.

It was a feeble consolation, given that my wife was, at that very moment, entertaining a man I despised. And, in the home I was still making monthly payments on, no less. I've got a price on my head, and my wife's boyfriend is sitting in my recliner and drinking my good scotch.

Turning out the light, I closed my eyes.

My head continued spinning. Tomorrow, I thought. Somebody is going to pay for all of this, *tomorrow*...

CHAPTER 60

Tomorrow came early.

My frenetic brain started right up when my eyes popped open at 5 a.m. Everything on my mind when I'd closed them may have been held at bay, but were right there waiting for me when I opened them again.

I was still on my back, which usually makes my snoring worse. But a quick glance to the side offered a measure of relief. Soltani was still there, asleep, undisturbed, unruffled, and with a childlike expression on her face. Wondering if the look would change once she found herself on my bed, I remained as still as possible.

The skeleton of my plan had started to take shape, though the finer details still needed to be fleshed out. My concept seemed a simple one; since we had no weapons to speak of, I intended to turn the groups of assassins against each other. Hopefully, that would neutralize the threats and prevent me from actually having to kill someone. Not that I wouldn't if I absolutely had to, but even if it was in self-defense my batting average with the Bangkok police was pretty low. And since I was going after their top commander, it was likely to only get worse.

"Hi."

The voice rose from the pillow next to me like a dream. My fingers were laced behind my head, and I had to look down to see her.

Soltani's big brown eyes and sparkling white teeth all smiled in unison. She didn't seem to be shocked or repulsed at the realization of where she was.

"I fell asleep," she said, pulling herself upright until she sat cross-legged facing me. "Please tell me I didn't grind my teeth."

"You didn't." I sat up against the headboard. "Sorry about last night. I got a phone call from my daughter, and when I came back you were out."

"How is she? Bridget, right?"

I smiled. "She's good."

Soltani rubbed her eyes. "You had a notepad with you last night. Were we going to talk about your plan or something?"

I wanted to tell her that she had romance in her eyes last night, and ask if she had a plan of her own. But I've never been a good judge of women's emotions, and I didn't want to risk gumming up whatever we might have had in the works.

"Yes," I said, thinking about how to best explain it. "These plans I make sometimes, they're kind of like penguin eggs."

"Penguin eggs..."

"Yeah, you know, like when the Emperor Penguin lays an egg. The little penguin chick doesn't come out right away, it takes a while. The male penguin carries it around with him for a long time. Same thing with one of my ideas... I have to sit on it awhile, look at it, think of its pros and cons, assess its risks and rewards, and then..."

"And then you hatch it?"

"Exactly."

Soltani grinned. "Okay, so tell me what you hatched."

For the next 45 minutes, I explained the concept in general terms and then went over the details and individual responsibilities with her. I kept waiting for a wrinkled brow or a look of resistance, or even outright refusal. But there was none. Only a few clarifying questions, and then she grabbed a pad and jotted down some notes of her own. It reminded me of briefing cops before a risky operation. Soltani was a true professional and it was obvious that she'd done this before.

We left the apartment at 9 a.m., then grabbed something to eat before kicking off the first step of the plan.

"Nothing opens until ten o'clock around here, so we have a little time to go over it again."

"First, we buy two sets of men's clothes," she said. "Then leave one set outside JR's door."

Nodding, I said, "Then we'll have to flag down a taxi and keep it on standby throughout the day."

"I was thinking about that part of the plan," said Soltani. "It'll be expensive, and we'll be hoping that the driver can be trusted."

She was right, but I hadn't come up with anything better. We could involve Foster and make use of his motorcycle, but I was still hoping we could avoid utilizing him for this part of the operation.

"I'm going to *sit on that egg* a little longer," I said.

We both chuckled.

It was ten on the dot when we got to BOYPLAIN clothing store. The trendy teen shop was tucked inside a shopping mall, on a main thoroughfare directly across the street from Police Headquarters.

The style of clothes would have been perfect for my daughter's friends, and I worried that none of the skinny jeans or tapered shirts could ever fit me.

"Over here," called Soltani, standing at a single 12-foot long rack. The sign above it was in Thai with the English translation beneath it: *Big-Tall-Portly*.

I chewed the inside of my jaw while Soltani laughed.

Astonishingly, I found a pair of black pants that fit. The second pair would be the same length, but with a narrower waist. Those would be for JR. The matching shirts were no problem, and I got two double extra-large black sweatshirts on a discount table near the front of the store.

As we left, Soltani leaned over and shoulder bumped me. “We can check off the first step of the plan.”

“Yep.” I gazed across the roadway to the imposing police building. “Now, all we have to do is find out where the colonel’s servant girl is and then kidnap her back.”

CHAPTER 61

We were on foot, traversing back alleys and little-traveled side streets to keep from being noticed. Since we'd only gone a few blocks to find the store, it was fairly easy. But tailing the colonel would require a vehicle and a driver, which, as Soltani had pointed out, came with its own risks. How to solve that problem dominated my thoughts as we scurried back to Monet House.

Leaving the narrower-waisted pants and one of the sweatshirts at Foster's apartment door, me and Soltani hustled back to the elevator. I wanted to avoid a face-to-face conversation with either JR or Foster at this point in the ballgame. I was the quarterback of this team, and as any good player knows, there can only be one person in charge on the field.

As Marines, they were both undoubtedly used to the concept of operational command and control. But they were also strong-willed men who saw this as *their* fight, not mine. And clearly, they did not consider me their leader.

Having to hash out, debate, and justify to them every decision I made was not part of my plan. To do that would be the derailment of the entire operation, and the kiss goodbye to any chance of getting Mai back.

My old football coach would have told them they had *pertinacity*. He used to say I had a bunch of it. Called it a blessing and a curse, and that one day I'd understand what he was talking about.

I guess that day had come. Probably a good ten years older than JR and Foster, I now found myself trying to manage their skills and determination without allowing their stubbornness to screw them out of what they're trying to achieve.

Anyway, I left a note with the clothes telling them to stand down for the time being, and that I would contact them when the time was right.

"Do you think they'll stay put?" asked Soltani.

With a shrug, I told her that I hoped so.

Stepping out of a service door into the back alley, I thought I'd stumbled into a sauna. The humidity and the temperature had gone up just in the few minutes we were indoors.

"We have everything, right?" I said to Soltani.

"It's all here." She held up my newly purchased outfit, and a brown paper bag containing Foster's first-aid supplies.

Halfway down the alley, a line of young kids snaked through the gates of the Pramahatai Suksa school. Two little girls played with a hand puppet shaped like a monkey as they waited. It reminded me of our driver in the park—the poor guy who not only lost his taxi, but also his fake monkey and nearly his life.

"Taxi," I said as we neared the end of Ruam Rudi 5 Alley. "The tuk-tuk we stole." I stared expectantly at Soltani. "Could it possibly still be...?"

She looked at me like I'd finally lost my biscuits.

Grabbing Soltani's hand, I turned left, pulling her along through the alleyway as it snaked around toward the park. The odds weren't good, a longshot at best. But then again, I was long overdue for a checkmark in the plus column.

Into the park we went, my head on a swivel knowing that every cop in Bangkok was looking for me. And if they didn't find me first, there was always Kingsbury's men. And if they missed their shot at me again, JR's bogus sister and the money launderers could be next in line.

"There it is," said Soltani, having figured out my aim.

The little tuk-tuk sat right where I'd left it, wedged between two trucks at the far end of the parking lot.

Soltani said, "I can't believe nobody noticed it."

"Are you kidding? These things are everywhere. They're like the homeless in San Francisco, people see right through them."

"Is it really that bad there?"

I could only lift my eyebrows and shake my head.

One more glance around to make sure this wasn't a set-up, and we jumped in. Brushing the shattered glass off the seats, I was overjoyed to find the keys still in the ignition.

She sputtered a little and then started right up. The gas gauge, a tad difficult to read because of the Thai symbols, appeared to be ample enough.

"This will make our surveillance a piece of apple strudel," I said as we pulled through an unmanned gate onto the main thoroughfare. "Like I said, nobody here pays attention to these tuk-tuks."

Soltani shot me a skeptical glance. "Not even when the windshield is broken out and the driver is a six-foot-tall white guy?"

I was closer to 6-1, but she still had a good point. We would have to stay as low profile as possible to keep from attracting attention.

It was nearly noon when we got to police headquarters. My heart sank and my stomach soured as I surveyed the sprawling complex.

"Which building is he in?" Soltani asked.

It didn't look the same. I mean, it was, but the cops had brought me in through another entrance. "Let me just..." I pulled the tuk-tuk to the end of the block and motored slowly west on Rama I Road. The place was massive. Turning across oncoming traffic, I pulled onto the sidewalk in front of a huge directory map with a legend in multiple languages. They didn't have a little red *you are here* sticker, so it took a while to get my bearings.

"Holy crap," said Soltani as she looked it over. "This place is like a small city. Police Clearance Center, Criminal Division, Information and Technology, Forensic Sciences, Support Division... They even have a police hospital. How are we ever going to find the colonel?"

I ran my finger over the map. My stomach clogged my throat and I was mumbling to myself as I did. "Police café, Institute of Forensic Medicine, Scientific Research, Police Bank, Central Investigation... That's it. I think that's it."

The map showed his building around the next corner, about 500 meters from where we were.

As we got closer, the trickle of familiarity became a waterfall. "There it is," I said, pointing. "The one with the yellow ribbon along the fence. Colonel Boontam's office is on the 4th floor. They took me through that gate into an underground garage."

Across a landscaped median and several lanes of traffic, sat a bank and a string of restaurants. There was also a bus stop where several other taxis waited under a row of shade trees. Backing into the line, I got a few curious looks from the other drivers but I had a perfectly unobstructed view of the parking garage's exit gate.

"Nice job, *Danny Boy*." Reaching over the seatback, she squeezed my shoulder.

The only other person to call me that was my old SFPD partner, Lou Cassidy. Cassidy had been laid up with a heart attack the last time we saw each other, and the conversation didn't end well. It's one of those things that even though I was right, I still felt like shit about it. Even after six months.

"Thanks," I said. "Now, I guess we just sit here and wait."

CHAPTER 62

My hope was that we would see the colonel stepping out for lunch, but there was no sign of him all day. Besides being disgustingly hot outside, the other tuk-tuk drivers were giving me the eye—American taxi driver whose only passenger all day is an American woman.

We had passed by a cool looking steakhouse called Neil's earlier in the day, and all I could think about was calling off the surveillance and treating Soltani to a candlelight dinner. But, having made that mistake before, I hesitated.

Soltani kept glancing over at me and checking her phone for the time. I watched her in my periphery, and I'd made up my mind not to suggest anything that could be taken as a come-on.

Finally, she let out a loud sigh. "How long are we going to keep this up?" she said. "I'm hot, and I'm tired, and I'm in the mood for a good scotch and a good dinner."

"Would you have an appetizer?"

She nodded emphatically. "Something fried."

"When you're bad, you're really bad."

"Why?" she asked. "What would you have?"

"I was thinking a microwaved Lean Cuisine lasagna and a Diet Dr. Pepper."

Soltani pursed her lips. "I had no idea *you* could be so naughty."

I chuckled. "What I'd really like is..." I held the binoculars to my eyes. "Wait, I think that's him. White Toyota, 4-door, some kind of hatchback or crossover thing. Exiting through the gate now."

"I see two people in the car," said Soltani.

"He's the one in the backseat. Probably has a driver. Must be one of his cops."

We would have had to hustle in order to get across the median, but his driver crossed illegally to our side of the street and continued past us heading south. Checking the time, I made a quick notation on my little message pad: *Left work – 5:17 p.m.*

They were moving along pretty quickly, weaving through traffic and passing cars at will. I was driving as fast as I could, but still managed to fall behind.

They could have easily lost me if they had turned, but I was happily surprised when the driver suddenly pulled to the curb and parked. The emergency flashers went on, and the driver got out and ran into a small eatery.

"He went into the restaurant," said Soltani. "Dink Dink Noodle Soup."

"Seriously?"

"That's what the sign says. Maybe he's picking up dinner."

I said, "The lazy dog is making the driver do it for him."

After a few minutes, the cop came out carrying a take-out bag, got in the car and drove off. The colonel sat in the backseat talking on his phone the entire time.

The Toyota turned left, passing under the elevated transit tracks, then turned left again, now heading north past Lumphini Park. Heavy traffic kept their speed slow enough for me to follow.

"They're moving over to make a turn," said Soltani, leaning onto my shoulder. "The little street on the left."

I followed in the rattling tuk-tuk, hoping we didn't stand out in the more residential neighborhood. Looking upward, I saw the street was lined with towering condominiums.

"This looks like the high rent district," I said. "Did you catch the street name?"

"Give me your paper," she said. "It's Chit Lom Alley."

I passed my message pad back and she wrote it down.

The Toyota pulled through a security gate at #1 Chit Lom, and stopped in front of the main entrance of The Park Condominiums. The modern concrete and blue glass building had to be more than 20 stories tall, each unit with a balcony looking out over the city. That, and the cameras mounted all around the building, confirmed that this place was no Section 8 housing project.

The colonel got out with his bag of noodle soup as the officer backed his way through a U-turn and then drove out the same gate.

We sat parked at the curb across the street.

"Should we follow his driver?" asked Soltani.

I shook my head. "I think he was only the colonel's ride home."

Looking up at the place, we both had the same question. She said, "I didn't picture him living in a place like this. With at least three women servants..."

"Right," I said. "And Mai had mentioned something about having to live in the basement."

"Maybe this is just where he stays during the workweek. Like one of those, *whatchamacallits*? A pied-à-terre."

I lifted an eyebrow. Soltani was a smart one, that's for sure. "Well, he definitely fits the profile: wealthy, arrogant, and probably corrupt as the day is long."

"If this isn't where he keeps Mai, then we're really no closer to finding her than we were before."

"It's only Monday," I said. "There's no way we're waiting until the weekend to follow him to his real home. Even if we did find it, she may not be there. She could be in a jail cell somewhere. There are just too many variables, we're too vulnerable, and we couldn't keep a leash on JR and Foster for that long anyway."

"I agree." Soltani leaned her head back and closed her eyes. "So what's our next move."

Stretching the kink from my neck, I said, "I think we need to go to my plan B and push this thing forward. We're going to have to force the colonel to tell us where he's got Mai."

Soltani sighed. "I was afraid you were going to say that."

CHAPTER 63

We waited across the street from the colonel's condo until well after nightfall.

"I've been thinking..." I turned in my seat to face Soltani. "The cops found Mai because the apartment manager called them. So we know they weren't responsible for planting the transmitter."

"We do?"

"Yeah, the police wouldn't have had to wait for someone to call. The colonel would have just had his men go in and get her."

"Right."

I continued, "And whoever is listening in, obviously isn't after me, otherwise they would have just killed me right there in the apartment. That leaves the Willoughby-Klehs money launderers. As far as we know, they're the only ones who want to kill JR."

"And they're hoping we lead them to him," she said. "So, at least we know whose bug it is."

"Exactly. Which leaves a big question mark about the guys in the park who came after us on the motorcycles."

"Leo Kingsbury's team."

"Maybe," I said. "We think so. But regardless of who they are, I'm trying to figure out *how* they found us. We were out on the street, in a tuk-tuk, following JR and Foster back to Monet House."

"Now you don't believe Leo was behind it?"

"Not so sure." Holding up three fingers, I said. "One thing is, he could easily have found where we were staying by tracking your phone. Two, his guys, if that's who they were, shot the hell out of that little taxi—with you sitting in it. I'm a guy, and I know jealousy, and believe me, Kingsbury wouldn't have his guys risk hitting you."

I had ticked off both points, leaving my index finger standing alone. Soltani stared at it. Finally, she said, "...and number three?"

"The third thing bothers the shit out of me, and I really, *really* want to be wrong." I took a breath and let it out slowly. "I can't think of anyone besides my secretary who knew where I was and what I was working on."

Soltani sat quietly. "Maybe they've tapped your cell phone, or even the phones in your office. Maybe she knows nothing about it."

"I hope it's something like that."

Soltani was silent again. "Why does that bother you so much? Do you have feelings for your secretary?"

A grin spread across my face. "Yes, I guess I do. But not like you're thinking. She's actually turned out to be one of the most trustworthy people in my life. And it would really break my heart to lose that camaraderie."

"Is there a way you can test her?"

"You mean give her information and see if it gets back to them? Yeah, I've thought about that. But it would take time, and we will need to lure these guys in quickly. Getting info to her, then having it passed to them all the way over here... The turnaround would screw up our timing." I sat in the tuk-tuk, staring up at the building and thinking. "Maybe there's a way for me to set the bait now..."

Taking out my phone, I checked the time. Soltani leaned over the seatback, watching.

"Seven forty-five here means it's five forty-five a.m. in California," she said.

It was too late. The phone was already ringing.

"Have you lost yo' mind, McKenna?"

"Probably," I said. "Sorry to wake you, again, Shanay. But things are starting to come together here and I really need your help."

"You still in Bangkok?"

I glanced at Soltani. "Yes, I'm still in Bangkok."

"You pick me up one o' them kimonos yet?"

"Not yet. But here's what I need you to do: As soon as you get into work today, I want you to use the office phone to call..."

Suddenly, I couldn't think of anybody for her to call. Sha Nay Nay was too shrewd. And if she was involved, she'd be able to sniff out the set-up. This had to sound legitimate.

"... my daughter," I said. "Tell her I'm going to be at the back gate of the U.S. Embassy at 9 o'clock tomorrow night."

"You want me to call Bridget," she said flatly. "And you want me to tell her that?"

It didn't sound as legitimate when she repeated it back that way. But at least my secretary, or special assistant, or whatever she was now calling herself, knew where I'd be. She had the information to pass on, if she was involved.

"You have lost yo' mind, McKenna. Li'l Bridget don't care noth'n about that."

"Okay, well, I just wanted her to know that I'll be finishing up after that and I'll be home with her birthday present in a couple of days."

"Uh-huh."

When the call disconnected, I sat there looking back at Soltani. Shaking my head, I rolled my eyes. "That didn't go too well."

"So I gathered."

"At least she has the information now. I figured the embassy was as good a spot as any. We can watch the back gate from our rooftop without being seen. If the two motorcycle guys are there waiting, I guess we'll know where the leak is coming from." I released a long sigh. "To be honest, I'm hoping they don't show up."

Sympathetic eyes watched me from the back seat. "Well," she finally said. "I doubt if the colonel is coming out again tonight. Did you want to get something to eat?"

"No thanks. I sort of lost my appetite."

"Wow, that's a first."

CHAPTER 64

I still had the phone in my hand, wondered if Sha Nay Nay could have possibly, even by accident, given out my location to someone. Just the thought of it made me feel sick.

Deciding to photograph the colonel's building—or pied-à-terre—as Soltani called it, I clicked off a couple of shots. The flash went off automatically, which was stupid because the light died after about 10 feet, leaving the street in the foreground hot white and the building dark as night.

It was then that I noticed the previous image. Taken two weeks earlier, I had asked the fictitious Elaina Teagan to hold up her brother's photo so I could take a picture of it. Apparently, I'd stepped back too far. Besides the print of JR in his dress blues, Elaina's face was also in my photograph. I'd never looked back at the picture, and hadn't noticed she was in it.

"Hey!" I said, holding the phone up for Soltani to see. "This is her. The sidewinder who pretended to be JR's sister."

Soltani studied the woman in the photo. "Where have I seen her?" she asked.

"Probably at the hotel in Arlington."

"She was there?"

I nodded. "Yeah, she showed up unexpectedly. Wanted to be there to greet her brother when I found him, or so she said."

Soltani's eyebrows flattened. "And that didn't strike you as a little bit strange?"

I flicked my hand with a chuff. "Forget about the past, will you? Anyway, we now have a good likeness of a suspect involved in, if not responsible for, the safe house bombing and the shooting of your protectee."

She shrugged. "What can we do with it? I can't very well send it to my agency. Especially now with Leo breathing down our necks."

I smiled. "What about our mutual friend?"

A minute later, I was leaving a message on Sarah Brooks' phone. I texted her the photo of our suspect and asked if she could run it through the government's facial recognition database.

We returned to the Monet House to find everything as we had left it. I checked behind the painting and the listening device was still in place.

With plans to get started early the next morning, we hoped to catch sight of the colonel on his way to work. Awkward goodnights were exchanged, then Soltani and I headed off to our respective bedrooms.

A minute later someone pounded on the apartment door. It was an unfriendly knock, and I instantly imagined the police. Slipping into shorts and a t-shirt, I went to the living room and peeked through the security lens. JR and Foster stood in the hall mumbling to each other.

Soltani emerged from her room, wrapped in a robe. With her hair down and her olive skin contrasting against the white terrycloth, I felt momentarily paralyzed by her beauty. Motioning hastily toward the painting, she quickly joined me in opening the door.

I hadn't considered what it looked like, but the two men's faces quickly went from surprised to a canny masculine nod. As much as I enjoyed the bit of machismo, I quickly shook my head. Me and Soltani squeezed our way into the hall, forcing the two of them backward—out of the device's listening range.

"The bug is still active," I said, leading the group to the end of the hallway. "We just got back and were about to go to bed. What's up?"

"What's up?" repeated Foster. "That's what we want to know."

I noticed that JR held the bundle of clothes I'd left. "And what in the hell are these supposed to be for?"

Foster had my note in his hand. "And what's this about *standing down*?"

"Easy, guys..." I glanced around as a reminder to keep it quiet. "Nobody's trying to put anything over on you."

Looking at my note again, Foster said, "*I'll contact you when the time is right?* Fuck that shit!"

JR still wore the worry about Mai on his face, but his expression was also one of annoyance. Foster, on the other hand, looked like he wanted to stuff me in a gunnysack with a couple of hungry pit bulls.

Soltani suddenly jumped in. "You two need to chill. If anything, you should be thanking us." She motioned to me. "McKenna has already been shot at twice and thrown in jail. He isn't making a single penny from this, yet here he is, willing to help get Mai back—a woman he only just met."

Her little monologue seemed to take the starch out of their shorts.

"I'm here because it's still my job to protect JR," she continued, "but Danny is here because he's a good person." Soltani paused, not unlike Sister Mary Benita used to during one of her good, guilt-inducing lectures. "Now, why don't you let him explain what's going on?"

All three of them turned, and six eyes bored into me. Soltani had done an admirable job deflating some of their hostility, but JR and Foster still looked at me like I was a know-nothing has-been. Besides, I wasn't prepared to lay out my entire plan just yet. In fact, I wasn't sure I'd even figured out where all the pieces go.

Sometimes when Doris feels she's being judged or criticized, she finds a way to turn the tables and put me on the defensive. I hate when she spins it around like that, but somehow it seems to work.

On our anniversary two years ago, I bought her a ring with her birthstone mounted on it. A sapphire. One day I came home and saw the ring on her dresser, minus the birthstone. When I asked her what had happened to it, she started talking about the time I ran my new power mower over a sprinkler head and busted the blade.

"What's *your* plan?" I suddenly said to JR. Then, before he could answer, I turned to Foster. "What about *yours*? Do you even know where Mai is?"

"No, but we know where she's not," Foster said. "I had a friend at the embassy check the police incarceration logs. Mai is definitely not being held in any jail. Meaning she's most likely at the colonel's house."

"Which is where?" I asked.

The two men looked at each other. "Not sure yet," said JR. "We were going to try following him."

I nodded, but it was a patronizing nod. "Follow him? From where? Do you know in which of the umpteen buildings within the police complex he works? Have either of you ever seen the colonel before? Do you even know what the guy looks like?"

It was classic Doris, but it worked. They both had the dazed look of a dog who had lost its tennis ball.

"Now..." I did the Sister Mary Benita pause. "I know what he looks like, because I've spoken with him before. I know where the colonel works, because I've been in his office. And I know where he stays, because I've followed him home."

JR blurted, "Then let's go there and get Mai."

Closing my eyes, I shook my head. "First off, the colonel has more than one home. His place here in Bangkok is a condo, and I'm sure Mai isn't there. Secondly, this isn't Iraq. We can't go house-to-house pillaging the town like we're searching for insurgents."

"Then what do you plan to do?" asked Foster.

"Have you ever been involved in a surgical strike?" I asked.

"Yeah," said JR. "Limited assault on a specific target, designed to minimize collateral damage."

I said, "Have you ever done a snatch-and-grab operation?"

They both shook their heads no.

"With any luck, that's exactly what we're going to do first thing tomorrow morning. Now get some sleep and meet us in the back alleyway at 0500 hours."

I motioned to JR. "Make sure you're wearing those clothes you're carrying."

They both nodded, then I heard Foster mumble under his breath, "And we fought in Afghanistan, not Iraq."

"Sorry," I said. "Tomorrow we'll be fighting in Thailand, so bring your duty weapon and be ready for action."

CHAPTER 65

Once JR and Foster had gone, we went back into our apartment. It was midnight, but the conversation in the hallway had infused me with nervous energy.

Soltani was wide awake too, so I put on the TV in the living room. We couldn't find anything in English, so we settled for a teenage reality show called *Secret Mission*. It did the trick, and we fell asleep next to each other on the couch—her legs draped over mine.

I woke up at 4:00 a.m. with my knee throbbing and a kink in my neck. Soltani had moved to the end of the couch where she lay curled in her robe. Limping to the sliding door, I opened it and stepped onto the small balcony. The sweatbox of a city hadn't cooled a single degree all night.

The airlessness was claustrophobic. I gazed down at the church parking lot across the alley and thought about jumping. Not that I'd ever really do it, but it felt good to imagine leaving all my problems here on the balcony; the separation from Doris, all the missteps with Bridge, my failing PI business, and the fact that in a moment of macho egotism, I had set an indelible timeline for this crazy plan to kidnap a Thai police colonel. Now the pressure was on, and I wasn't even sure if I was equal to the task.

The screen door slid open behind me. "Big day today, huh?"

I nodded as Soltani joined me at the railing.

Aware of her body sidling up against mine, I reached my arm around her shoulder. I tried to make it like, we're just two buddies in this together. She didn't recoil. In fact, she leaned her head into me.

"What part of this are you most worried about?" she asked.

"Disappointing you." It had come out without thought or filter.

Soltani pulled back enough to look at me. "Do you mean that?"

I nodded.

After a few seconds, she leaned her head back against me. "Don't worry about that. I know this thing will all come together."

"How can you be so sure?"

Playfully nudging me, she said, "Because I trust you, Danny."

It had been a long time since a woman made me feel important and reliable. In any case, the nervousness was gone and I felt ready to take charge of this operation.

At five o'clock sharp, we were in the alleyway with JR and Foster. Me and JR both wore the black pants and shirts I had purchased.

JR said, "I hope there's a good reason I'm wearing a sweatshirt in this heat."

I felt his pain. "Unfortunately, it's all they had in black."

"And the significance of wearing black?" asked Foster.

"The two men who followed us from the church and shot at us in the park wore all black."

The Marines looked at each other in confusion.

"We are going to be those two guys," I said. "At least as far as the colonel is concerned." I held up the bag of first-aid supplies. "And I'm going to bandage my face for added realism."

Foster snapped his fingers. "You're going to be the one whose face was burned."

"So, what's the play?" JR asked.

We huddled in the alley as the sky began to lighten above a tangle of electric lines.

"Foster... you and Soltani will take your motorcycle and follow me and JR over to Chit Lom Alley. The colonel's condo building is at number one; Soltani knows which driveway. We'll park the tuk-tuk around the corner from his place and the four of us can stage there. We wait there until the colonel's driver picks him up. When that happens, Foster will set the motorcycle down in the street in front of the exit gate as if you've been in an accident."

Foster lifted an eyebrow.

"Don't worry," I said. "It's just for show. Anyway, you're going to lie down next to it like you're hurt."

Nods circulated around the group. JR said, "And they stop their car to help."

"Right." I motioned to Soltani. "But you'll be there, just in case. Stand in front of their car, wave your hands, whatever it takes to get the driver out to help."

Foster said, "So, we have me on the ground, and presumably the driver is out of the car helping me. I'm assuming he's a cop?"

"Yes, although we don't know if it's the same or a different cop each day."

"And this is where I get the drop on them?" asked Foster.

"That will be the tricky part," I said, looking around the huddle. "We'd rather not have the colonel out of the car. Once he sees you drawing down on his driver, he'll either be reaching for his own weapon or calling in for help. We need to gain control quickly, before either of them has a chance to radio for assistance."

"How do we do that?" asked JR. "I mean, are you and me still with the tuk-tuk around the corner?"

"No, we'll have joined them at the front of the building by then. As soon as Foster makes his move, you and me are on the colonel. We jump into the backseat, one on either side of him, sandwiching the son-of-a-bitch between us. I'll jab him with the syringe and it'll be lights out for Colonel Boontam."

Foster gave a wry grin. "Oh, so you found the *ketamine*."

I held up the first-aid bag. "You and Soltani will need to work fast, too. You'll want to disarm the driver, take his radio, and handcuff him to the steering wheel. I'll run back, get the tuk-tuk, and pull it up next to the police car. We'll transfer the unconscious colonel into our vehicle and we're gone."

"Wait," said Soltani. "The cops already have photos of you in the stolen tuk-tuk. If the officer sees you in it, they'll be combing the city for us. Maybe we should put him into the trunk of the police car instead."

"Good idea, I like that better."

The lightening sky caused me to check my watch. It was nearly 5:30 a.m., and we needed to get this show on the road.

JR had another question. "Once we get the colonel, what do we do with him?"

"Again, we'll have to move quickly. The only place I can think of is Church of the Holy Rosary."

JR and Foster looked at me like I was crazy. "That priest is going to flip his shit," said JR.

"That'll be my department," said Soltani. "I'll keep Father Su busy and out of the sanctuary while you guys drag Sleeping Beauty down to the dungeon."

"It's the perfect spot," I said. "When he comes to, he'll have no idea where he is. And since the basement is concealed beneath six feet of stone, no one will hear him if he yells."

"*When* he yells," said Foster.

I checked my watch again. "Okay," I clapped my hands. "Time to put this thing in motion. I don't want to miss what may be our only window of opportunity."

A minute later, Foster's motorcycle sat idling in the still morning air. He patted the seat behind him. "C'mon Deputy Soltani, let's roll."

CHAPTER 66

We arrived at the Park Condominiums just before 6 a.m. Motioning toward the exit gate, I continued slowly past and then pulled the tuk-tuk to the curb at the next corner. Foster and Soltani followed on the motorcycle.

The city was starting to come to life, and the smell of coal fire cooking added a new layer to the sticky, brown air. Watching from about fifty feet away, we had a clear view of cars coming through the gate—none of which were police cars. But that didn't mean the colonel wasn't in another vehicle. We had to check all of them.

After another thirty minutes of watching, the reflection from the rising sun made it difficult to see the occupants. We decided that a better vantage was across the street in a parking lot rimmed by a thicket of trees and bushes. I had Soltani set up there, adjacent to the exit. Foster took his bike about 50 meters further down the block, so we had the gate pretty well triangulated.

An hour passed and there was still no sign of the colonel. Me and JR left the tuk-tuk and slowly migrated closer. We planted ourselves near a street vendor selling fish balls and bags of cooked rice. The location would give us quick access if the colonel suddenly appeared.

I had my eye on Soltani, too. Partially concealed by the shrubbery, she was using my binoculars to scope out the block. It was 7:45 a.m. when she lifted a hand with a *thumbs-up* signal.

Looking behind me, I saw the silver compact turning onto the street. It had all the markings of a police car without the lights on top, just like the car that drove him home the evening prior. Foster saw it too, and his bike coughed to life down the block. I was about to grab JR and head back to our stolen taxi when I stopped.

Soltani was now waving a hand in the air with a closed fist—the tactical signal to hold or stop.

My head whipped around again, and behind me I saw a second police car making the turn onto Chit Lom Alley.

The first car—the one without emergency lights—pulled through the gate and stopped at the front door of the condos. The second car drove slowly toward me, turning at the last moment onto the side street where I had left the tuk-tuk. As it was turning, I saw the two cops inside intently scanning the area.

"We got problems," I said to JR under my breath.

Glancing down the street again, I saw Soltani emerge from the underbrush and onto the roadway to wave off Foster. It was clear to me, as it was to the others, that our tightly choreographed plan did not include, nor could it accommodate, two more *hostiles*. Especially armed ones with radio communications.

My immediate thought was, *what in the hell are they doing here?* I made my way back to the intersection, trying not to appear as if I were a wanted suspect who was lying in wait to kidnap a police colonel.

Anyway, my answer came right away. The patrol cops were there to investigate a suspicious tuk-tuk with a shattered windshield. They were already out of their car, alternately checking the taxi's green and yellow license plate, making notes, taking photographs, and radioing headquarters with the information. Some *do-gooder* had no doubt called it in. Which meant that seconds from now, the cops would know the tuk-tuk was stolen and had been involved in the Lumphini Park shooting.

Son-of-a-bitch!

Since I had already been connected to the tuk-tuk, the two officers would surely call for reinforcements and begin a thorough search of the area for me. Which also meant, I had only minutes to get the hell out of there.

At that moment, Soltani signaled again. Pointing toward the gate, she was trying to alert me that the colonel had come down. Foster was doing lazy-eights on the street out front, as Colonel Boontam met his driver at the door and climbed into the back seat.

The electronic gate sprung open and the police car pulled onto Chit Lom. As the security gate eased closed, I visualized my window of opportunity closing along with it.

This was the end of my plan. It was also the end of Mai, and without a way to escape, it was likely the end of me.

Foster pulled his motorcycle up next to me and turned off the engine. In a dejected but somewhat consoling voice, he said, "Do you know what's the first thing to die on the battlefield?"

I shook my head.

"The plan."

CHAPTER 67

"Slide forward on the seat," I said to Foster. "How many of us can fit on your bike?"

"Uh... two?" he said.

I motioned JR over to us. "We'll have to make it three."

Soltani was there, listening, grasping the exigency of the situation. Somehow, she sensed my desperate lunge for some form of a plan B. "Go on!" she said. "I'll take another taxi to the church and make sure Father Su is out of the way by the time you get there. Good luck." She punctuated it with a wink that implied, *I know you can do it.*

At least one of us had confidence in me.

Climbing aboard Foster's Yamaha, I felt like a piece of jerky lodged between a couple of molars. Strangely, nobody in Bangkok seemed to find three grown men riding on one motorcycle the least bit strange.

Thanks to some impressive tactical driving, Foster caught up to the colonel's car at the intersection with Phloen Chit Road—a major expressway beneath the elevated transit tracks.

Without a clue of what we were going to do, we followed along toward Central Investigations. Hundreds of scenarios jockeyed for position in my mind as I clung tightly to the first-aid bag with one hand and the seat strap with the other. One truism remained at the forefront: any attempt to take the colonel once he reaches the police compound will be a suicide mission.

Though I couldn't read many of the cross streets as we whizzed past, I knew we were getting closer. Then, I spotted a landmark that I recognized, and my stomach turned inside out. The large-scale map of police headquarters.

The colonel had arrived. The clock had run down and the fourth quarter had come to an end. The game was over.

"He's signaling to turn," said JR. "No, wait, he's pulling over."

Leaning over Foster's shoulder, I felt a wisp of optimism. Another recognizable landmark. "Dink Dink!" I called out. "Stop behind them. Close, but not too close."

"What in the hell is a *dink-dink*?" Foster asked with an air of annoyance.

"It's a noodle soup restaurant," I said. "His driver stopped there to pick up dinner last night. It must be the colonel's go-to spot."

Then it hit me. Last night's driver got out, leaving the colonel in the car while he went inside to pick up his dinner. If that's the routine they usually follow, it may be our one and only opportunity to...

But what would we do with him? *Four* men on the motorcycle, and one of them is unconscious? Bad plan.

It's really hot out, I thought. And the asshole colonel wouldn't stand for the A/C to be shut off while he roasts in the backseat, which means the keys will still be in the ignition. It was a guess on my part, and I put the odds at about 7-to-3 in my favor. *Good enough!*

"I'll take the colonel," I said. "JR, you drive the car. And Foster follows on the bike. On my signal!"

We were stopped at the curb where a dozen other motorcycles were parked, which was a good thing because Foster's Yamaha blended in perfectly. But working against us were the heavy black sweatshirts me and JR wore, and the bandages on my face.

Even worse was that the noodle soup eatery was directly across the street from Central Investigations—the same building where the colonel worked. The guy was a well-known figure in Bangkok, and certainly within the massive police department. If our little snatch-and-grab operation was inadvertently seen by somebody—a plain clothes detective, a uniformed cop, or even a civilian employee—the jig would be up.

Then there was the issue of timing. How long did it take to pick up a container of soup? Had they called it in ahead of time? Was it a daily thing that they had ready and waiting for him? Or, as I was hoping, would they have to ladle it into the takeout container while the colonel's driver waited? The difference was, maybe, 15-20 seconds at the most. But each one of them counted.

The driver's door cracked, then inched open. Out stepped the police officer—a well-polished young man in a crisp uniform.

JR and I were off the motorcycle, hemming and hawing in place while we furtively watched.

With his bike idling next to us, Foster unconsciously patted the outline of a handgun tucked into his belt as he eyed the driver. His was a tool of last resort that I prayed would never see the light of day.

The restaurant's glass doors were no more than twenty feet from the police car. Counting his steps, I figured we'd start our approach when he was at the halfway mark. That way he'd still have his back to us, and he would be inside when we made contact with the colonel.

Counting his steps to the midpoint: "Three... two... one... go!"

CHAPTER 68

Right on cue, Foster eased his motorcycle up to the colonel's car while we followed behind him on foot.

The door to the noodle restaurant had just closed when we reached the colonel. Sitting in the backseat, his head was down as he thumbed his phone's keyboard. It was perfect.

He didn't even look up when JR slid into the driver's seat. A half second later, I jumped into the backseat next to the colonel. That, he did notice. At first he recoiled, leaning away to get a look at me. Without changing his already dour expression, he glanced from me to JR and then back to me. By that time, I had the syringe out, the cap off, and the plunger in my hand.

Before the colonel could react, I jammed it into his thigh so hard and deep that I thought I'd hit his femur.

"You," he said, as if trying to place my face. He didn't even glance at the needle sticking in his leg. "The American."

The next several seconds were a jumble. Not exactly what I had anticipated, it was like a tornado had been unleashed inside the car.

The colonel's little slit eyes blinked twice, then he reared back and headbutted me. His greasy forehead caught me square in the nose, and besides the excruciating pain, I could feel his stir-fried hair in my eyes.

My reaction was a quick uppercut, which hit him under the chin like a mule kick. I heard and felt the clack of his teeth.

JR had turned to see if he should help.

"Drive!" I yelled.

Feeling the thrust of the car jerking forward, I had to fight through the pain and starbursts in my eyes to see. The battle for survival was definitely on, and the two of us fighting in the confined backseat felt like two sumo wrestlers in a bathtub.

Trading punches, I tried to cram my thumb in his eye but had to settle for the soft, fleshy area beneath his Adam's apple. It provoked a gurgling sound like the last of the dishwater down the drain. My hopes that he would give up or pass out were only met with renewed resistance.

The son-of-a-bitch was struggling to reach his holstered handgun, but I had an arm bar on his wrist. As we vied for position, I felt saliva from his open mouth straining for purchase on my forearm.

"Stick him with the needle," yelled JR.

Between gasps, I answered, "I did."

"It didn't work?" He turned to glance over the seatback.

"HELLO! Apparently not." Then I realized that the sedative was probably intended for intravenous use. Pumping it through muscle and fat, as I had done, would take longer for the colonel's body to absorb. I had imagined it like one of those wildlife shows where the park ranger shoots the dart into the bear and he drops like a rock. Instead, I only managed to piss off the bear.

The next noise I heard was the sound of a gun leaving a leather holster. Believe it or not, it's as distinctive to a cop's ear as the crack of a golf club striking a ball is to a golfer.

The colonel had managed to pop his weapon loose, and now I was bracing for the next sound... a gunshot.

At that moment, JR swerved to avoid stopped traffic ahead. He hit the curb, then the car bounced up and over a raised median. The force of the impact jarred us hard, and the colonel's gun clattered down to the floorboard.

We both reached for it at the same time, and in that split second I saw the colonel's head bent forward just above my elbow. With as much explosive force as I could muster, I drove the flat part of my elbow into his face. The bony knob struck pay dirt, and the sound that came out of him was like an old man's snore.

Between the elbow strike and the ketamine injection, enough pain and drugs had now worked their way into the colonel's body to have an effect. He went completely limp, and his eyelids dropped. Poking him a few times to be sure, I finally had my sleeping bear.

The timing couldn't have been better. A quick right turn and JR navigated us off the main boulevard and down the alleyway behind the Holy Rosary Church.

Soltani had left the back door to the sacristy open. Between JR's injury and my screwed up knee, lugging the unconscious bear wasn't as easy as I'd hoped. His high-gloss black shoes left a double helix track in the alley, up the two steps to the door. It was like an arrow to the cops who would now have heard from the colonel's driver and would be going all out to search the city for him.

"We need to get rid of that car!" I said. "Hell, it could have a GPS beacon for all we know."

A rumbling sound echoed down the alley, and I looked up to see Foster on his bike.

He pulled up next to us and I asked, "What happened after we left?"

Foster shook his head. "It looked like a freak'n cage fight going on in the backseat, I'll say that much. Surprised the cops didn't get a dozen calls about it."

"I guess the drug wasn't super fast acting," I said.

"Yeah, I should have warned you that the effects of subcutaneous and intramuscular injections take longer." Foster turned off the bike. "You definitely clowned that police driver, though. He came out with his bag o' soup, and was like, where did he go? Dude will probably get fired for losing his boss."

"He eventually radioed it in, right?"

Foster nodded. "Eventually. I think at first he didn't know if the colonel had driven off on his own. But yeah, some other cops came and they started asking around if anybody saw anything. That's when I beat feet. So where is he now?"

"Me and JR dragged his fat ass into the sacristy. Next we're going to have to roll the son-of-a-bitch down the stairs to the basement. But we've got to get rid of the cop car."

Foster said. "I'll take care of that."

He left in the police cruiser and me and JR went back to work on the colonel. After a good fifteen minutes of pushing, pulling, rolling and dragging, we got Colonel Boontam into the cellar.

After another fifteen minutes, the secret door slid open and down came Soltani and Foster.

"The priest believes that I stopped by to thank him," said Soltani. "Has no clue that we're down here."

Foster said, "I dumped the cop car inside a garage over on Sathon Road. Nobody will notice it for weeks."

Soltani said, "Depending on where he's got Mai, we'll need to start thinking about our transportation there and back."

Foster said, "Got that covered. Just down the block from where I left the police cruiser was a TN Car Rental. I'm the only one with a local license, so I picked us up a blue Toyota Fortuner—an SUV that seats seven."

"Excellent." My head, still hazy from the punches it had blocked, was trying hard to absorb it all. Stepping toward Foster, I gave him a high five. Though he seemed more of a fist bump kind of guy, he slapped my palm anyway.

"What now?" asked JR. "What do we do with the colonel?"

"Uh, I guess we just sit here and wait for the jackass to wake up."

CHAPTER 69

We took the colonel's gun and cell phone and tied him in a sitting position against a heavy timber beam. And just for added humiliation, I used his own handcuffs to secure his arms behind his back.

Essential to my plan was that the colonel only saw the two of us dressed in black. He'd never seen Soltani and Foster, and I wanted to keep it that way.

The man awoke with a jerking flinch, causing me and JR to jump as well. The colonel had been out for nearly an hour, giving us time to go over the rest of my plan. But now that he was back with us, it was time to get busy with the *dirty work*.

As if the crucifix staff hadn't been through enough already, it was about to become our main implement for extracting the colonel's information. JR used a prayer candle to heat the end of it, just as I had done before his wound cauterization.

How and where JR would use it was a mystery to me. This was his part of the show, not mine. Besides, I didn't think I had the stomach for torture. Maybe I would have felt differently if the man had stolen my daughter. In any case, the colonel watched through his serpent eyes as JR heated the section of pole until it could roast s'mores.

Turning abruptly, JR plunged the white hot staff toward the colonel's face. He stopped within an inch of his eye, then stared at the colonel without a word.

"What do you want from me?" the colonel stuttered.

"You know what I want." JR adjusted his grip, as if he were about to ram the thing through to the colonel's brain. "The only one I have in my life is Mai, no family, nobody else. Nothing in this world to keep me from torturing you to a slow and painful death. So, believe me when I tell you that I *will* do it."

The colonel looked from JR to me and back again. "Who?" He screwed up his face like he couldn't remember. "Oh, you mean that piece of garbage that ran off? I thought *he* was her boyfriend," he said with a nod in my direction.

"And I give a shit what you thought, why?" The staff in JR's hand wavered back and forth over the bridge of the colonel's nose.

"You're right," he said. "It hardly matters. You Americans are all the same. You come here to visit our country, and you bring your drugs, and your diseases, and your pathetic excuse for a culture."

JR pressed the metal tube so close that I'm sure the colonel could feel the heat of it.

"Easy with that, boy. Yes, it's true, I've brought the girl back to complete the terms of her contract."

"Contract." JR's jaw tightened. "I'll give you ten seconds to tell me where you have her, or this thing goes into your eye."

Again the man scoffed. "The piece of garbage is an employee, boy. She means nothing to me."

JR reared back. "Call her a *piece of garbage* again..."

"Okay, okay, yes, I know where she is. I can take you to her."

"You're not taking me anywhere. You'll tell me exactly where she is. And, by the way, your ten seconds are up."

The colonel flinched again, jerking his head back against the post. "Ayutthaya!" Then, regaining his composure, "It's a town about 80 kilometers north of Bangkok. I have a villa there. This girl you want, the piece of garbage, she's a member of my staff."

"Tell me the address."

The colonel gave JR the address. "But you won't need the numbers to find it. My villa is the biggest house in the whole region."

"I bet it is," said JR. Then he jammed the hot poker into the center of the colonel's forehead. It sizzled and smoked, as the colonel's eyes crossed beneath it in shock.

An earsplitting wail echoed through the underground vault. As JR pulled the staff back, a scorched and blistered circle about the size of a dime remained on the colonel's forehead.

"I warned you not to call her that again," said JR.

Ouch! Smelling the burnt flesh turned my stomach, and the wimp in me had to look away. Using it as an excuse, I went to the far corner and texted Soltani the Ayutthaya address. Told her to grab Foster and meet us there in an hour, give or take.

"What do we do with the colonel now?" asked JR.

"Eighty kilometers..." I tried to visualize the Bangkok map. "It'll take us at least an hour to get there. We'll have to take him with us."

What was to follow had been preplanned. Me and JR had rehearsed the dialogue with each other while the colonel was still unconscious, but I wanted the old bear to think that he'd overheard it by mistake.

"On your feet," I said, untying the man from the wooden beam. With the colonel's hands still cuffed behind him, I knotted a gauze strip around his head to cover his eyes. This was so he wouldn't see his surroundings, and would never know that he had been held in the church. Then I jerked him by the uniform lapel all the way up the stairway.

JR slid the cabinets back and went through the trapdoor ahead of us. His instructions were to make sure Soltani and Foster were nowhere around, so that the only voices the colonel could hear would be JR's and mine.

Leading the man out to the alley, I laid him face down across the backseat floorboard of our rented SUV.

"Wait a minute," said the colonel as he strained to lift his head. "You're going to make me lie back here for the hour-long trip?"

"An hour on the floor is the least of your problems," I said. "You'll be lucky if you live through the day."

Removing the vial from the first-aid bag, I drew up the last of the ketamine. The colonel struggled to turn his head, and the gauze slipped down allowing him to glimpse up at me from the floor.

"One shot of this, and it's Bedtime for Bonzo."

The colonel's brown face turned deep red and his eyes narrowed to slits. "*Dai yang sia yang*."

I looked down with a smirk. "Come again?"

He huffed, as if an explanation was hardly worth his effort. "You must lose something in order to gain something. It's a Thai proverb."

Holding the dripping syringe at port arms, I said, "What I'm going to gain is the girl, Mai. So, what is it that you think I'm losing?"

The colonel bared his teeth like a dog. "You are going to lose your life, because I'm going to kill you myself."

With that, I jabbed the needle through the colonel's pants, and into his ass so hard that it almost hurt mine. This time he flinched, then let out a grunting breath.

I saw JR's eyes in the rearview mirror and gave him a wink—my signal to start the act.

"After having to fight the asshole earlier, I decided to give him a double dose this time," I said.

JR winked back. "Good thinking. How long till he's unconscious?"

I shoved the colonel with my heel. "I think he's already out."

The 1.3 cc dosage had been computed for a man weighing 200 lbs.—just as the last one had. Also like the last dose, it had been administered into the muscle instead of the vein. Me and JR now knew that the ketamine would take at least a few minutes longer to get into his system. We also knew the colonel was lying there, still conscious and still listening.

"Should be enough to keep him out of the way tonight," said JR. Another wink into the mirror. "What time does our ride pick us up?"

"Nine o'clock," I said. "We're supposed to meet on the street, at the embassy's back gate."

With that, the hook was set.

CHAPTER 70

JR maneuvered through afternoon traffic like a guy who's lived in Bangkok before. Then I realized he had.

We pulled into the suburb of Phra Nakhon Si Ayutthaya at 6:15 p.m., and the colonel had been right; the property was massive. Set behind a gated entryway, I saw the driveway curling up through a lush grove of banyans, palms, and monkeypod trees. In the distance sat a well-manicured lawn the length of a golf fairway that led up to the estate.

The black metal gate was at least 8-feet high, held on either side of the driveway by huge, natural stone pillars. Clearly designed to appear high security, it was actually not. There were no cameras, no guards, and beyond the stone pillars, there was no fencing. Only the thicket of trees and shrubs served to demarcate the property. I took these as modest signs of encouragement.

Soltani and Foster had arrived on the motorcycle before us and were parked beneath a shade tree about 50 meters from the entrance.

"He must feel comfortable out here," said Foster, leaning into the car's window. "Not much in the way of security."

I slowly nodded. "It would seem so, but he must have someone keeping an eye on his workers." I glanced through the trees toward the residence. "It'll take the rest of us a while to get up to the house in this heat."

"The rest of us? Foster looked disappointed. "You want me to stay here and watch the colonel. In the corps we call that *voluntold*."

"When he comes to, I think he'll pose a bigger threat than anyone we will encounter inside." Gazing down at the snoring lump on the floorboard, I added, "And since we're out of the knockout drugs, you may have to tune him up a bit so he stays quiet. Just keep his face on the floor and don't let him get a look at you."

"Yeah, I can do that."

There were other reasons, too, that I didn't tell Foster. He was armed, and I still didn't know for sure if he would go into the villa with a *shoot first and ask questions later* mentality. Foster was also the only one of us that would probably be staying in Thailand when this was over—at least for a while. To this point, he had not been seen by any of the aggressors and was not on anyone's radar. I wanted to keep it that way if I could.

Before we started for the house, I went to the back of the SUV and took a crowbar from the flat tire kit. It wasn't much of a weapon, but at least it was something.

Unseen from the front gate was a large irregular shaped pond that took up the entire west side of the property. Once we broke through the tree line, me, Soltani, and JR had to work our way around the lagoon.

It was taking longer than I'd planned, especially in the humidity, and I realized that the colonel would be coming out of his dormancy any minute now.

It took us another 15 minutes to reach the two-story Balinese style home. Tan colored, with dark wooden accents and steeply sloped rooflines, the place looked like a palace. Warm lights glowed from the windows, and the smell of cooking food danced in the air.

"The basement," whispered JR as we approached across the lawn. It was dark now, and a cultured stone walkway up ahead of us curved to the top of an outdoor stairway that led downward against the side of the house. A small, grate-covered window sat only inches off the ground, emitting a weak glow.

A heavy padlock hung from a chain that wove between an eyebolt on the door and one on the frame. Placing the end of the crowbar through one of the eyes, I torqued it as hard as I could. The soft wooden jamb easily gave way, and the threaded bolt popped loose. I chuckled at its inferior mounting, juxtaposed to a chain and padlock that were heavy enough to secure Fort Knox.

Yanking open the door, we were met with a rush of stale air. The squalid little room held a sink, a toilet, and three mattresses lying side-by-side on the floor. On one of them sat a young woman, naked, frightened, and holding her thin brown arms crisscrossed over her breasts. She was not Mai.

I hesitated, then felt Soltani wedge past me in the doorway. "Do you speak English?" she asked the girl.

"Little," she said, holding up a thumb and forefinger.

My breathing was shaky, and I could hear JR swallowing hard next to me. The girl was about the size of my own daughter, though probably older. We turned away while Soltani found something to put over her.

My blood was boiling, and I knew JR felt the same. Now, a part of me was hoping the colonel would get squirrely, and Foster would put the bastard down like a dog.

When I turned back, Soltani was sitting on the mattress next to the girl, gently stroking her hair and softly offering reassurances.

"Does she know if Mai is here?" said JR.

Soltani held up a hand, and continued speaking to the girl, too quietly for us to hear. Eventually, the young woman pointed upward toward the massive residence directly overhead.

"Mai is upstairs with the other young woman," said Soltani. "The colonel's wife and mother live here as well. They have two grown children, but apparently they're both away at boarding school."

"Any guards?" I said.

Again Soltani and the girl conversed in hushed tones. "There are usually two," said Soltani. "Both are men, but she doesn't know if they are armed."

JR's breathing increased. I saw his jaw tense and his eyes grow as wild as a rabid animal. Turning, he yanked the chain and padlock from the dangling eyebolt.

Soltani asked, "Do you want me to stay with her or go with you guys?"

I thought for a few seconds. Although a third person could be useful, Soltani still hadn't been seen, and was a complete unknown to the colonel and his men. "If you don't mind staying here," I said.

The heavy chain rattled behind me, and I turned to see JR poised in the doorway. "You ready to do this?" I asked.

"Never been more ready for anything in my life."

CHAPTER 71

The basement stockade was isolated from the rest of the house, so me and JR hobbled back up the exterior stairway—me babying my bum knee and him with his convalescing injury.

Avoiding the main entry in front, we continued around to the back of the house where a service door opened to a kitchen. Pausing to listen, we heard nothing.

I checked the handle and found it unlocked. Signaling to JR, we both moved to one side in preparation for a tactical entry, albeit with primitive weaponry. Silently but quickly, we pushed open the door to the kitchen where a middle-aged woman prepared food over a modern grill. She glanced up with a bothered expression, as if two new dinner guests only meant more food was needed.

Holding my finger to my lips, I motioned her toward us. "Do you speak English?" I whispered.

Her response was in Thai, which told me what I needed to know. Gingerly ushering the woman out the door we had just entered, me and JR continued through the kitchen. We paused at the opposite end of the room in front of a closed, sliding bamboo door. A hallway branched off to the right.

Listening at the door, I heard muffled conversation and clinking dinnerware. I hesitated, wondering if the hallway to the right would eventually work its way around allowing us to flank whoever was in the dining room.

I turned to JR. "You go that way," I said.

He nodded, then started down the hall.

Bracing myself, I gripped the crowbar tightly and slid open the door. I probably had an excess of adrenaline, because the door flew open with so much gusto that it hit the bumpers inside the wall and bounced back into me. At that point, it came off the track and rumbled to rest cockeyed against my shoulder.

The several people inside looked back at me in shock, and I couldn't tell if it was because of the uninvited white guy with the crowbar or that their nice bamboo door was now broken.

"Nobody move!" I yelled as I visually took in the scene.

The dining table stretched to the far end of the room where two Asian women sat—one elderly and one I guessed to be in her late 40s.

Closer to me, a man in a suit sat with his back to me. Short and thick, and with a pineapple face like General Noriega, he was my pick for the problem child.

Another man, younger and thinner, was on a chair against the wall opposite me. Not at the table with the others, I made him for the second security man—maybe a trainee.

Along the back wall, behind the seated women, stood a built-in serving buffet. It looked to be made of sandalwood, which matched the wide-plank flooring, crown molding, and window trim in the room. Two young women stood in front of it, both wearing green aprons over simple brown blouses and pants—obviously the two remaining service girls. Though both had their hair pinned up behind their heads, I was pretty sure one of them was Mai. She was holding a flat tray stacked with skewered chicken satay.

The big guy with his back to me started to stand, and I shoved him down into the seat with the curved end of the crowbar. He let out a slight growl as his girth slammed onto his chair.

The younger guy against the wall seemed stunned, his eyes wide and his back straight as a ruler.

The two women seated at the table whispered almost silently to one another. My guess was that the younger one was the colonel's wife, and the old bird was either her mother or mother-in-law. In my mind, they were on the low end of the threat scale.

Again the big boy started to push up from the table, and this time I slammed his head forward into his green papaya salad.

I had to assume the two men were armed—probably off-duty or ex-cops working under the colonel. Crouching quickly, I groped the man's waist for a gun. Before I could work my way around his ample paunch, I became acutely aware of his partner across the room. Saw him in my periphery, standing now.

"Stop!" he said. "Take your hands off of him and step back."

Nobody talks with that much authority unless they have a weapon pointed at you. True enough, I looked up to see the young buck gazing at me over the sights of his pistol—a .45 if I wasn't mistaken.

"Drop the pipe," he said.

"It's not a pipe, it's a crowbar." Not sure why I felt the need to correct the kid, but if he's going to speak English he ought to know the difference. I let it clatter to the floor, just the same.

By the way, I thought to myself, *where the hell is JR?*

CHAPTER 72

Just when I began to wonder where JR had gone, I heard something across the room. I initially thought it was the younger of the two guards, getting ready to drop the hammer on me. But to my relief, it was JR's frame filling the doorway. In what could only be described as amazing, he swept into the room whirling the chain and lock like Bruce Lee.

Everybody's eyes were on him, as he whipped it downward toward the guard's gun hand. It struck the man hard on the forearm, coiling around it like a serpent. The gun went off in an earsplitting explosion that thundered around the room. Suddenly, pandemonium struck.

I fell to the floor, thinking I'd been shot. The two women seated at the table screamed, and the big guy tried to jump to his feet. He wallowed there for a second, half seated and half standing, one arm flailing for balance.

Thankfully, I hadn't been shot. But my knee was once again out of commission. Apparently my entrance through the now broken door, the squatting to search Noriega, and my dive to the floor when the shooting started was more than it could endure.

I spotted Mai out of the corner of my eye. She had somehow come around the table during all of this, probably to help me to my feet. But then I saw that her attention was not on me, it was on the big son-of-a-bitch who was still floundering and growling like a wild animal with his paw caught in a trap.

As I struggled to stand, putting all my weight on the other leg, I saw why. Mai had stabbed the guard's hand with a satay skewer, pinning it to the table. His partner across the room was bellowing in pain—the chain and lock still wrapped around his mangled forearm. The man's .45 had dropped to the floor and skittered under the table, leaving only the flailing Noriega still armed.

Then there was the sound I'd now heard for the second time in one day. As Noriega yanked his pinned hand free from the table, he grabbed his pistol with the other. Shucking it from the leather holster, I knew what was coming next. Unlike his partner, this man would give no warning. There would be no attempt to gain our compliance, or to secure us with handcuffs. There would only be gunshots, none of which I would even hear because I'd be dead before the sound reached my ears.

In that fraction of a second, my life did not pass before my eyes. There was no revelation about the hereafter or the meaning of life. Only the image of Bridget. The fact that I had missed her thirteenth birthday, and I would never get the chance to make it up to her.

The Irish boiled up inside me like a nuclear reaction and I threw myself into Noriega with everything I had. Maybe he'd shoot me and maybe he'd kill me, but I was determined to make him pay with his own pain.

Almost as if I were swimming a sprint, I swarmed over the top of him—my arms digging and gouging like a paddleboat. More screams rang out around the room, and food flew in all directions from the table, which was now beneath us. I was on top of the man, but he had my neck in a vise grip with his thumbs pressing into my windpipe.

I felt my eyes bulge and heard my blood pumping in my ears, but I took it as a good sign that both of his hands were on me instead of the gun.

I kneed him in the nuts and he kneed me back. Suppressed whimpers of pain eked out of us both, and the fight continued with no sign of letting up. We slid off the table and I felt the old lady crumple under the weight of us. Another muffled scream.

On the floor now, I found myself on the bottom with Noriega pounding me with his fists. I did my best to dodge the blows, and though the majority of them were glancing, many connected. I was tired, really hot, and the headshots were beginning to take their toll. In addition, my kidney hurt from something I had landed on—probably the old lady's dentures.

Then as my sweat-drenched sweatshirt slid up, I felt something cold and metallic in the small of my back. Reaching backward, I groped around beneath the area of my kidney. The cost of this effort were two unblocked punches that landed on my face, nearly putting me out. One of my eyes immediately puffed up like a glazed donut, and I tasted blood in my mouth. But I had a hold of what I was reaching for.

Whether it was Noriega's gun or his partner's, it hardly mattered. I swung it with the force of a missile launch, and connected with the side of his head just above his left jaw. The butt of the gun struck with a crack that reverberated around the room.

The man rolled off me like a dead whale in the surf, as I lay there gasping for air. Turning onto my side, I felt the coolness of the wood flooring against my distended eye. Through my good eye, I saw the old woman—still on the ground—staring at me with a panicked look. It was as if she thought I'd come after her next.

When I got to my feet, I saw that JR had the younger guard at gunpoint on the chair. Two guns pulled, and two guns recovered.

Not bad. I breathed a little sigh of relief.

Mai raced across the room to JR and threw her arms around him. His expression was also one of relief.

"Need rope," I wheezed.

Mai found some heavy twine in the kitchen, and as JR held his weapon on the two men, me and Mai secured their hands behind their backs. Noriega started to tune back in just as I tied the last knot. With most of his piss and vinegar gone, he kept still and quiet except for the sound of his dog-tired breathing.

"Should we tie up the women too?" asked JR.

"Not Samira." Mai motioned toward the other servant. "She's my friend."

JR smiled. "I meant them."

The wife had helped the older one onto a chair, and they both sat together in petrified silence.

It hardly mattered at this point. We had won the game by a couple of touchdowns—recovered the girl and knocked the shit out of the bad guys. I was ready to dump the colonel somewhere along the road and head back to Bangkok.

Suddenly, my head snapped around at the sound of pounding on the front door.

"In the name of the Royal Thai Police, I command you to open the door!"

Son-of-a-bitch!

CHAPTER 73

The police showing up now was definitely *not* a good thing. In fact, it rivaled my knee for the *Bad Timing Award*.

I wondered if the colonel had somehow escaped from Foster, and had managed to phone his men. Maybe someone in the neighborhood had seen the four suspicious Americans loitering around the colonel's home. Had these cops checked the back of the house already? Could they have found Soltani and the young girl in the basement? Then my mind settled on the most likely scenario: the cook we had shooed out the back door had probably alerted them.

Wheeling around toward the group, I knew we had to work fast. Pointing to JR, I said, "Gag the two security men and keep them quiet upstairs."

Then to Mai, I said, "Tell the wife that we are holding her husband hostage at this very moment. If she has any hope of seeing the colonel again, she will make up a reasonable excuse for the cops at the door to get them the hell out of here. One wrong word and her husband dies."

I quickly glanced around the trashed dining room. It looked like Thailand Buffet—meets—Hurricane Katrina. Damage assessment: two broken chairs, a cracked wall mirror, one bruised old lady, and a bent satay skewer on a bloody tablecloth.

"And you," I motioned toward Mai's friend, Samira. "Try to clean up this mess as best you can."

Whether or not Samira understood English, she seemed to grasp her instructions. Immediately, she bundled the immense tablecloth—dinnerware and all—and dragged it off to the kitchen.

Mai was still translating to the two ladies when I interrupted. "You go to the door with her," I said to Mai. "Validate her story to the cops, and we'll try to stay hidden in case they search the place."

The sandalwood theme continued on floors and walls throughout the house, and large mirrors hung on every surface. There were windows of cut glass, 15-foot high scalloped ceilings with recessed lights, and marble pillars that rose up high overhead. We passed through the dark living room, where a gigantic double staircase curled up opposite sides of the room to meet in the middle on the second floor. In the center was an enormous arched window looking out to the pond.

Assisting JR with the two gagged and bound security guards, we manhandled them up the stairway to a back bedroom. The old lady was taking her sweet time, so I pulled out Noriega's .45 and motioned to her with it. Amazingly, the old bird managed to kick it up a notch.

JR corralled our hostages in a bathroom that was three times the size of my sailboat. A tub that could fit all five of us sat against the wall. Its smooth, dark wood appeared to have been hand-hewn from a single gargantuan slab of timber. At that moment, I wanted nothing more than to get rid of my damn sweatshirt, jump naked into the tub, and take a cold bath.

Once JR had seated the captives in the bathroom, I eased back out the door. Traversing the bedroom, I paused at the hallway to listen over the 2nd floor railing. A lot of good it did me, because they were all speaking in their native tongue. At least they were still at the door instead of searching the place.

As I started back toward the bathroom, my swollen eye prevented me from seeing a bench at the foot of the bed. My foot stubbed into it like a crash dummy into a concrete wall. It was upholstered, which thankfully padded my knee. But I tumbled over it, landing on the hardwood floor with a loud thud.

From that point on, the voices grew louder and I knew the officers were now inside the house.

Hopefully, they were like some of the cops I used to work with—smelled the food and were trying to wangle an invitation to a quick bite or doggy bag for the road. With any luck, they were at the end of their shifts and as eager to get out of there as I was. Or perhaps they knew it was the colonel's house, and were trying to score points with the big boss by going all out for his wife.

Then I heard the clippety-clop of their shoes coming up the stairs. Sons of bitches weren't after a picnic basket full of sticky rice after all.

Their conversation grew louder still, as they moved from room to room along the hallway. Mai and the colonel's wife scurried along with them, jabbering in high-pitched voices. I imagined they were trying to turn the cops around, telling them everything was fine and dandy.

Inevitably, they would reach the back bedroom and check our hiding place inside the bathroom. We were already running low on twine, and definitely running low on luck. I glanced at my watch and we were also out of daylight. This thing had to wrap up quickly, or we wouldn't make it back to Bangkok in time.

A squeak rose from the floorboards on the other side of the door, and then footfalls making their way toward the bathroom.

I had my ear to the door, listening. Turning, I looked at the scene the cops were about to encounter; two of their own, tied, gagged, and lying side-by-side in the bathtub. And an old lady curled on the floor in the corner.

JR had moved to one side of the door, and I stood on the other. For the next ten seconds, nobody breathed. I closed my eyes.

A break, please. All I'm asking for is just one freak'n break here.

CHAPTER 74

I had pulled the window curtain, so the only light into the bathroom would have to work its way around the two policemen in the doorway.

Number 1 stepped inside, reaching for the wall switch as he did. Number 2 was close behind. They hesitated as light illuminated the scene before them, then moved toward the bathtub to help their comrades—almost like, what happened here? Did the old lady tie you up in the bathtub?

The reality struck the two cops a fraction of a second later and again they hesitated. But it was too late, they had passed the point of no return and me and JR were now behind them.

Turning quickly, Number 2—who was the closest to me—stared directly into my eyes, then into the barrel of the gun I was pointing at him. Apparently, it wasn't an easy decision for him as he stood there with his hand on the butt of his weapon. His intense, button eyes held fearlessness, or loyalty to the colonel, or professional pride. Whatever it was, his expression gave no clue to his intentions.

I knew there was no way I was going to shoot him, but I didn't want him to know that. On the other hand, I'd already been through the wringer with Noriega and I didn't have another knock down-drag out fight in me tonight.

Meanwhile, JR had his gun leveled on Number 1, and thankfully he was more compliant than my guy. Ultimately, they both ended up with their hands held high while we relieved them of their pistols, two-way radios, and cell phones. Using their own handcuffs, we interlocked all four men together with their backs facing inward.

The colonel's wife was still nervously hovering in the hallway at the top of the stairs. Forcing her into a closet with the old woman, we warned them not to come out for 30 minutes or they would be shot. Now it was time to leave.

We gathered Mai and her two servant girlfriends, as well as Soltani—who had remained below decks, unaware of our tribulations taking place directly above her—and headed down the long curving driveway to the gate.

Foster was seated in the SUV with his boots on the colonel's back.

"Did he give you any trouble?" I asked.

Foster shook his head. Then eyeing my pummeled face, he said, "But it looks like the servant girls sure worked you over."

Struggling a painful smile, I said, "I'll explain later."

Foster climbed out and I took his place on the back seat. The three girls slid in next to me—all of us sitting with the colonel facedown and underfoot.

JR drove and Soltani took the front passenger seat, while Foster followed on his bike.

Breaking out the tattered map I'd bought at the 7-Eleven on our first day, I scanned the space between Ayutthaya and Bangkok. It was mostly farmland—miles and miles of irregular green plots followed along the snaking river, sporadically broken up by a small village.

"Here," I said, leaning up to hand the map to Soltani.

My finger pressed into a spot marked as a Buddhist Temple—one of a million in Thailand. It was right off Udon Ratthaya Expressway, the main artery into Bangkok.

She held it up for JR to see, and fifteen minutes later we turned off the highway. Without speaking, Soltani motioned toward a sign welcoming visitors to the temple.

"That way," I said, pointing past the parking lot.

A rutted, two-lane road stretched out before us with endless vegetable fields on either side, fading into the steamy black horizon. After another half mile or so, our SUV rumbled off the pavement onto a sweaty dirt road that followed an irrigation ditch. We kept going until the ground became a path—no more than a couple of tire ruts in a sea of shallow grass.

JR stopped, and I realized we had finally arrived in *The Boonies, East Jesus, Bumfuck Egypt, The Middle of Nowhere.*

"This is good," I said. Then I tapped JR on the shoulder, silently motioning him out of the car.

Together, we dragged the colonel by his ankles out and onto the dirt. While he was facedown, I refastened the gauze to cover his eyes and then we stood him up. We walked him a couple of hundred yards into the middle of a green onion field and left him in the dirt with his hands still cuffed in the back.

I'm sure he thought we were going to kill him, because he didn't move or make a sound. As we turned the SUV toward the highway, I looked back to see the tan hump of the colonel's body lying still in the field. With any luck, it would take him a good 30 minutes to find his way back to civilization.

Just enough time for me to line things up for the night's big finale.

CHAPTER 75

"Let's get these damn things off of us," I said as I pulled the heavy sweatshirt over my head and clawed the bandages off of my face—which I actually needed after the head-butt and punches. JR removed his sweatshirt as well, tossing it onto the floor beneath the driver's seat.

Our return into Bangkok was an uneventful hour, driving through the country's bread basket on a wide highway. It felt a lot like a trip down I-5 from the Bay Area to Bakersfield. Our co-pilot, Aafreen Soltani, kept an eye on the map while I kept an eye out the back window and Mai chatted contentedly with her friends.

As the lights of Bangkok grew brighter, I went over a checklist in my mind; The people in the house only saw me and JR—*check.* The colonel can't identify anyone besides me and JR—*check.* The colonel overheard me and JR discussing details about the meeting behind the embassy tonight—*check.* The colonel wants more than anything to see us dead—*double check!*

A silent smile washed over me, as we drove along. But for some reason, I felt as if I was still missing something. Unable to determine whether or not it was an actual oversight, I reassured myself that it was only residual anxiety from the past few days.

I turned to Mai. "What's going to happen with your friends?"

"Achara and Samira are sisters who come from Phayao Province," she said. "They will have to find a way back home in the north."

"We can take them," said Soltani. "How far is it?"

I leaned over Soltani's shoulder to study the map in her hands. "Uh, that would be *no,*" I said, sliding my finger along the Nan River northward until just before the Laotian border. "It's got to be at least an eight-hour drive."

"Ten hours, actually." Mai put her hand on Soltani's shoulder. "Thank you, Ms. Aafreen, but Mr. McKenna is right. Their village is very far away, and we will have our hands full trying to make our escape from Bangkok tonight."

"Tell you what we can do." I thumbed through the last of the Baht in my wallet. "We can take the girls to the Hua Lamphong station, and I'll buy their train tickets for them."

There were prayerful bows all around the car, ending with Soltani who wore a sagacious smirk. Leaning close so only I could hear, she said, "The benevolent benefactor to the rescue again."

I feigned a hurt look. Sure, maybe I wasn't willing to go to the ends of the earth for these girls—victims, by all accounts—but given the direness of our circumstances, I think freeing them from slavery and then buying their train tickets home should still score a jewel or two for my heavenly crown.

After dropping the girls at Hua Lamphong and accepting many more prayerful bows, we began the final 15-minute drive to Monet House. Foster left his motorcycle in his usual spot in the garage, and I had JR park the rented SUV on a side street a couple of blocks away from the apartments.

We all met there, under the glare of the streetlights, to go over the last of our plans. It was just after 7 p.m., and I knew this had to happen like clockwork or it would all blow up in our faces.

"Pack everything you need and we'll lock it all in the SUV," I said. "Once the first shot is fired, it's going to be a shitshow. At that point, we need to hustle back here and be ready to roll."

I gestured toward Foster. "I want you to be free and clear of this mess. Can you pull a shift inside the embassy tonight?"

He shrugged. "Well, not a shift. But I can be inside when the shit goes down, as if I just happened to drop by for a routine inspection."

"That'll work." I motioned to JR. "At some point, the colonel will figure out what happened and every cop in the city will be looking for us. We need to get to the airport before that happens."

"No problem." He lifted the keys. "It's 25 minutes, door-to-door."

"Okay, let's get to it." I slapped my hands together, a quarterback breaking a huddle.

But nobody moved. The team stared blankly back at me, as if they had missed the play call.

"What?" I looked from person to person.

When I got to Foster, he said, "Not try'n to be a dick or anything, but what the hell is supposed to happen?"

JR nodded his agreement.

I turned to Soltani who kind of cocked her head. "The plan *is* a little murky," she said. "I mean, I get that you and JR dressed like the two men who shot at us in the park. And I'm guessing you wanted the colonel to think you and JR were them? But how is that going to help *us?* And what about the people who bugged our apartment?

JR said, "Yeah, and what about the Willoughby-Klehs crew who shot me? We're super thankful that you found a way to free Mai, but I've still got a price on my head."

Soltani turned to me. "And so do you."

Closing my eyes, I pinched the bridge of my nose. Then I checked my watch and let out a sigh. Time was getting tighter.

"Look," I said, "I know this scheme of mine isn't wrapped in colorful paper with a pretty bow on top. But we don't have time to go over every tiny nuance right now. Suffice it to say that I've considered all the things you've brought up..."

An admission that I didn't actually have it all figured out was right there on my lips. But as I surveyed my little team, I realized that they needed a leader right now. They didn't want to hear about *maybe*, or *hopefully*, or *with any luck*.

It was *go time!* And they wanted the confidence of knowing it would all come together. That everything would be okay.

"You're right," I said. "This isn't the kind of thing we can leave to chance. All of our lives depend on this plan working, and I promise you that it will. This ends tonight!"

CHAPTER 76

Satisfied with my pep talk, we all went our own ways to pack our bags.

As had been the case, I was still tentative when opening our apartment door since we never knew who had snuck in or if they were still there. But the place was empty and nothing appeared disturbed. Not even the microphone behind the painting had been touched.

Soltani suddenly brushed up close and whispered, "Follow me." Then she turned toward her bedroom.

A number of things raced through my mind... well, actually only one thing. But I knew time was of the essence, and however I might have impressed her with my calm leadership, this was probably just a reaction to the stress she's been under. Kind of like a man and a woman who survive a crash and end up on a deserted island together. Under other circumstances she might not fall for him, but in that situation she can't resist—especially if he's done something heroic.

Leading the way into her room, she reached around me to shut the door behind us. Her conspiratorial expression seemed both giddy and naughty at the same time. I checked my watch again.

"I think I know what you're going to say." Putting my hands on her shoulders, I eased her onto the side of the bed where she sat facing me. "This has been a whirlwind couple of days, and we're all feeling a little, oh, I don't know... frisky?"

The deep V burrowing into Soltani's forehead made me second guess myself. Could I have misread her?

"Frisky?" she stared at me. "What?"

"What..."

"What?"

"What..."

"Frisky, like what? What did you think I was going to say?"

I swallowed. "Because... I mean, you seemed..."

"Seemed what?"

Quickly, I needed to think of something. Then an idea came to me. "You know, frisky, like you were wanting more involvement." Her face relaxed a tiny bit. "I mean, I felt badly leaving you in the basement with Mai's friend. I'm aware of how capable you are, and I would never want you to think I'm, you know, a chauvinist, or one of those meathead guys who's like, 'Me strong like bull—you stay in basement with girl.'"

Soltani rolled her eyes and shook her head. After letting out a breath, she said, “I was going to say, now that the others are gone, what, *exactly*, is the plan?”

“Oh that,” I said, wiping the curtain of sweat from my forehead. “So, yeah, you and me are going to have a conversation in the living room that will be picked up by the hidden mic. But that will be the last thing we do here. Right now, we need to load our things into the rental car.”

We all rendezvoused at the SUV five minutes later. Exchanging hugs and handshakes, I said, “We've still got a half hour to kill before we meet up on the rooftop terrace. Plan on getting up there a little before nine, and we'll have a front row seat for the show.

In the hallway outside our empty apartment, I briefed Soltani on what to say. She followed me inside, and we both took a seat on the sofa in front of the wall painting. It was coming up on 9 p.m., so the timing couldn't have been more perfect.

“When do we leave?” Soltani asked in a clear voice.

“Soon,” I answered. “Jonathan and his buddy will be on their motorcycles. They'll meet us at the back gate of the U.S. Embassy at exactly 9 o'clock. From there we'll head to Hua Lamphong station and take the 10 p.m. express train to Chiang Mai.”

“Then we had better get moving.” Soltani gave me a wink, which I wasn't about to fall for again.

We left the apartment for the last time, and took the elevator to the roof. JR and Mai were the only ones up there, huddled at the parapet, looking out over the city lights.

I had put the duffel bag containing all of my things in the car, with the exception of my binoculars which hung around my neck.

Motioning to JR and Mai, I said, “Over on this side. We'll be able to see down to the embassy gate and watch the whole thing.”

The four of us gazed over the west side to a mostly dark street. The only real lighting came from the spotlights encircling the embassy wall. Checking the time, I saw that we still had fifteen minutes.

The idle time gave my mind the room to start screwing with me. Although I had covered all the bases, I felt there was still something I was missing. It would come to me eventually, but I hoped it wouldn't be too late by then.

Even more upsetting was that one element of my plan counted on Shanay to betray me. She was not only my secretary, assistant, executive whatever, but I literally trusted her with my life. She was the only one I told where I'd be at precisely 9 p.m., so if the men who tried to kill me show up there at nine...

It just *couldn't* be her.

“Something’s happening,” said JR. “There, on that rooftop.” He motioned down to a carport attached to a private residence. It was well below us and off to our right—directly across from the embassy’s back gate.

Pressing the binoculars to my face, I twisted the viewfinder until the scene came into focus. A man in a tan police uniform had climbed onto the carport carrying a long narrow case. In my experience, it could only be one thing: a police sniper with his rifle. I watched as a second policeman joined him—his spotter.

I adjusted my binoculars to the end of the street where two figures sat in a black Suzuki Swift—the same unmarked police car I’d seen near the embassy when we arrived in Bangkok.

“They’re cops,” I said.

Mai looked at me with dread in her eyes. “What does that mean?”

“It means that the colonel made it out of the cornfield in time to alert his men.”

She turned to JR. “That’s a bad thing for us.”

“No,” I said. “That’s actually a *good* thing for us.”

CHAPTER 77

At 9 o'clock exactly, two motorcycles turned off of the main street and started down the alley. Bringing the riders into focus, I saw that they wore all black and one had bandages all over his face. It was as if a sledge hammer hit me in the middle of the chest.

"It's them," I said aloud but to myself. "Damnit, they showed up."

JR and Mai seemed confused, but Soltani understood. I felt her hand in the center of my back. As I let the binoculars drop on their lanyard, Soltani's hand slid to the base of my neck where she kneaded it like pizza dough.

"Maybe it wasn't your secretary who tipped them off," she said.

Turning away, I forearmed the moistness from my eyes so she wouldn't see. "I hope you're right."

This development was devastating in one regard, but it was a positive in terms of my plan coming together. JR and Mai were still in the dark, so I took a second to fill them in.

"The two on bikes are the men who shot at us in the park," I said. "We think they are connected to a deputy chief in the Marshals Service, but we don't know for certain. In any case, one of them was badly burned and his face is bandaged."

I handed JR the binoculars, and he and Mai took turns watching the men as they paused their motorcycles, holding their position at the end of the alley.

"That's why you had us dress in black," he said. "And that's what the bandages on your face were all about. You wanted the colonel's policemen to think these two guys are us."

"Right." I nodded. "After what we've done to the colonel, he wants us deader than dead. Probably gave his men a shoot-on-sight order."

Soltani flashed a perceptive smile. "And after the motorcycle guys caught the Molotov cocktail in the face..."

I nodded again. "They were already well armed killers, but now it's personal. They'll want revenge."

Mai listened with a questioning expression. "There were others though. The woman who posed as JR's sister; she was with the money launderers who tried to kill JR..."

"They also bugged our apartment hoping we'd lead them to JR," I said. "So, we used that to our advantage. If the device still works, they'll think you and JR are meeting us there." I pointed down to the back gate.

Everyone was all smiles. And though I tried to wear a confident grin in return, I was more concerned than ever. Beside the possible Shanay double-cross, the Willoughby-Klehs money launderers still hadn't shown up. That was the whole ballgame. And then there was the gnawing feeling that I'd missed something, except now I knew what it was. I'd covered every angle but one—the colonel hadn't seen anyone else in our group, but he had seen our rental car—the Toyota Fortuner. At the time, I hadn't thought that would be an issue, but now I wondered if I'd live to regret the misstep. After all, the man didn't rise to his position by being stupid.

"There," said Soltani, who now had a hold of the binoculars. She motioned toward the middle of the block. "Three men and a woman."

I grabbed for the binoculars, which were still around her neck. Nearly strangling Soltani, I yanked them to my face and gazed down at the Pramahatai Suksa school. The four-person hit squad who had blown up the safe house in Greenbelt and shot JR at the Bangkok hostel had deployed in the school property, ready to finish the job.

It was a tactically sound move, which put them right where they needed to be without anyone knowing they were even there. Another confirmation that these assassins were professionals.

The motorcycles began moving again, at almost walking speed, into the alley toward the embassy. They were going to pass directly in front of Elaina and her crew.

Something caught my eye and I adjusted the binoculars. The pedestrian gate into the embassy opened and two figures stood in the shadows of it. It took me a second to recognize them, and my troubled face melted into a smile. Finally, the last guest had shown up to my party.

"Your buddy..." I motioned toward the gate. "He's a smart guy. Foster figured out the plan and he's making sure the main player is front and center."

Colonel Boontam stepped into the light with his radio held up to his mouth—undoubtedly giving his men the *green light*.

Sirens sounded and lights flashed from the grill of the unmarked car, and a second later all hell broke loose.

All at once, Elaina's group opened fire on the motorcyclists and the police snipers opened fire as well. It was unclear who they were shooting at, though I suspected it was all of them.

One of the bikes went down right away, but the second accelerated through the alley at high speed. In the binoculars, I saw that it was the bandage-wearing burn victim. But he wasn't trying to get away, he was out for blood.

The street was filled with gunfire and smoke, as weapons were turned on the cops and on opposing groups.

The colonel was in the street with his pistol in hand, apparently hoping to head off the racing motorcycle. From our rooftop balcony seats, it looked like a game of chicken. Then, as the bandaged biker opened fire on him, the colonel ran back toward the gate.

Unfortunately for him, the gate was closed. Foster had stepped back inside the embassy grounds, locking the gate behind him. I could imagine the colonel as he pleaded for Foster to let him in, but the dark figure on the other side stood firm.

Colonel Boontam was now stuck in the middle of the alley while the bike sped toward him. Flashes of gunfire erupted as both men exchanged bullets. The colonel spun and wobbled as if he'd been hit, but he didn't go down. Instead, he stood there firing his pistol at the cyclist like a mid-street jousting.

As the distance closed between them, the burn victim's magazine went dry. He tossed it to the ground as he bared down on the colonel.

In the bike's glaring headlight, the colonel's face had the ferocity of a grizzly. He stood his ground, firing toward the driver until his magazine was also dry.

The speeding motorcycle slammed into the colonel, throwing him up, into, and over the driver.

The motorcycle barreled forward on an erratic trajectory. The driver was probably dead before he careened off of the approaching police car and splattered himself against the embassy wall.

The colonel, on the other hand, lay in the middle of the street. Mangled and covered in blood, it looked like he was trying to talk to the cops who had come to help him.

About 50 yards away, the other gun battle was starting to wind down. Through the lens, it looked like injuries had been sustained on both sides—the 4-person assassination squad getting the worst of it. The street was littered with injured or dead, not the least of which was the woman posing as JR's sister.

Sirens cut through the smoky air, and it sounded like they were coming from every direction.

Glancing back toward the embassy, I spotted Sergeant Foster in his uniform. After escorting the local police colonel through the embassy compound to the back gate, and then locking him out, Foster had watched from a safe distance as the event unfolded.

The colonel, if he lived through his injuries, would never know that the Marine sergeant who had given him access through to the back gate was the same man who only hours before had held him down with his boots.

And though I felt no sympathy for him, there was a part of me that still had to come to terms with Elaina. In reality, there was no *Elaina.*

But it hurt to know that I had a hand in the beautiful young woman's violent comeuppance, even if she was a trained killer who used me to flush out her victim. In any case, she would never know that the dead motorcyclist was not JR.

"Time to get moving!" I said.

The four of us started back down to the rented SUV, which had been parked on a side street well away from the activity. On the way, I took the opportunity to put JR's mind at ease.

"Should the woman posing as your sister or any of her crew survive, the Willoughby-Klehs Corporation will no longer be hunting to the far ends of the earth for Jonathan Teagan. As far as they're concerned, he died on a motorcycle behind the embassy tonight."

Mai hugged him tightly, as if they could both finally stop looking over their shoulders.

"Now we can start living again," said JR.

My plan had worked out well, and I was also on an emotional high. Taking a risk, I reached over and pulled Soltani next to me as we walked. A brotherly squeeze was all I dared, but she didn't pull away and that felt good.

We came around the corner and the bottom dropped out. My temporary euphoria drained onto the street like radiator fluid, and I stood there in horror.

Several cops were gathered around our rental car as it was being winched onto a flatbed tow truck.

This was the one oversight that had nagged at me all day, and I knew at once what had happened. The colonel had seen the SUV at some point—probably as we were dragging him from the church—and he had broadcasted its description once he freed himself.

"All of our money, our identification and our passports," said Soltani. "They're all inside the car."

CHAPTER 78

The three of them looked at me with despair in their eyes. Not blame, thankfully, but the bitter foreboding that none of us would ever make it out of Bangkok.

Soltani leaned up to my ear. "What are we going to do?"

I thought about telling her that on the bright side, our apartment was paid up through the end of the month. But her pleading brown eyes told me it was not the time for levity.

"The embassy," I said, indicating back in the direction we had come. "It's the only place I can think of to go."

By then the alley was choked with ambulances and police cars. Hordes of onlookers packed themselves as close to the bodies as possible, taking selfies in front of the grizzly scenes. Even the emergency workers smiled for their phones before the backdrop of blood and gore.

Mai saw my shock, and nonchalantly said, "It's a Thai thing."

We mostly kept our heads down, staying in the middle of the road away from the police and medics. Glancing up briefly, I saw that we were nearing where the motorcycle had crashed against the embassy wall. My hunch that nobody could live through such an impact was confirmed when I saw them zipping the mangled corpse into a body bag. The man's face no longer required bandages, but a hand trowel and some superglue.

Next to me, an old woman who had been excitedly watching the activity, bent down to pick up something off the street. She held it high in her hand and shouted something to one of the cops.

"His phone," Mai repeated in English with astonishment in her eyes. "The motorcyclist must have lost it when he crashed."

Apparently the cop hadn't heard the woman, because he kept working with his back to us.

"Grab it!" I said to Mai.

Without missing a beat, Mai reached over and snatched the phone from the old woman. With only a word, Mai offered a quick half bow and then turned to me. "I told her we would take care of it for her."

Dodging through the evidence-strewn battlefield a little faster now, we made it to the embassy's back gate. It was locked, and two rifle-toting Marines were posted just inside.

Mustering all the command presence as I possibly could, I strode up to the gate. "We're here to see Sergeant Foster."

After a briefly coded communiqué over the radio, one of them opened it and escorted us to one of the half-dozen embassy buildings within the compound.

All lights were on and there was a buzz of activity, which seemed odd for the late hour. Then I realized that multiple shootings just outside of the embassy would have definitely stirred things up.

Our escort sat us in some kind of meeting room with tables and plastic chairs set in a U-shape, then he stood like a sentry next to the door—almost as if he was guarding a group of prisoners.

Pulling out both cell phones—mine and the motorcyclist's—I set them in front of me on the table. I turned mine on, and just as it came to life, the Marine spoke.

"Due to security, we ask that you keep all phones and electronic devices turned off while inside the embassy." His words carried a tad more authority and command presence than mine had, and I quickly shut it down. But not before I noticed a missed call from Sarah Brooks.

I shoved both phones back into my pockets just as Foster walked into the room. "I'll take it from here, Taylor."

Our guard nodded, turned sharply and walked out.

When the other Marine was out of the room, Foster turned to me. "Well played, McKenna. Your little scheme went down as slick as snot."

"All except the rental car," I said. "It was impounded with all our stuff inside."

"I know." Foster pulled up one of the chairs and sat backwards on it. "Colonel Boontam told me they had found the suspects' 'getaway vehicle' on the next block. Obviously, he had no idea who he was talking to." Foster laughed. "Anyway, I knew your stuff was in there, so I made a couple of calls to help you out."

The breathing was a little easier, now that we had some hope.

JR and Mai stayed entwined with one another while laughing and talking with Foster. Deputy Soltani, on the other hand, seemed lost in her thoughts.

"Everything okay?"

She hesitated and glanced at JR. Then in a hushed voice, she said, "I'm concerned about his status as a protected witness. He's safe as long as everybody thinks he's dead. But the whole protection program is predicated on witness testimony. If JR testifies, they'll know he's alive, and he'll be at risk again."

It was a dilemma I hadn't considered, but it made perfect sense. My guess was that a new life with Mai outweighed any notion of civic duty, and he'd much rather take his chances living as a dead man.

"What if we had JR give some kind of sworn statement or affidavit against Willoughby-Klehs, and then we backdated it?" I asked. "We could say that he gave it to us before he died."

"Maybe..." Soltani's endorsement was underwhelming. "But it wouldn't be enough to get him into protection. My concerns have more to do with his safety than the prosecution's case against the money launderers."

"I guess in the end, that would have to be JR's call."

She nodded, "Yeah, you're right."

A few minutes later, in walked my third grade teacher. Well, not actually Sister Mary Benita, but the embassy woman who reminded me of her.

"Greetings, I'm Ruth Billings from American Citizen Services here at the embassy. Sergeant Foster has explained your situation to me, and has asked me here to assist..."

Billings stopped suddenly, narrowing her focus on me. "I know you," she said. "McCormick, right?"

"Uh, McKenna. Danny McKenna." I glanced around nervously at my classmates.

"McKenna, that's right. Jailed for not wearing underwear."

The others stared at me as I tried to melt into my seat.

"That... no, that was a mistake. I wasn't charged. They let me go."

"Right." Billings shrugged. "Anywho, so, y'all are going to need replacement passports. We've also been contacted by the U.S. Marshals Service, and we've been made aware of your situation," she nodded toward JR. "It's all a bit out of the ordinary, but I think we can get you folks taken care of."

CHAPTER 79

I was eager to check my phone messages. Even more, I was curious to know what was on the dead motorcyclist's phone. My hope beyond all hope was that Shanay's number would not show up, and that somehow the data would clarify how he and his partner knew we'd be at the embassy gate at 9 o'clock. But rules are rules, and the last thing I wanted to do was piss off the Marines by using my phone.

The waiting was tedious. We'd been in the room for hours, it was nearly light outside, and other than taking our passport photos, nothing had happened.

Mai was asleep with her head buried in her folded arms. Soltani had moved her chair and was leaning back against the wall with her eyes closed. Foster read a magazine while JR sat waiting.

"Me and Soltani were just discussing your future," I said, scooting my seat next to his. "She's primarily worried about your safety, but also your ability to receive protection from the Marshals."

"You mean, because I won't testify?"

His question was an answer in itself. No testimony equaled no protection. I nodded.

"It's not that I don't want to send all those bastards to prison, I do, but my life and my future mean more to me."

I nodded again. "I get it, believe me."

"Besides, testimony is just my word against theirs. The key to the whole case was the evidence I had."

"I wondered about that," I said. "But you said, 'evidence I had' as in the past tense. What happened to it?"

"Couldn't get to it." JR sighed. "I hid it, and they were waiting for me when I went back for it. Started shooting at me, and I barely got my ass out of there."

A frown came over me. "Wait, are you talking about your parents' house in Berkeley?"

"Yeah."

"On Tanglewood Road?"

"Yeah, why?"

"I was there." Deciding not to admit that I was with his fictitious sister, I left it at that. "If you don't mind me asking, what *was* your evidence?"

JR managed a wistful smile. "All their records, wire transactions, bank accounts, off-shore transfers, everything. Even the names of the shell companies they used."

I shook my head, imagining the treasure trove of criminal intel the feds could extract from that. No wonder they were salivating to get the kid on the stand.

"Yeah," he continued, "I had it stashed at my folks' house inside a box in my bedroom."

My lungs seized as the breath caught in my throat. "Where in the box?"

JR looked at me quizzically. "It was taped to the back of my service ribbon. The one I got for my time in the Embassy Security Group. It's a USB flash drive with a shitload of storage capacity. Has everything downloaded onto it. Why?"

"I have it."

"What do you mean you *have it*?" said JR.

Soltani's eyes sprang open and she sat upright in her seat. Foster's magazine fell to the table. They all waited for my response.

"When we thought... when *I* thought you had gone missing, I went to your parents' house and searched through your things. I found the service ribbon and your transfer papers, which were what ultimately led me to Bangkok. Anyway, I was actually inside your house when the shooting started. I think whoever it was—well, now we know who it was—saw me through your bedroom window and mistook me for you. During all the shooting, I must have accidentally slipped the ribbon into my pocket."

"Where is it now?" asked JR.

Again, they all listened intently. Even Mai had awakened and was now turned in her seat.

As I opened my mouth to answer, the door swung open. A Marine held it for a man I'd never seen. In a crisp gray suit, he immediately gave the impression of a political bigwig. Maybe the Ambassador, I thought.

Soltani's seat sprang forward. "Leo! What are you doing here?"

Leo? Leo Kingsbury? The boss with whom she had an affair? That Leo?

Suddenly glad I hadn't answered the question of where I'd put JR's evidence, I sat there sizing up the jerk. His hair, perfectly in place, was almost the color of an unripened pear—the pigment that only comes from pool chlorine or bad hair dye. He was a gym guy; I could tell by the way he filled out his suit. And then there were the straight white teeth—probably caps.

Kingsbury stood stiff as a board, taking in the room, and then his gaze settled on me. Our eyes locked for only a couple of seconds, but it was a second longer than it should have been. Enough to let me know that he knew who I was, and was also sizing me up.

Why was he here? I wondered. Had he been behind the attempts on my life? Were the two motorcyclists who met their demise in the alley tonight his men? Did they have evidence that would connect him? Had he come to take their phone before I could even look at it? These were all questions that crowded my mind in that fraction of a second.

Kingsbury motioned to Soltani. “I’d like to talk privately.”

She was behind me, and immediately jumped to her feet. As she reached the door where Kingsbury stood, he gazed past her toward me.

“Both of you,” he said.

CHAPTER 80

The embassy guard who had brought Kingsbury in led the three of us to an interview room next door. He unlocked it then stepped into the hallway outside.

I felt the weight of the assassin's phone in my pocket and was determined to maintain possession of it, come hell or high water. *They'll have to pry it from my cold, dead hands.*

The door closed and it was just us three. The man turned and extended his hand. "Leo Kingsbury."

A stilted handshake. "Hi."

"You're the San Francisco policeman," he said.

It wasn't exactly correct, but close enough. I nodded. "And you are Assistant Deputy Chief of the Marshals Service."

"Yes." He released his grip. "First and foremost, I'd like to thank you for your help in our investigation. Deputy Soltani has told me that she could not have recovered our protectee without your assistance."

Oh man, this guy was a slick one. Never gave the slightest clue that he wanted my head on a stick for stealing his girlfriend.

"Secondly," he continued, "I'm confident that you will furnish us with a full chronology of your involvement in the case, and, of course, release to us any and all physical evidence you may have recovered."

Soltani had been watching quietly. I couldn't quite read her face, but it seemed like a combination of shock and skepticism. Finally, she spoke up.

"Leo, why are you really here?"

Now he looked surprised. "Didn't you get my messages?"

She shook her head. "I thought my phone was being tracked, so I removed the battery."

Kingsbury considered her explanation for a second. "Well, you did contact me a week ago disclosing that you had left the country in pursuit of a protectee. And at that time you expressed some concerns about your safety here in Thailand, did you not?

Soltani scratched the side of her head. "Yes."

"Aside from violating protocol and departmental orders, you put me in a bit of an awkward position. Not only are you an employee of the Marshals Service, but you are under my command. After several phone calls and messages to you went unanswered, I felt it was incumbent upon me to see to your security and safe return."

"It's okay, Leo. Danny knows about our relationship."

Kingsbury rocked back a step. Whether it was Soltani's familiar use of my first name or the fact that she'd shared their little secret with me, he was definitely stunned.

As he stood there processing it, I watched his eyes for a tipoff; anger, rage, lust. But there was only sorrow.

He palmed the air. "That's certainly a nonissue in this context. You made it clear that whatever we had is over, that it's in the past. I'm here in the professional purview of my position. Nothing more."

"Fair enough," said Soltani. "Well, as you can see, I'm okay, I'm safe, so..."

He lifted his chin. "I have a Marshals Service jet on standby at Suvarnabhumi. Your emergency passport is ready and you've been cleared to leave. We will be wheels up in less than an hour."

Soltani motioned toward me. "Can we bring--"

Kingsbury was already shaking his head. "Sorry, no. The aircraft is authorized for Marshals Service personnel only."

Walking out into the hallway, the three of us loitered awkwardly for a second. Then Soltani leaned over to give me a hug. It was stilted and brief, like the kind one might receive from the Queen of England.

"I'll be in touch," she whispered.

They headed down the hallway without looking back. I watched Soltani until she turned the corner and the sound of her shoes on the tiled floor faded into silence.

Someone had pulled the plug before the last scene of my movie. Far from the ending I had hoped to have with the beautiful deputy marshal, it was the one I was apparently dealt. Following the Marine guard back to our waiting room, I tried to get my mind off of Soltani and back to the situation at hand.

I can scratch Kingsbury off my list, I thought. The guy might be a pompous stiff who's likely still in love, but he didn't give a damn about the phone in my pocket.

Kingsbury clearly didn't care about JR either, otherwise the kid would have been *"wheels up"* with them. That told me that Kingsbury had already made his decision, and that JR was not long for the Witness Protection Program.

Three of us had left the room, but only one returned. Foster, JR, and Mai stared back at me as I came back in.

"That was Soltani's boss," I said. "He's taking her back to D.C."

"What about you?" asked JR.

I shrugged. His question was open to interpretation, and could have meant my future with Soltani or simply my travel plans. Since I had no idea about the former, I only addressed the latter.

"As soon as I get my passport, I'll book the earliest flight back to the Bay Area."

"How long have you been on this?"

"What, the case?" I ticked off the dates on my fingers. "Today is day sixteen."

The door opened and Ms. Billings came in with our new passports in hand. "Daniel McKenna, Mai Nakhon, and JR Travis." She passed them out, handing JR's to him last. "Figured we'd stick with your new name."

Wishing us all good luck, Billings left—hopefully never to be seen by me again. I set down my passport and turned to JR.

"What about you guys?" I said. "What's next?"

JR shrugged. "Don't really know yet. Probably have to find a new place where we can start over."

I got that he still had some lingering security concerns. Even if he did know where he was headed, it wasn't information to be shared.

"I wish I could give you something to start out with," I said, "but my wallet is completely tapped out."

JR smiled. "You know I worked as an accountant."

I nodded.

"And you know my father was a shrewd businessman."

"Yeah, I gathered that."

"So, you don't think that I'd really just walk away from all my inheritance, do you?"

I lifted my eyebrows. Now that he mentioned it, the scenario did seem unlikely.

"I set up joint accounts with my dad a long time ago. He insisted, and I had all the connections to do it discreetly back then. So, thank you for the generous thought but we'll be okay no matter where we end up."

He and I shook hands and Mai gave me a big hug that conveyed her gratitude for having been liberated from the colonel's grasp.

Starting for the door, I diverted to where Foster sat. "How long until you get out?" I asked.

"Of the service? Another few months and then I decide whether or not to reenlist again."

My hand landed heavy on his shoulder lapel. "If you ever need a job reference, or for that matter even a job, give me a call. McKenna Investigations in Oakland."

He stood and shook my hand. "Thank you, sir. I will."

Picking up my passport, I offered a last goodbye and left the embassy.

CHAPTER 81

The ticket counter was a madhouse, but the airport was clean and modern and air conditioned.

They had an afternoon flight to San Francisco with a scheduled layover in Hong Kong. It was the earliest departure, but it was also going to be horrendously long and horrendously expensive. What did I care? I'd already charged so much on this trip that another sucker punch to my credit card barely mattered.

As I handed the agent my passport, a slip of paper fluttered to the floor. I picked it up and stuffed it into my pocket while the ticket agent tapped furiously on her computer keys.

After getting through security, I sat down in the huge, egg shaped rotunda and pulled out the piece of paper. It was a note from JR.

Remembering that I'd set my passport on the table during our goodbyes, I assumed that JR must have slipped the note inside when I wasn't looking. It read:

> Detective McKenna,
>
> At a time when I had no family to help me, you stepped in and risked everything to return Mai to me. You kept us both alive, and you did it all without expectation of payment. As a show of our eternal gratitude, I'd like to reimburse you for your time and out of pocket expenses. Please text me the name of your bank, their SWIFT code or wire number, and the number of the account where you want the money wired.
>
> Thank you again for everything, and all the best in the future.
>
> JR & Mai

It was an unexpected godsend. Just the *shot in the arm* I needed. There were still so many unanswered questions, but now, at least there would be money in the bank to cover my losses.

With time to kill before my flight, I fired up my cell phone. There were calls from Shanay and the one I'd missed from Sarah Brooks.

I listened to Sarah's first: *"Hey McKenna. Getting back to you about the chick's photo you sent me. They could only measure half of the nodal points needed for a match because of poor lighting and the angle of her face. But something about her looked familiar to me, which was weird. Maybe an old case I had. Can't remember, but it will come to me eventually. Sorry for the strikeout. Let's get together for a drink when you get back."*

The fictitious Elaina was likely dead now or at least permanently out of business, but it would have been nice to know who she actually was. Had I taken a better photo of her, we might have learned more about the woman and her motives. Even so, any professional assassin would probably have had her face scrubbed from every databank from here to Mongolia.

Next was Shanay's voicemail message: "*Gimme a call, McKenna.*" There was nothing more to it than that.

Taking a breath, I dialed her number. Too exhausted to figure out the time change, I tried to prepare myself for her wrath if it was late at night on the West Coast.

"That you, McKenna?" Shanay said.

"Yeah, it's me."

"Everything all right with you?"

"Uh-huh, why?"

"Just got a bad feel'n about something and wanted to check."

I pictured the two motorcyclists in the alley, armed and ready to kill me. Tipped off to my location. "What kind of bad feeling?"

"'Bout that wife o'yours," she said.

"Doris?"

"Unless you got another wife. Anyways, I called li'l Bridget to give her that message like you told me, and *she* answered."

"*She*, Bridget?"

"No, *she*, your wife. C'mon, try to keep up with me, McKenna."

"Okay..."

"And she... your wife... told me to give *her* the message. So I did."

"Uh-huh." I couldn't figure out where Shanay was going with this. None of it really mattered, because the trap I'd set had been for her, not Bridget or Doris.

"So I'm axi'n myself; why does McKenna's wife, all of a sudden care what he's doin' or where he's gonna be at a certain time?"

I felt my pulse accelerate a little as Shanay's point became clearer. The more it started to sink in, the harder it was to catch my breath. "Are you telling me you think Doris sold me out?"

"I don't know nothin' about nobody sell'n you out. All I'm say'n is I got a bad feel'n when I heard him."

"Him? Him who?"

"Him. The chump she's been sleep'n with."

I winced at the ugly image I still hadn't actually faced, myself.

"Heard the dude talk'n to her in the background. You know, like he was try'n to find out where you were."

My brain was in a pool of oatmeal. I couldn't connect the dots, or maybe I didn't want to. Could Mike Prowse, that ass-kissing Internal Affairs son-of-a-bitch have something to do with this?"

Sitting there in silence, I tried to work backwards in my memory. I had gotten a call from Doris after the embassy had already contacted her about my arrest. So, she would have known then that I was in Bangkok.

Squeezing the timeline out of my gray matter, I tried to recall when it was that I talked to her again. Was it the next day when Doris called to say that Bridget was worried about me? I remembered that I was whispering because I was with everybody inside the sanctuary. During the conversation, I must have mentioned where I was. Then, within minutes of leaving the church, me and Soltani were shot at. Could Doris or Mike Prowse have tipped off the motorcyclists to our whereabouts?

"You must'a had some kinda hunch," said Shanay. "Or else, why would you want me to call Bridget and tell her..." She paused, and I had a bad feeling about what was coming. "Wait. You wasn't test'n them, you was test'n me."

I felt sick in the pit of my stomach. She had been more loyal than anyone else in my life. "Shanay, I swear I never believed that. We weren't sure why these guys were trying to shoot me or how they knew where I was, but I had to figure out where the leak was coming from."

"Hmmm." She was quiet for a long time, and I suspected that she was hurt. I guessed that she didn't trust many people, and I should have been more reverent of her allegiance.

"I should have been upfront with you from the beginning," I said. "And I'm really sorry I wasn't. I promise that I'll make it up to you."

"Uh-huh. And how you gonna do that?"

I sighed. "A bonus. I'll give you a salary bonus for taking care of things while I was gone and to show you how much I appreciate your hard work."

"Now that's what I'm talk'n about."

We finished the call, and I could tell that we were all good again. What wasn't *all good* was Doris and that prick of a boyfriend she was seeing. There wasn't really any hard evidence to connect Prowse to this Bangkok mess or to the people who tried to kill me. It was all just circumstantial, and weak circumstantial at that. But it was definitely enough of a coincidence to pique my curiosity.

I took the second cell phone out of my pocket—the one belonging to the dead assassin. It was locked, of course, and I had no way of knowing how it was set up. I probably should have cut off his finger and pressed it to the phone like they do in the movies, or scanned his lifeless face to unlock it.

My guess was that whatever passcode this guy used, had to be pretty simple. So, having plenty of time to kill before my flight, I started messing with the keys.

I'm definitely not the techy type, but after only 15 minutes, I had cracked his code: 1-2-2-1. Wow. Call Steve Wozniak.

A lot of good it did though. Only a few calls had been received and even fewer placed, most of them began with foreign country codes that I was unfamiliar with. Only one call was made to a U.S. number, and I did not recognize the area code.

The overseas connection surprised me, because other than one case that I worked at SFPD, my exposure to international crime was zero. It made me wonder if these guys were mercenaries or freelance assassins that shady corporations like Willoughby-Klehs could hire.

It wasn't as if I'd ever be able to ask them. They were both dead and I had survived. Beyond that, their lives were a mystery to me and probably always would be. Just as I may never know for sure if my wife's new boyfriend had anything to do with them. I never say *impossible*, but of all the scenarios, Mike Prowse's involvement seemed the most far-fetched.

And then there was the flash drive sitting in a box on my sailboat. By all accounts, it held information that had caused this entire mess. The information that people were willing to kill for, and what the federal government was willing to offer immunity and protection for. If that talking suit, Kingsbury, actually believed I would turn it over to him, he was sadly mistaken. At least not until I had a chance to look at it myself.

In any case, my job had been to find Jonathan Teagan and I did. The rest of this mess could wait until another time. Another lifetime, for all I cared. At this point, all I wanted was to get home.

A little ice cream shop in the airport rotunda caught my eye, so I wandered over and celebrated my good fortune with a waffle cone and two scoops of chocolate chip.

Next door was a high-end women's clothing store. The dearth of customers seemed an indication of the exorbitant, airport prices. But as I walked past the window with my ice cream, I spotted a colorful silk kimono displayed on a mannequin.

At 3:25 p.m., I boarded my flight back to the Bay Area. Carefully tucking my shopping bag into the overhead compartment, I took my seat beneath it.

I had picked out a red and black kimono for Shanay. Kind of a cross between a judo *gi* and a bathrobe, the thing was 100% silk and had a dragon stitched on the back of it.

The second kimono was for Bridget. I'd missed her birthday and I didn't want to return empty handed. I also didn't want to show up with a Barbie or My Little Pony. She was thirteen now; no longer a little girl, but not quite a woman.

The robe I'd bought for her was light blue with white trim, and had tiny trees with leaves stitched in gold. Something about the print reminded me a little bit of the painting in our Bangkok apartment, but I tried to put that part out of my mind.

As the plane took off into the hazy sky, I took one final look at Bangkok. Taking a deep breath and slowly letting it out, I was leaving behind all that had happened to me there.

Smiling to myself, I was glad to be going home to my peaceful life on my little sailboat in my little marina. Most of all, I was looking forward to seeing Bridge. I'd been carrying the weight of a lot of mistakes with her, and I wanted to make things right.

Maybe for once, I'd done okay with my daughter's gift though. The kimono was beautiful and delicate, just like her.

See these other Phil Ribera novels:
(Available at Amazon.com)

San Francisco File

Book #1 in the Danny McKenna detective series

Ensenada File

Book #2 in the Danny McKenna detective series

It's Only a Badge

Book #1 in the police memoir series

Barkers & Bones
Portrait of an Undercover Narc

Book #2 in the police memoir series

Malfeasance

Book #3 in the police memoir series

Sadhana
Two Lies–One Truth

Fictional family saga set in India

www.ingramcontent.com/pod-product-compliance
Lightning Source LLC
Chambersburg PA
CBHW060316260626
47160CB00007B/2630

9780996210386